Madder ran with a high, easy gait that left the plain a blur far below us. The wind of our passage blew through my mind and body. I was one with the sky that spread not only above but all around us. On and on we ran and always the plain stretched before us without end.

The memory of that first ride will run forever in my blood. I can close my eyes and feel again that escape from earth into speed and space, like Dance except it was not interior to me, not mental at all, but *real*. "Between," windriders called where we rode: between earth and sky. It cannot be described to those who do not know it. It is worth any price.

I nodded to myself understanding that a windrider rode alone. I threw back my head and laughed aloud.

STEPHANIE T. HOPPE is by profession an attorney and is counsel to an agency of California state. About herself, she writes:

"I am aggressively, possibly unpleasantly Western, the fifth generation of my family born in San Francisco. Here the sun rises from the land and sets in the ocean. Spring is short, summer harsh, autumn non-existent, and winter green. The hills are old—and frail and scar easily from overgrazing or ranch house subdivisions. These things are to me the basis of reality—and of my writing.

"I have travelled; my family lived in Sweden during my high school years. I returned to California with a Swedish accent and an inability to understand football or supermarkets, which I have to this day. I have a romantic teen-ager's view of the major historical and religious monuments of Scandinavia, Germany, France, Italy, the British Isles and Washington, D.C.

"In recent years I have spent my free time camping and hiking in the desert mountains of eastern California, Nevada and Utah; those days and nights lend depth, harshness, and space to my easy view of life on the coast."

The Windrider is her first novel. She is working on others.

THE WINDRIDER

Stephanie T. Hoppe

DAW BOOKS, INC.
DONALD A. WOLLHEIM, PUBLISHER

1633 Broadway, New York, NY 10019

DAW Collectors' Book No. 618

For Frank

First Printing, March 1985

1 2 3 4 5 6 7 8 9

PRINTED IN U.S.A.

CHAPTER

1

In the cool, dark cave of the shadow cast by an ancient nut-pine tree we lay together, Jily and I, murmuring of love—and proving love; caressing arms intertwined, sleek and white, so like, female with female as we were, and close kin besides.

Laughing, Jily rose and stood above me. Her whiteness glowed in the shadow. I shivered at the sight of her in her beauty. I thought she laughed for joy, as I did; that she could not be still for delight.

From the ground Jily took up her silken gown. With an arch sidelong look at me over one graceful shoulder, she drew the gown around her, and then she sprang away from me into the blaze of afternoon sun.

I leapt to my feet, tangling in my own discarded clothing. I snatched up something as I ran and huddled it over my head: my short, Dancer's tunic, unadorned. I cared nothing for display even then; I wanted only the heart of a thing—*that* I did want. I went after Jily.

High, high above the world Jily ran, a white spear against the golden sunlight and the darker gold of the drying grass: a vision to haunt my dreams. But she was real. Laughing, she glanced back, teasing . . . inviting. I ran and gained on her. Diving headlong just as she gained the ridge, counting no cost, I reached to grasp the slender column of one flying ankle and brought her down. Laughing, we tumbled together, and then flung ourselves out upon the sweet-smelling grass and the hot earth, gasping for breath.

There, then, the others found us lying fully dressed and apparently chaste, side by side: Aymar and his lot. Drowzy and dreaming I disregarded them. Instead I stared up into the vast summer sky, where afternoon thunderclouds towered, billowing white, ever slightly shifting shape, sailing inexorably onward over Empire in a slow, stately dance.

From that high ridge where I lay on my back looking up, there seemed only sky around me, and I seemed myself to sail among those towering clouds. They might be steeds—beasts to ride such as legends Conquered Peoples told of. The beasts I knew were poor creatures. I could walk as fast and far as they; of course I held power over them, whenever I wished to exert it, as I did over all people also. Even these cloudsteeds I could control—ride—for there was no limit to my will: I, Oa, daughter of the Gandish Empire of the Thousand Years. Presently I would exert my will. . . .

Just now, languid after love, I only closed my eyes and felt the afternoon sun beat down upon me, warmly, loosening, and the earth thrust hard against my back. Lords of Earth we Gandish were, not of dreams or illusions . . . or of cloud figures. I smiled to myself while I drifted in the sweet smell of the ripening grass.

There came to me also, faintly but unmistakable, that still sweeter, far more intoxicating scent of Jily after love. My Jily. And my love. The heat of desire washed over me. I turned my head and opened my eyes to look at Jily.

She lay at her ease beside me, the long, sleek lines of her body set off by the shadows where the soft, filmy stuff of her gown gathered. Her white skin glowed through the pale blue fabric with an otherworldly light. She lay at her ease, but not resting. Her blue eyes, very pale and open wide, stared up into the face of Aymar, crouching in the grass at her head. I had forgotten that he had come after us up to the ridge.

Aymar leaned forward over Jily, his handsome face flushed. "Love, thou loosener of limbs—" he whispered to Jily. His fingers boldly stroked her cheek, just where the curve of it sharpened with such haunting grace.

Jily! Silently I willed her to turn from Aymar, to look only at me, but she never moved, only smiled and smiled up into Aymar's eyes. He was her full brother, sibling of the same birth, but at the look they gave one another, I stiffened, and the heat in my blood turned icy cold. By my will I forced myself: Jily I would not doubt. Had she not sworn she was mine a thousand times these last months? Sworn off, just as I had, male and female alike, out of love for me alone? The rage that flooded through me I directed at Aymar.

In a single convulsive movement I came to a crouch and leapt. I caught Aymar off guard, and he went sprawling.

A spate of laughter came from the others. Like a pattering of rain or a sudden gust of wind sending dry leaves swirling, their noise was. Intent on killing Aymar, I paid the others no heed.

But I had brought no weapon to tryst with Jily, and Dancer that I was, adept as none other of the Imperial kin in this latter time, I had barely reached my full growth and could hardly consider myself a match for Aymar in an unarmed contest. He was a male in his prime—and something of a Dancer himself. I did not closely consider anything beyond my rage, however.

And Aymar felt my blows. "By Gandda!" he swore, as we did by the eponymous hero of our Imperial House, who served us for god in big things and small. "Oa! You shall regret this also!" Aymar hissed through clenched teeth, coming after me in earnest.

"Also? With what else?" I laughed in his face. Of course we were adversaries, we who were both such near heirs to Empire. I could not be sorry there was now also Jily between us: as prize she sweetened the contest. I fought in earnest myself.

I kept free longer than I could have hoped—and hurt Aymar worse—but in the end, as I did not flee, he trapped me, catching my head against his chest, imprisoning my arms between our bodies, holding me in a hard, loveless embrace. Some sharp-spined ornament of his dress cut my cheek.

I cursed him. I could hear for myself my voice sounded childish, muffled against his hard, male body. Again came the sound like rain pattering or dry leaves—both impossible at the height of summer; this time I knew it was rather the laughter of the others who had come with Aymar to interrupt my solitude with Jily. I fell silent, the same willful pride now restraining me that had earlier driven me to attack.

Aymar released me gingerly, keeping tight hold on my arms, his every muscle alert. I lifted my head, thinking he was rightly wary of me: in the long run I would rule him along with all the others; it pleased me to think he knew it. Aymar could take me—now—in an unarmed fight. I would not often go unarmed. And the wielding of power in Empire, beyond the weeding out of young heirs, depended on far more than physical prowess. Females had held the Dynasty before. I need not doubt that I also could. For I thought I was like none before me, female or male.

Aymar shook me slightly, to see what fight remained in me, reminding me that for now he held me. I would not raise my eyes to meet his and so acknowledge his hold. Instead I fixed my gaze on the ornaments he wore pinning his stola at his chest. One held a lusterless stone that just missed the pale shade of blue called Imperial. It was the gleaming, rayed setting of that ornament which had scratched my face when Aymar pressed me against him. I scowled, seeing it. Aymar shook me again.

"Oa—child—have you yet had enough?"

Gritting my teeth, I picked among all the hot words that came to me for the most cutting. Then I sensed Aymar's attention left me. He let me go. I looked around where he did, down the long slope toward the palace and the city. A messenger came, an old slave wearing the gold-hemmed stola of the Dynast's personal service, gimping along awkwardly, looking put out at the long climb to the ridge.

It could be any one of us he came for, with a summons to high honor—or to death. I glanced around, briefly seeing with the salve's alien eyes: half a dozen of us, each with the flattened features, the pale skin and blue eyes that marked our race, the skin around our eyes delicately tattooed with pale blue lines to mark our rank within it. Jily reclined on the grassy ground, looking beautiful and very remote, her eyes closed. Her beauty was ever her claim to rank; the smooth, glowing skin around her eyes was scarcely marked. Aymar and I stood erect, flushed from fighting. Even with our eyes open our tattoos stood out clearly, they were so many. I had some of mine by birth; he had won all of his. Of much less account than either of us were the others, the escort with which Aymar always surrounded himself. They sat in the scant shade of a stunted nut-pine on little folding chairs their slaves had carried that were carved in the shapes of fantastical beasts. There was a low table set out among them, offering sweetmeats and wine in flagons nestled in ice saved from winter to melt now unregarded in the heat of a summer afternoon.

The old slave came to a halt and stood before us, swaying, head lowered, breathing heavily from the effort he had been put to. I saw after all he hardly looked at us. He was accustomed, no doubt, to the many scions of the Imperial House, all the ranks of the heirs of Gandda as well as the lesser kin, sent off here or there to claim or rule distant dominions, never knowing what whim of the Dynast would recall us to what fate; mostly he kept us in the Imperial capital kicking our heels. So many we were, hundreds altogether; too many, playing at love or at intrigue—playing often all too earnestly.

Aymar shifted his weight and fingered the clipped, blond curls of his beard, growing impatient to know the slave's errand. The slave lifted his head, looked past Aymar, and looked at me.

"The Dynast," he said, "requires Oa."

This slave was a captive who had grown old in the Dynast's service and knew not to use the titles of so-called honor of the Conquered Peoples. We trueborn went by our names alone; they were honor enough, we thought. And I did not doubt that this summons the old one brought me was to honor. I cast away from me all thoughts of Jily. In this ambition love had no place—Aymar had more. Him also I thought now finally to leave behind me, however. Without a word I strode swiftly to the path that cut the steep slope of the ridge, leaving the weary slave to hobble far behind.

Below me spread the Gandish Empire of the Thousand Years—the heart of it, at least. The slope swept steeply down to the palace, the ancient, low, rambling edifice of courtyards and wings that was near a city in itself. Beyond it the Imperial City straddled the river Flod. The establishments of the other Great Houses, trueborn like us of Imperial House Gand, dominated the near side. Across the river where the roads began, sprawled the teeming warrens the Conquered Peoples had thrown up over the generations of our rule: markets and thieves, manufactories, administrators, law courts, and all the rest, a world in miniature, where every language was spoken and anything could be had.

East of the city, out of sight beyond a low range of hills, began the Middle Plain, the rich heartland of Empire, which stretched for days' journey, populous and productive, cut and crosscut with roads and canals: what supported us in our luxuries but where we could hardly bear to go, so restricted in movement and hemmed in did we feel there. Vast as Empire had grown, it was not yet spacious enough for us the trueborn. This west bank of the river, the ridge where I had gone with Jily and all the land beyond, we kept empty for our pleasure.

Unhindered by the city, the Flod ran also west in a broad, shimmering sheet, into the desert, toward those mountains behind me so distant they were but shadows on the clearest day. Into those mountains the Flod ran, and disappeared there. In every other direction the Empire stretched near the ends of the earth. But not to the west, not through those mountains.

The oldest legends recounted that we, the trueborn, had come from the west following Gandda, and that after we passed, the mountains rose behind us to shut off our return. The legends were garbled with age, and in no time had any Dynast felt bound by the scarcely comprehensible warnings of legends. Scouts had probed the nameless western mountains. High and barren as they were, they proved so near impassable and promised so little reward, the great effort their passage would require was never mounted. Nowadays we seldom looked to the west, not because we cared that it was forbidden, but because we thought there was nothing there—and we were content the land should be empty at our back when we looked east over our empire.

Presently I came so far down the slope the cultivated grounds outside the palace walls enfolded me. People thronged there, some trueborn, mostly lesser folk, members of the Conquered Peoples. They looked much like the trueborn, except that they bore themselves with consciousness of their abject status. For their failure to stand up to us, they no longer ruled themselves or any of the world. Though I wore only a Dancer's tunic, bare of ornament save a thin trimming of Imperial blue, the white silk rumpled and stained from the grass and the heat, from tumbling Jily and fighting Aymar, my bearing alone cleared my path.

The main palace gates stood wide at this hour. Inside was also a crush: trueborn, Imperial kin and officers from the hereditary armies or provincial administrations, all in court robes. Some might have had business with the Dynast or with palace officials, but most came to watch each other. All saw me, of course; young as I was, there were no few who turned to look after me closely.

I went directly to present myself to the station of the outermost chamberlain and was conducted at once, respectfully, to the inner palace. At the second station slaves of mine waited with my audience robes. Hurriedly they pulled the heavy draperies encrusted with jewels and embroidery over my limbs. I stood stiff with impatience at the discomfort and the foolish display; I submitted—for now. Last the slaves held up the stola marking my rank and laid the silk softly across my throat, letting it fall to the floor behind me in long, blue-striped streamers. Fringeless the stola was—that one dignity, seal of adult status, I was not yet entitled to. I thought this day would bring me the offer of that—that and more.

My slaves were permitted no farther. The Dynast's own servants led me deeper into the labyrinth of the inner palace. Here was quiet, all stir muffled in the swathing of rich carpets and tapestries, these oldest halls dimly lit through garden courts shaded by ancient trees.

In one doorway I glimpsed Kastra, unmistakable in her multi-hued, long-fringed stola, her lithe Dancer's stride unmarked by her advanced age—*she* had full right of access here. She paused and looked at me unsmiling. I no longer owed her pupil's reverence, and I gazed back at her levelly, without bowing.

Kastra had taught me Gandish Dance, which was something rather different from the lighthearted play and celebration among Conquered Peoples that went by the name of dance. Nor was Gandish Dance any mere wildness in release. Gandish Dance was rather both an ordeal of violence and a deep discipline; it was equally of mind and will and flesh; it focused the entire being of a Dancer . . . upon the Dance. Its origin, together with our own and Gandda's, was lost in the legendary West. In these latter days of Empire well established and easy living, the Dance had become something of a formality, just to be got through to claim full adult status. Even in these days none denied the utility of it at weeding out those unfit to hold even the name of trueborn; the finer testing of higher rankings by very large Dances had fallen out of use.

I had first gone to Kastra as a very young child, declaring on a whim and a dare that I would learn from none but the foremost Dancer of the Imperial kin. Kastra took me on and schooled me long and unmercifully. I kept coming back, determined that neither she nor the Dance should get the better of me. In that hard discipline I learned what I thought none had in generations—more than Kastra meant to teach me, certainly. I meant to hazard my future on it.

I passed Kastra by and went on with my escort through halls filled with the riches of a hundred lands, plunder and tribute for the rulers of all Earth, a sort of material record of the Gandish Conquest by the Imperial armies, which were thrusting their way even then with broadsword and pike to the very ends of the earth. The hereditary armies were the invention and origin of Empire, that of the Red and of the Gold and the others, continually growing by natural increase and capture, through generations molding the soldiers, male and female, to service.

Now long unseen at this heart of Empire, the armies hardly seemed the powering force of it any longer. Dance had taught me to think of power as something more subtle, as relations and tendencies rather than death and tribute. Making my way now into the innermost reaches of the palace, I seemed to feel such currents of power and intrigue move about me like palpable forces, as real as the waters of the Flod or the winds on the ridge. I shivered with anticipation but no fear. It was what I was born to and prepared my whole life for.

Bowing low, a slave opened for me the last door.

It was the garden room I came in to, a large, high-ceilinged hall where the Dynast collected the strange plants sent him from every corner of Empire. I had not seen it before. Great trees there were, with enormous fleshy leaves, and strange twining vines with flowers that gave off disturbing aromas. The hall was kept very hot and humid—uncomfortably so, I thought. I had heard the Dynast found this wet, heavy air easier to breathe in the disabilities of his extreme age. He had been old for generations' time.

At the end of an avenue left between the plants, on a dais, stood a great carved chair. In it sat the Dynast. His figure was shrunken but his presence overflowed both chair and hall—I felt it at once—and I was as always unnerved by the contradictory evidence presented to my sight and my instinct. The Dynast's counselors and favorites stood around him: wizened elders of the Great Houses and a sprinkling of others. Imperial kin and slaves could be equals here, all deciding the fate of thousands in a single gesture.

My mother, whom the Dynast greatly favored, sat very near him. I had heard the rumor that he himself had fathered me, her only child. From the vantage point of my youth, looking at his enfeebled age, I found it difficult to credit him with paternity. Certainly some male of the Imperial kin had sired me. Mingled blood even of other trueborn Houses diluted the fragile Imperial coloring, and I had the extreme pallor of the Dynast himself, skin and hair so pale as to be near transparent. Even if the Dynast had not sired me, his blood ran very directly in my veins, for he acknowledged my mother his granddaughter. I supposed I would never know for sure; my mother did not discuss with me her liaisons, which were many.

While I now waited for the Dynast's notice, my mother leaned forward and spoke into his ear. I could not but think of the last time she and I had talked—a conversation that ended in a quarrel. She had dared to advise me. My headstrong will would be my downfall, she said in her enragingly clipped and precise tones. I might have every ability I claimed, she allowed, but I was young and did not well control myself and overreached myself in everything. So much I took. Then she warned me against Jily. That I refused to hear. Now I wondered uneasily if she thought she had cause to warn the Dynast against me.

I measured her warily. She looked as cold and as austerely beautiful as ever, tall and white, her flat Gandish features without flaw—her beauty was neither opulent nor accessible like Jily's. I was very like her, not so beautiful but probably more striking, my high, wide cheekbones strongly angled, eyes ghostly pale, skin utterly colorless. I was larger and stronger than my mother, less graceful, more forceful in both features and gestures. Her determination and will I had in full—and then some. I lifted my chin now in defiance even of her. She looked at me unsmiling, and with a sinuous furling of the heavy folds of her court robes, she stepped back from the dais.

The Dynast turned his great, heavy head, so out of proportion with what remained of his body, and fixed his eyes on me. "Oa," he said in a rasping, whispering voice, which carried to me easily across the hall, for all the others who had been talking in muttering low voices fell silent. "Come forward, child."

Across the length of the hall the gaze of those ancient, colorless eyes gripped and held me. For once I felt myself truly to be the child I still officially was, though I had not accounted myself so for several years, nor allowed anyone else to do so. Thus we were raised, we of the Imperial kin, without check save the natural competition of our kind.

Even the Dynast would rule only so long as he actually kept hold of the substance of power.

I stepped warily between the plants, for some of them were reputed poisonous and looked it. I held my head high, as high as I could, more awed than I had expected to be by this first individual audience I had ever been called to. The heat of that hall made me feel faint. My skin itched from the heat and from the chafing of the heavy ceremonial robes. My very breath felt stifled within me. The Dynast seemed able to see to my innermost being. I had not the skill even to judge his assessment.

"I've ordered the Great Hall prepared for a performance of the High Dance ten days hence," the Dynast said, his rasping voice sounding disembodied and fateful.

I waited, telling myself I could take so much for granted, and it was not enough.

"I shall like to see several score Dancers, both postulants and initiates—"

My heart started to beat faster. So many! A long Dance it would be, the ordeal of the testing stretching a full night and day, perhaps several. None had been tested that hard in recent years, that I knew of, nor invited to Dance again after their first testing. Truly the Dancer that could weave so many into the single culminating pattern could claim all honor. And if this Dance succeeded at all, it would likely kill, taking a victim to seal the survivors to that Dancer in the commanding role in the mysterious binding without which, it was said, none could be Dynast. I lifted my head higher, the better to catch my breath in the heavy air. Well might I breathe more quickly—but not for fear of *my* death!

I had practiced the commanding role of the High Dance most carefully. My mother had gone out of her way to advise me it would be ridiculous for me to attempt it, as well as unnecessary. I must survive in some role, of course—and she trusted I would—but I need not risk a large failure. I did not know the power of the High Dance when Danced by many, in concert, she warned. Of course I did not: uninitiated I had never even seen the High Dance, but only practiced the various roles separately.

Kastra herself talked often of my gawkiness after my

recent rapid growing; she admitted the slight rawness of my movements had its own style, however. I thought her actions spoke loud enough of my readiness when she brought a slave to the practice halls to teach me the Death Points. Even Dancing alone I gave him a clean death, snapping his neck at my first attempt. I knew I was ready. When I told Kastra she had no more to teach me, she did not gainsay it.

Now I fairly trembled with the eagerness to hear that the Dynast would give me my chance. But he delayed, watching me—testing me. I doubt I ever knew half the tests he set for me as for every near-heir. Many I had passed: witness the numerous fine lines of tattooing across my eyelids and temples. There had been Dynasts who had had fewer lines of rank, in early times anyway.

The Dynast grunted. Then, slowly, he listed the names of those he meant to invite to Dance: many of my own years, ready like myself for initiation, just those I expected. Then he began to list those already adult—heirs all of them, mostly near-heirs, and the highest ranked among these. I marked each name and tried to assess what difficulty the person would add to the Dance. Then the Dynast spoke Jily's name.

I caught my breath. Jily's rank was too low. Her beauty made her rank irrelevant for most purposes, but for such a ceremonial event as the initiation of near-heirs she was no fit choice. I stared into the Dynast's motionless face and fathomless pale eyes around which the fine blue lines of his tattoos shimmered through the translucent dry skin. A sudden fear came to stifle my breath worse than the hot, heavy air of the hall.

The Dynast said, "And I wish to see you, Oa, Dance the commanding role. If you will."

So he offered me everything I wanted—but poisoned. For I understood that somehow he would arrange that Jily would be the one who would come under my hands if I could bring the Dance to the culminating figure, and that I would kill her.

In that moment I first plumbed the depths of my love for Jily, when I learned that to gain my ambition I must agree to kill her.

Could the Dynast arrange it? I did not know. I had never heard the like, but there had to be some chance of it, that he spoke of it at all. Could *I* take the chance that he was bluffing? Long and deeply I stared into those eyes so like my own except that I could not probe him as he probed me. By that one difference he cornered me. Slowly I nodded. I had to. I could not, in a single moment, forswear my ambitions.

"If you will . . . ," the Dynast said softly.

I said, "I will Dance."

But I did not truly agree. Mentally I kept reservations and conditions. I would not kill Jily, I swore to myself, though I did not see how not. And I showed the Dynast no reverence in my answer, not from pettiness, but because his very setting of this elaborate test went in itself no small way toward confirming I was all I claimed. Shaken as I was, I marked this acknowledgment he made.

Doubtless the Dynast saw all I thought. He smiled faintly, enigmatically, as he dismissed me and my mother again bent over his chair. Somehow I got from the Presence.

I had gained my object, but I was near wishing I had not.

CHAPTER

2

All manner of persons waited in the outer halls to question me: lesser kin who made their way precariously in the shifting currents of intrigue among the high ones; heirs also, who aspired to rival me. I saw none of the near-heirs, those whom *I* counted fellow contenders for that highest prize of all, the dynastic succession. That near-heirs watched me, however, I had never doubted; I did not think it so small a matter as I had an hour before. Now the great prize was suddenly so much closer to my grasp, I first saw how great were also the risks that ringed it.

All the persons I saw I had already the power to deal with. I used my power: I threw them off and went alone to my own apartments. Suspicious for the moment of everyone, impatient of all interference, I dismissed even my own slaves once they had freed me of my court robes.

I could not rest. I poured wine from the carafe set out for me and, glass in hand, gulping the astringent young vintage, I paced my rooms, which I had lately made nearly as spare as a practice hall.

There were carpets, to be sure: the floors and walls were thickly covered to hide the rough construction stone and to insulate against both summer heat and winter cold. For furniture I had in the outer room several low divans and hassocks, between them a low table where the wine was set out between some seedcakes. The inner room held a bed and a large chest for clothes, and opened onto the garden, high-walled, stone-paved, planted in somber greens under a single large nut-pine that shaded the entire small expanse. Among the lower branches of this tree twisted a vine which bore the only flowers I permitted in the garden, white trumpets that gave off Jily's own haunting scent. When she and I first became lovers I had remembered the vine from my visit a few years before to the cities of the Southern Shore, and I had sent for one, which I had since cultivated with indifferent success.

That flowering vine had been the one frivolity I had allowed myself since I entered deeply into the austerities of Gandish Dance. With true Dancer's intolerance, I scorned display and superficiality. I wanted only the very heart. My own heart it seemed the Dynast had just showed me—and displayed his power there. I might now think Jily also a frivolity, one I could ill afford: by means of her I was truly caught.

Back and forth I paced, outer room to inner room to garden and back, and I found no ease. Once or twice I thought to go to Jily—and could not, not just yet, not until I settled with myself if I could kill her. Or could refrain from killing her.

The sun set. The garden slowly darkened, together with the unlighted rooms. Still I paced and probed, and what I saw was only more clearly the insolubility of my dilemma. For whichever course I chose was poisoned. If I grasped the ambitions for which this High Dance was the first, indispensible step, I would ever know I had my rank at the price of yielding up Jily, or at least of being willing to do so. And if I chose rather Jily . . . why, such foolish fondness as it would seem would make even Jily scorn me. And what I might have to pay in the future, just to live with myself, I could not even guess, save that it would be much.

I stopped short finally, fists clenched for the very lack of an opponent in the flesh, raging at the way the Dynast hemmed me in with the substance of my own will. I turned to the door to call for lights, and then, on impulse, turned back. I wanted distraction. I wanted escape, from very Empire. I would go out, into the city, across the river, even.

Quickly I fastened a purse at my belt with money to pay for entertainment and beside it a knife to protect it, a small, slim-bladed knife that I could easily hide in my hand, good for close work. I meant to go to places I knew across the river where my Imperial features would not necessarily keep me from harm. I swung a plain cloak around my shoulders against the evening cool and slipped quietly through back corridors of the palace. Labyrinth though it was, I had learned most of its tricks very young. I left by a side door; unobserved, I thought.

I walked along the wide streets that sloped to the river in tunnels made dark, though the evening was still early, by the trees that met overhead. The long blank outer walls of great houses hemmed me in on either side. There were few abroad this early, few enough that I soon sensed that I was being followed.

I was not surprised. Many would know by now the High Dance was called—a large Dance, in which I was offered the commanding role. The news would set the rankings among heirs, which were never well settled, into flux. More than one might think themselves served by picking me off before I Danced—incapacitating me or even killing me. Near-heirs tried each other so relentlessly, I sometimes wondered why the Dynast bothered to set us tests.

I walked on with loose, easy strides that let me feel free, grinning to myself. Some would have said I was foolish to go out alone this night; I thought only I had not needed to go so far as the other side of the river to find distraction. As I walked, I planned: this cousin who followed me was one who would not get off unmarked.

A score or more of persons came out from Lus House just as I passed the main gates. In the light of their lanterns, the Lusians' red hair flamed like additional torches. I slipped among them, inconspicuous as a shadow with my pale, Imperial coloring. I worked my way through them into the darkness of a many-trunked tree: a simple means of ambush, which sometimes worked, and did this time. The Lusian party moved down the street; looking back, I saw come into the open, heavily cloaked and unrecognizable, the shadow of my trail.

I dropped my own cloak under the tree and drew my knife and came out noiselessly on the back of him who searched for me. Male I thought he must be, so much larger than me the figure was. I puzzled that I could not recognize him either by bulk or walk; he should be very close kin. I had to wonder how far I had threatened; as I jumped I supposed I would soon find out.

I got him mid-stride, off balance, and pulled him over backwards, twisting to come down on top of him. He began to recover from his surprise even while he was still falling, and flipped the weight of his fall with no small skill to catch *me* off balance. He did not try to escape. He was after me, more earnestly than ever Aymar. I saw the glitter of perhaps a knife or a garrote, quickly gone. I knew I had to fight now. I felt no unsettling rage, only cold certainty and calmness. I did not reckon my chances foolishly, either: I had my Dancer's quickness, and I was armed. I used the knife without hesitation.

I heard a grunt. Struck, my opponent slowed. Then I had him, his back to the ground, my knee in his belly, knife in hand ready at his bared throat. With my other hand I swept the hood from his head. In the dark I found only darkness, no pale glimmer of the Gandish face I had expected. He was no kin of the Imperial House. He was not trueborn at all.

"A slave!" I exclaimed in astonishment. I examined him as well as I could. "Without livery. What're you doing on this side of the river?" I prodded him with the knife point. "What're you after?" I demanded. I guessed he was only a thief who had tracked me by chance. I prodded him again.

"A Dancer, aren't you?" he said then. "To move so fast and silently. I've heard of Dancer's skills. But none had any longer, I also heard. I should have known. It was too much money they offered me."

I frowned, hard put to follow his words, which were distorted by bitterness as well as alien accent, understanding, however, here was something other than I had yet thought. My captive spoke very boldly for one who was not trueborn, who had attacked a near-heir, or meant to. Was he a slave at all? "A hireling assassin!" I exclaimed. "A Gamorgen."

That *was* something new, that my kinfolk no longer dared come against me in person. Those elders who said the trueborn were growing soft might have had the right of it. But they should also know that one adept at Gandish Dance had reflexes a Gamorgen assassin envied. I could be pleased I had brought down such a one, one of the guild killers of the walled city of Gamorg.

"Who?" I demanded. "Who paid you?"

He grimaced at the bite of the knife. But after all I only goaded his pride. "They paid," he said through clenched teeth, "enough for my silence if they're not to get anything more."

I spat in disgust and felt about the assassin's clothes with my free hand, seeking tokens, clues, but finding only clothes, layers of harsh, cheap fabrics sour with travel and wear. Then my groping fingers caught on something that prickled them with a pain oddly familiar. I tugged, but the thing would not come free. I felt a clasp and fumbled it loose and drew it forth: a jeweled ornament.

From the end of the street came voices and lights, a party moving my way. I glanced along the dark tunnel of the street, fingering the jewel, wondering if I alone was worth the trouble and risk of bringing a hireling assassin into the city, and across the river at that. Was this a larger conspiracy—a true treason against the Dynast? I had no basis for deciding, save my assessment of my own worth, and I was not so sure of that as I had been a few hours earlier. I hesitated.

The Gamorgen was alert for his chance, and twisted suddenly in my hold, breaking my grip with an ease that astonished me. I reached after him, slashing out with the knife. He hissed in pain but got free, and scuttled off into shadows. Again I hesitated, uncertain even now whether to call out. In himself the assassin did not matter a great deal: he was one small datum, like a single gesture in a complex Dance. What mattered was what he came from and lead toward; he would likely go to his death without telling that.

The revelers up the road neared, loud and boisterous. I decided I did not want to be found with only a tale of a fled assassin to account for my disarray. I could already hear the questions and exclamations; I would rather deal with another assassin. Hastily I sheathed my knife and grabbed up my cloak and myself fled into the darkness, away from those who approached; as it happened, toward the river.

Nearer the Flod there were shops and eating places in huts and stalls between palaces of the trueborn, open for evening trade, which was picking up. I slowed my pace and headed less obtrusively onto the stone quay that fronted the river. To avoid my kin I paid my coin for passage on a public ferry, one of those guided by a cable and powered by heavy sweeps, each of which required numerous slaves to operate, or as many of the little draft beasts we had.

Light lingered on the river, illuminating my pale face enough to show my rank. People stepped back to leave me room, well knowing the sort of sport that interested my kind, and not wanting to become embroiled. I hardly saw them. Instead I saw my kin, the heirs of Empire who sought what I also sought. In my mind I measured as well as I could which would move against me in this fashion. I could not see my way clear to any answer.

A sudden sharp pain in my left hand brought me back to the crowded ferry, the plash of sweeps over the darkening waters of the Flod. I looked down, opening my clenched fist, and found there the ornament I had of the assassin: a blue jewel set into a brooch of rayed design, itself set in a circle of glistening blood where I had clenched it so hard as to break the skin. No wonder I had felt a familiarity. My cheek still bore the memory of that prickling pointed setting. This very afternoon I had seen it pinned on Aymar's breast. Yes, hiring a Gamorgen was just Aymar's sort of plot. He was a fool! Others might think him my match, or more; I thought scornfully I could handle him as easily as I did his hireling assassin.

Abruptly I pulled back my arm, meaning in my scorn to throw the ornament into the river and be rid of it. But then

I changed my mind and thrust what I held within my cloak, another use for it coming to me belatedly with the thought of Aymar's sibling Jily. Jily! At the thought of her my limbs grew weak. They were so fond, she and Aymar, of course they were fond, being siblings of one birth, and that not a very high one, so they were more to each other than they might otherwise have been. I would like some means to wedge my way between their sibling closeness. Perhaps this ornament would provide it. But of course the thought of Jily brought me back to my dilemma. My breath came hissing in anger as I set my face to the fast approaching shore.

The tavern by the riverbank where I first went was crowded with the trueborn. I thought in disgust I might as well have stayed on my own side of the river, and I left without finishing the first drink I ordered. I looked in upon some others of the places I usually frequented and found them much like the first—full of reminders of matters from across the river. I wanted something different. Anything.

I wandered some distance out along the Northern Road where the poorest and most desperate folk of the city lived, drinking in one after the other of their gathering places, finding the setting ever less Imperial, the liquor ever fouler—and fewer trueborn—the farther I went. I drank the liquors of the Conquered Peoples, evil tasting as they were, sliding burning down my throat. They were not watered, but I could not get drunk.

I tried to pick a fight, but the folk steered clear of me, returning fair words for insults. Perhaps they suspected a trap, that my kin would suddenly emerge in force if I was threatened. Or perhaps they were warned off by something in my face, that was more forbidding even than usual in my race.

I turned then to the whores. Some of them seemed shy of me also, but at last I hired a boy, a youth who was probably my own age—old enough, but not too old. He led me through such squalid byways off the Northern Road that I wondered for a time if he meant to lead me into a trap to rob me. I kept going, thinking I would then anyway get the fight I had wanted, and which I would still just as soon have as the boy.

In the end he took me to a more substantial-looking building than I would have thought existed in that quarter, where he had a room furnished in something of the Imperial style, with tribute rugs and hangings. By lamplight they looked well enough, though doubtless they were shabby castoffs. All that was needed really was a bed. That was provided, on an Imperial scale. I guessed the boy was not unaccustomed to dealing with the Imperial kin: he had that dark-skinned look of Southern mystery that attracted us. The very predictability of my attraction gave me pause— this boy could be bait for wider intrigues than his own. I stopped in the doorway, narrow-eyed, surveying the place and the boy. "What's your name?" I demanded.

He looked back over his shoulder at me out of his great, dark, doe eyes. "Sezny," he said, "if it please you, lordly one." I questioned him further. He said his mother had come to the capital from a Southern city. He had been born here, of no particular father, it seemed, and lived in this quarter all his life. While he spoke he slipped off his richly colored but rather threadbare tunic. Then he came to take mine.

I watched him come toward me, naked, dark, and sleek, with an animal grace enhanced by his exotic color. I smiled a little with pleasure at the sight and thought after all I did want him. I reached to untie my cloak and felt the ornament I had taken from the assassin hidden in the folds of fabric. I drew it out, meaning to lay it aside, not looking at it—looking only at Sezny.

I saw his gaze shift, distracted perhaps by a glitter from the jewel in my hand, then fix and widen in surprise. I stiffened and my free hand flew by instinct to the knife at my belt; my left hand, but that was little matter, for the first thing a Dancer learned was symmetry.

"How do you come to be familiar with this?" I hissed, remembering very clearly how I had thought he looked to be such as would attract the notice of Imperial kin, wondering what chance might have brought me so directly to another of Aymar's minions. Sezny's dark gaze flew from the jewel to my face, looking fearful.

"No!" he said desperately. "I mean you no ill, lord. I swear it!"

"But you know exactly who I am. And what this is." I gestured with the jewel.

"Yes." He licked his lips. "I can't give you proof," he said bitterly. "But look around you. See just how little I have. I've gotten no reward. I don't enter into their conspiracies. But I have to accept what comes, just to survive."

I relaxed a little, near being convinced by his manner.

Sezny continued eagerly. "I do know *you*—know of you, Lord . . . Oa. When I heard your name in the tavern, I thought I had rather go with you than any other of your kind. You have the reputation to go freely and carelessly—openly—not to hide to a whore's poor quarters to plot against your betters."

"*Who* has plotted?" I asked softly. "The one who owned this, I take it." Again I gestured with Aymar's jewel. And a Gamorgen. And who else? How many? Male or female?"

"Several," Sezny said uneasily. "Always different—except the female. It was she who found me first. She saw me in the Old Market one day and bade me attend her in the pleasure gardens by the river. Later she came here, with the others, saying they wanted a place to talk in secret. They thought I was of no account—save as I might pleasure them, of course, when they were done with their plotting." He went on, but I ceased to attend after his first words.

"A female," I whispered. "A very beautiful one, no doubt." Jily.

A dozen different occasions came vividly to my mind, including that very afternoon when I stood in the open air of the ridge in back of the palace hearing the Dynast's messenger summon me; Jily's gaze flickered past me to Aymar with a look of something other than idle flirting. Jily had betrayed me, with Aymar, with Sezny, with countless others. I could have known it any time. I could no longer avoid admitting that I knew.

Something of what Sezny was saying penetrated my consciousness and I understood *why*—how for Aymar's advancement, at Aymar's behest, Jily did all that she did. From the outset, I guessed, she came to me only to see what she could make of me for Aymar's use. If ever *he* decided she was not molding me to sufficient pliancy, she would throw me over openly. Love! There was no love involved, save mine.

My mind scrabbled at the chance of revenge the Dynast's offer contained: I wanted to ravage Jily for her faithlessness. Then, at the thought of laying my hands on her sleek, lovely body, my limbs grew weak with love and longing, and I even thought that perhaps she could explain her part in this plot if I gave her the chance. Perhaps she plotted not *with* Aymar but *against* him, for my sake. . . . Even as the thought came to me I knew it for foolishness. Aymar had always held Jily. I had never come between them. In that he was my match, and just now I accounted that equal with the dynasty. Even now I loved her, and my will was utterly clouded over with my love. I cried aloud at the wrench it was in my flesh.

Sezny came nearer and touched my face with a shy caress. I fixed my gaze on him finally. With great clarity I saw him, and in a sudden fever of impatience I threw off my tunic and led him toward the bed.

I had sampled love in some variety on both sides of the river, females first, and then males after I learned the Dancer's tricks of control that guard against unwonted conception. Sezny was one of the best I had yet found, male or female—or perhaps my need to be pleased was greatest that night. He seemed to have a trick of building, by a glance and a touch and a word, a whole world, tawdry perhaps and fragile, but complete while it lasted— and *mine*. His dark eyes glowed with practiced invitation as he pulled me on top of him, and I rode him to good purpose.

But the time came we could neither of us move anymore. Sezny fell asleep, his limbs intertwined with mine and the tangled bedclothes. I could not sleep. Sated though I was, so soon as I was not immediately occupied with Sezny the very different touch and smell of Jily swam before me, and I ached with wanting her.

I ached, and aching had to acknowledge Jily's very

betrayal only strengthened her hold on me. I was fixed, powerless, between wanting to kill her for her betrayal and hungering for her living; between killing her at the Dynast's bidding and forswearing all ambition. Long hours I waked that night while Sezny slept in my arms, learning in the example of my own flesh what power surely was—when it was not mine.

It was no easy lesson to one raised as I had been, a near-heir of the Imperial House.

Dawn came slow and gray to find me still waking—and undecided. Ten days the Dynast said: ten days must pass, of which the first was not yet even begun, before any choice I made could be sealed by the deed and put behind me. For ten days I must consider . . . and reconsider . . . no! I would not tolerate it. Abruptly I sat up, pulling myself free of the weight of sleeping Sezny's body.

Sezny stirred at my movement. I glanced down and saw his dark eyes open, blank and incurious. He murmured something in a tongue I did not know and when I did not answer curled up more tightly into himself and slept on. I slid off the bed and retrieved my tunic from where I had flung it. I pulled it over my head and belted it with the silken sash of Imperial blue.

I *had* reached a decision, I discovered: by my very need to have the decision made at once. I would yield nothing. I would allow no exactions of myself. I would take the only course I saw open to me in which I could act unhindered by others' will. Flight, some might call it, or refusal or forswearing: the words seemed muddled, irrelevant. Impatiently I shook them off. I would face this challenge as I had all else that had ever come to me, but in my own time and my own way. My course came clear. Did not the Dance itself teach that anything that could be separated out or thrown off was not the heart? I would throw off all I could, and then I would see what I would do.

Once more I glanced toward Sezny, lying sleeping on his bed. I would not wake him, I decided, but I lingered a moment just to look at him, at the grace of his young form, and the mystery of his dark color. He was lovely and he had pleased me greatly. I remembered also, however, how fearful he had been and easily cowed, and I frowned. He was flawed like all of the Conquered Peoples. He could not understand that I must *act*, nor could he share my fate, and so he might as well sleep.

I turned from him and took up the purse I had carried, and then set it down again with what money it still contained, for Sezny. Aymar's jewel I also left. I had done with it. My knife I took, however, and my cloak.

I went out into the chill dawn and made my way quickly through near-empty streets to the riverbank. I worked my way downshore beyond the stone quay where small boats were moored or drawn up onto a sandy, unfaced bank of the Flod. I slunk among the shacks and boats with Dancer's steps, moving more smoothly than shadow in half light, so not to be seen by any who might be waking.

I soon found what I wanted: a light sailing skiff such as my own that was moored across the river where I would not go. It was a working folk's craft, not so finely made or fitted out as mine, but serviceable. I checked that sails and rigging were in order and pushed the boat out into the water. I climbed into it and sculled it gently out into the river, where the light of the new day was stronger. The water, licked by a rising breeze, was a pale blue, the same color as the vast vault of the sky at this hour: the Imperial blue of my own eyes. But for the wind and me, all was still, as if I were the only one in all Empire who moved.

I set the sails and turned the tiller, and the boat purled away smartly, downriver before the dawn breeze, westward whence my forebears had come but none had ever returned—to that one place remaining on earth, if any existed at all, free of Empire: the land beyond the forbidden mountains.

That was my decision. I was, of course, very young and saw things as absolutes; and perhaps not the less clearly for that.

Slowly the sun rose. Under the midday heat, with the city still in sight, the wind failed. The sails hung slack and the tiny craft drifted at the great river's own slow pace. I leaned over the side to drink of the muddy river water, cupping my hands to carry it to my mouth. About my growling, hungry innards I could do nothing. I felt light-headed from hunger, from the heat and the glare, from long waking and too much drinking, and from the high emotions of the preceding hours now run down into a single slowly drifting boat, rocking slightly from my leaning out to drink.

I trimmed the sails. It was no use, there was not even a whisper of air moving. I grew bored. I had never taken my boat out save during those hours when the wind blew briskly. There was no point to sitting in a boat drifting. I had not known a boat could drift so silently, so slowly.

I looked behind me where the Imperial City, low and sprawling on either side of the wide river, was dissolving into a shimmer of heat. It hardly looked real. Nothing seemed very real to me any longer: not the past, certainly not the future and whatever destination I might find among fragments of legend. I had thrown off much! Only my will—or mere stubbornness—remained; I would not turn back. Anyway, now I could not, not until a wind came up.

Uncomfortable and restless, I called upon the inner disciplines of Dance to channel my thoughts and energies, but found they did not avail against the heat and tedium of the afternoon. At last I lay down in the bottom of the boat among its former owner's poor belongings and slept.

For several days I traveled thus along the Flod, stopping nights to hunt for small beasts on the river shores or to steal from the crops of the smallholders settled on the east shore to grow fresh food for the city. One night I was caught, tripping a snare set for rather smaller marauders, from which I could not at once free my ankle. Two small, dusky females came to investigate the commotion I made. When they saw the pale glimmer of my angry face and knew what I was, they dropped to their knees to free me with trembling frightened fingers and then remained bowed over, not daring to look at me while I hobbled away. I went hungry that night, nursing my ankle while the boat ran on through the darkness.

The next day I discovered I had come to the end of the inhabited places. Long ago all the land on both sides of the river had been inhabited by a peaceful people who tilled the land. But the trueborn required wide open spaces and, centuries since, when my forebears first came out of the west, it was said, they enslaved or killed the former inhabitants, and all the land west of the river Flod became wasteland and desert. Even now that the conquering Imperial armies neared the far ends of Earth, the Dynast kept his capital at the edge of the desert and required all who had business with him to come to him.

So far the river had run south as much as west, but now the land to the east rose in barren hills that forced the river ever more strongly westward. The nameless mountains, shadowstuff as seen from the city, rose solidly before me, directly in the river's path. The river ran on, dropping quickly, accelerating its pace until it ran in a wide trough between high bluffs, straight at the mountains, which soon seemed to tower directly overhead. Then I heard the roar of cataracts.

Years before I had gone with some others overland to view the cataracts where the river ran at the mountains and disappeared from view in an awesome gorge. Now, as the boat swept ever more swiftly beyond my control around a last curve, and the vista of roiling water stretched ahead of me at my own level, I saw how little I had appreciated the sight that time from the bluff top.

I sat frozen, staring, hypnotized by the sight of that upheaval and the roar of it. My nerve failed but it did not matter: the river was carrying me on inexorably. Wryly I thought one last time of my mother's warnings, and knew I had truly overreached myself beyond recovery, for it was obvious to me I could avail nothing against this immensity of the river.

Even while I acknowledged my situation, I wrenched my hands free of the hold the sight exerted and lashed myself to the boat with a line. I was barely done when the boat ran in upon that flashing turmoil. The fact was beyond question; only the manner in which I faced my fate was still to be seen.

I faced it boldly. I sat erect as the little boat rocketed forward on the waves, thrusting me high above the angry river. At the soaring sensation, I even thought I rode the river, and I cried aloud in exultation.

The boat dropped suddenly and smashed against rock,

tilted and half filled with water—all in an instant—and then whirled on. The roar and flash of the waters engulfed me.

Briefly an eddy cast me up and spun me in place with what remained of the boat; the mast and rigging were gone and beneath the curving green of solid water tumbling over it the gunwale looked to be splintered. Wonderingly I lifted my eyes and saw back the way I had come.

Rock rose sheer and high to confine the great river on either side. Far back where I had come a narrow slit alone remained of the world I had known—Empire. There was a thin strip of sky and a dab of browning, sun-dried grass. Already I had come a great distance into the mountains, to the end of the run of cataracts that we had seen from outside; not to the end at all, I could see now.

Momentarily the river roared louder. The eddy where I spun, failed, overwashed, and I was swept on beyond a curve into the bowels of the mountains, which seemed to close overhead. Drunk on speed and fury I refused either fear or regret. I bethought myself I had chosen this course. I rode the black water, breathlessly, a long run into oblivion.

CHAPTER

3

Oblivion receded from me by such imperceptible degrees I could not have said when I was again conscious. I sensed that much time had passed, however, and long distances. I lay in darkness. I felt dazed—hurt—and thought there had been worse. Where—? I stared about me.

The darkness was not absolute. There was movement in it, vague and shifting, a figure. I realized; a person hunched at some scuffling, meaningless task. I rose, or tried to. "What—?" my voice croaked hoarsely. The figure turned. I hardly noticed, startled by the sound of my own voice, hissing and timbreless. What—?

I remembered. I had forsworn Empire. I had fled down the Flod. I wondered if I had died and come to one of the underworlds the Conquered Peoples talked of, such as no trueborn set any store by. For the trueborn there was but the one life, the life of Empire. With death it was over. When I had renounced my rights of birth, I had taken no thought I might have altered my death thereby. I remembered the cataracts of the Flod. . . . I might well have died there.

But was I dead? I had no memory of dying, and I began

to remember more: being beaten and battered by the river and rock and storm, not always in darkness. I remembered times of light. Days there must have been, when I drifted . . . yes, I had drifted, the water was salt, it burned. Ocean. I must have drifted beyond the end of the world into the salt sea that ringed it. Storms had come, wind and wave had driven me far over Ocean. Still I had not died, I thought. I had clung to some boards—the wreck of my boat, perhaps—refusing to die. I remembered the pounding rhythms of storm, the hateful, endless beating of Ocean all through my being. But I had not come to dying, no; I remembered I had been taken up. Suddenly I remembered with great clarity.

In the midst of the pounding roar of storm the sky had opened and a dazzling light spread over the stormy waves. Clouds standing on the very waves towered unimaginably high all around me, majestic, all-powerful, like gods sweeping across the skies. One bore down on me, bending very low to take me up. A long, pale, wedge-shaped head thrust forward from the mass of the cloud and wild, wide eyes fixed on me. Long legs flashed in a bright beam of sunlight, whirling like pinwheels, skimming disdainfully above water and ground, insubstantial cloudstuff, but alive, coming ever nearer. It was about to take me up, that cloudsteed— surely it *had* taken me up. . . . I looked around me, bewildered, at the darkness where I lay. How had I come here?

A face thrust suddenly close to mine: a swarthy, shadowed, thin-featured face lined from old pain and striving; a face that looked to be one of such as could inhabit the underworld of a Conquered People; slyly calculating, full of trickery and greed. I turned my face away. So near the other's was, I felt his breath warm and moist against my neck, and I knew he must be a living being like myself. He was the one I had seen hunched at some work. He muttered, louder than before, words that sounded alien in my ears. If I had not died and come to an underworld, still I had passed the ends of the true world. I had crossed Ocean and come to some other place, where I could not expect to find any who spoke the true language. But where—?

I peered past the denizen of the darkness, probing the darkness itself, and found it was ever less as my eyes became accustomed to it. I lay in some small, confining place, as I had already had some notion; beyond it was daylight, or perhaps only twilight. In my weakness the light seemed unreachably far, though it could not have been more than three paces' distance to the door of the shelter. Around me was a clutter of goods and tools, roughly made of leather and wood, poor-looking things. There was a smell of unwashed flesh and badly tanned hides. And that was all. Finally I looked more closely at my companion. He bent over me, talking still, excitedly. I shook my head and frowned.

He slid an arm under my shoulders. I stiffened, resenting his touch, too weak to resist whatever he willed. He held a container to my mouth and tilted it so a liquid ran out and I had to swallow it, though it felt like knives sliding, scraping, down my throat; it tasted only of pain. Anyway I knew I did live: by the pain I could be sure of it.

Still supporting my shoulders, the stranger reached behind him and brought forward another container, a leather bag from which came a rich smell of cooked meat. He fed me small pieces of meat and made me drink some of the broth. Despite the pain I began to eat more eagerly. Too soon he took the food away. I protested, and he leaned over me, speaking very fast. I thought, though, that I heard a word of the true language, then another—but none that made sense to me. "Raun," he concluded—his name.

"I am Oa," I said, disdaining to hide my name, slurring the sounds together into a single syllable as we did in the Imperial City, slurring even more perhaps, from weakness, though my voice was already stronger than it had been.

"Oa!" Raun repeated, leaning forward again, smiling with a boyish delight that stripped the years from him. I had taken him for old with his lined face, but now I saw he was young, a man grown, but not so many years older than I was. "Oa," he said again and again. He spoke whole phrases I could understand: a lordly name . . . years . . . waited for *you*. . . .

He had some notion who I was! It could only mean I lay

still within reach of Empire. At that thought, I knew how much I had wanted to be quit of Empire.

"—sea-glittering eyes," Raun said. "Close kin to Ocean . . . lord of Ocean—"

Ocean! Ocean was to me only a mindless heaving grayness, which had carried me helpless and tormented me. Didn't Raun know I was a lord of Earth and Empire—or had been? But he said nothing yet of Empire, and he touched his fingers gingerly to the lines of rank tattooed around my eyes, as if they were strange to him.

"—message," he said, "power . . . tell me . . . give me. . . ." And more. His bottomless black eyes, hounding, hungering, seemed to drink my very life. His words swirled around me, disconnected, clearly demanding. And yet he seemed also to fear me or revere me; he thought I was—or could be—a power in his world. If I would be what *he* willed.

It was Empire all over again, all that I had gone to such lengths to be free of. I flung myself away from Raun convulsively, crying out in refusal—and from the pain of my battered body when I moved. I would take my death, I thought wildly, before I lived any life this stranger willed. Around me the darkness increased. I was now dying, I thought as I sank back into oblivion.

I woke to a rustling noise and a stronger light. I lay naked under a leather covering in a small hide tent. I remembered it—and Raun. Turning I saw Raun also waking, sitting up and disentangling himself from another covering of skins. He grunted with painful effort and used both hands to pull his leg free, intent wholly on himself, without thought for me.

There was light now to see him clearly. He looked commonplace enough in daylight: a young, slender, male, face soft from sleeping, with lines of pain still showing in it, lighter against weathered skin—no denizen of any underworld, or even of any very strange world.

Raun stood up to pull a garment over his head. He was tall, disproportionately so for the slightness of his build. His body seemed somehow wasted. Then I saw his hip and thigh were slashed with four parallel scars the length of my forearm. The gashes had healed into thick ridges of dead-white flesh with hollows between them so deep it seemed to me the bone should be exposed. The muscles of that leg had shrunk. The leg below the wound was wizened. It was an old wound, long healed, and the distortion of it was what had twisted and wasted his entire body.

Raun's head emerged from the neck of his tunic, and he saw me staring. He pulled the tunic down over his knees and said bitterly, "You see . . . earth's creatures do with no hindrance from lords of Sky! You can't tell me the . . . favorites of Ocean are used in this way."

I understood almost all he said. I guessed then he had spoken the true language all along, if strangely; in my weakness I had not deciphered it. I saw his eyes were not at all ordinary: black, large, and deep. I scowled, remembering his demands of the dark night; what he said now was more of the same. "I'm hungry," I said.

He studied my face a moment in silence, then turned away to shrug his tunic into place. "If you're no lord of Ocean, then you must be housebound like me," he said. "You can fetch your own food."

"Housebound!" I said, echoing him, so astonished as to be distracted from archaic word which meant "trueborn." Thus the oldest legends in Empire called those who had followed Gandda—the heroes of the first days, who founded the Great Houses that ruled Empire. But in the daylight that came through the half-closed opening of the tent, it was clearer than ever there was nothing of the trueborn about Raun, dark, surly, misshapen, and impoverished as he was. And sly—he had not at all given up his demands of me; I could see he was only biding his time. "Housebound," I repeated scornfully. There was some mistake. I must not be understanding as clearly as I had thought. I said, "You look to me to be a slave from the Conquered Lands, and you may as well serve me."

He stared at me, his black eyes hard, with no slavish yielding in them. "Housebound," he said, bitter and angry, as if the word were an insult. "Yes, I am—and conquered, too. And so are you."

He went out, leaving me having spent the small store of strength I had built up upon the vain quarrel. Hunge nagged me more than disability, however. When Raun did not return, I stood up, weak and hurt as I was, pulling myself erect by one of the poles that held up the shelter. I stood shakily, breathing hard and painfully, feeling more aches and bruises I had not yet known of. My body seemed whole, if badly battered. When my head stopped spinning I looked about for clothes. Not finding my own I supposed they must have been lost in Ocean, and I put on a leather tunic like that Raun had donned. The garment was stiff and ungraceful and none too clean, but there seemed to be nothing better. I walked outside unsteadily and stopped short in amazement. Grasping the stiff leather of the tent, I stood blinking in the strong light that poured down the grassy slopes of a bowl-shaped valley, the pale, drying grass of late summer making the land seem naked under the enormous, brilliant sky. I might never have left the steppe where the Imperial City lay.

I turned full circle but did not see what I more than half expected, Empire's sprawling city proclaiming itself something to be reckoned with. Instead, in every direction, stood rough leather tents like Raun's, hundreds of them, I thought, packed closely, separated by narrow paths trampled into channels of soft dust. The tents were small and poor for the most part, dun-colored like the dry earth, no interruption at all to the spread of the open land.

There were people, as poor as their camp, all ages and both sexes dressed as I was in clumsy tunics slashed at neck and knee for ease of movement. They were Raun's fellows, I saw at a glance: housebound, as he would have it, in that ancient, honorable name of the trueborn. Let them have the name, I thought. For I had done with it.

No one turned to see to me, as if I were one of them, or of neither more nor less account than any one of them. Where they were looking, with quick, nervous glances, was up toward the rim of the valley. I followed their gaze 'th my eyes, and I forgot my aches and hunger.

'loud rose beyond the ridge into the morning sun, ' high into the sky. I thought at once of the won-'ng steed I had seen coming to take me up. This 'r, was dark and ominous, and it gave off a 'ar, like Ocean building up to a storm. Ocean could not be far off if Raun with his crippled leg had carried me from it. So he claimed and had likely done. The cloudsteed could only have been a trick of my mind when it was hard driven.

The dark cloud rose higher, the thunder grew louder. I shivered, clinging to the tent for support. In an instant, I thought, something vast and unspeakable will wash over the ridge into the valley. I faced it.

A greater darkness that seemed the base of the cloud crested the rim of the valley and rippled down the slopes like sheeting water.

"The lords of Earth," the people in the camp sighed as one, in a voice faint beneath the roaring thunder.

What came was beasts. The dark mass split into countless individual beasts, incomparably larger and wilder-looking than any animals in Empire. The cloud was the dust raised by their passage. The noise was the pounding of their feet and their bellowing voices. By their power and mass these beasts seemed the very essence of the darkness and weight of earth. Lords of Earth! In Empire we of the Great Houses were wont to style ourselves so. These beasts could better claim the name. I lost all sense of myself in the vastness of the spectacle.

The mass of beasts turned to circle the ridge, and a single file broke away from the others; these, I saw as they neared, were altogether different from the beasts in the mass of the herd. They were larger still but neither gross nor heavy. They moved gracefully, seemingly skimming above the ground, delicately—mockingly—acknowledging its existence by dips and rises in their flight paralleling the undulations of the earth's surface. Their long legs whirled like flashing pinwheels, setting their feet in a single line beneath them. They were of many colors: gray and white of clouds, dun and brown of earth, striped and blotched and speckled. A long fringe of hair ran the length of their necks and backs and down their tails and hind legs, and stood out from the wind of their passage.

They ran toward the camp, standing out ever more distinctly from the tumultuous backdrop of the herd behind them. Cloud and wind taken flesh, they seemed: the fellows of the steed I had dreamt. *But these were real.* I could not doubt it, for all I was so lightheaded that the scene wavered a little in my sight.

The creatures reached the outskirts of the camp, and I saw the scale of them was even larger than I had thought. Their backs topped my head by a considerable measure, and their long necks and tails arched still higher as they ran.

Then I saw lumps upon the long necks were riders. They crouched at the bases of their steeds' necks, their own bodies all but hidden in that crest of flowing hair that blended with the riders' own long hair. I leaned forward, as if I, too, rode.

Of course I did not. Raun appeared at my side and gripped my arm, hissing, "Get back into the tent! Quickly! Get out of sight before the windriders see you. You shall give your message only to *me!*"

"I have no message," I said angrily, clutching the tent with desperate fingers so he could not thrust me away where I could not see the steeds. Windriders, he said. And they rode windsteeds.

I succeeded in my aim. Raun's grasp remained tight on my arm, but he no longer tried to hustle me away when the long, slender legs of the windsteeds flashed by our very faces, and swirling tails writhed in the dust all around me. High over my head haughty faces rode the crest of the excitement into the camp—windriders.

The windriders jumped down, greeting the camp dwellers disdainfully—as well they might. Obviously they were a people apart, born to a higher fate. I stared in great wonder at their very appearance. They wore tight-fitting leather leggings and shirts that showed off their lean, muscular bodies. There were males and females both, with dark-tanned hawk faces exaggerated by hair pulled tightly back into long braids, which whipped about as they moved, like the tails of the windsteeds.

One after another they strode by with never a glance for me. Then came one for whom even such as they made way. The newcomer topped any I had seen by more than a head, and his build was proportionately massive. Everything about him was on a grand scale. Great matted hanks of black hair, braided in layers, framed his face in a tangle that fell below his waist and, together with a full, black beard, shrouded all his features save his glittering black eyes. He came toward where I stood with Raun, and he stopped. Harshly he said, "Does Raun then think to set up in his own House within mine?" I started at the rumbling, stormy strength of his voice, and drew my breath in sharply when I saw he watched Raun's hand on my arm.

Raun stiffened. With elaborate care he said, "Ajanna, my brother, my chief. I rejoice in your safe arrival."

"It appears you didn't expect me, that you make free with my housewomen," Ajanna answered—playing with Raun, perhaps. Doubtless a dangerous game.

Wondering then if the game was to claim *me*, I lifted my head and opened my mouth to protest. Still I could not easily follow the sense of what these folk said, though I was becoming used to the sound shifts and archaic words with which they distorted the true language. I delayed, uncertain, and my gaze crossed Raun's and I saw his was fixed on me greedily. He was very eager to hear what I might say. Brothers he and Ajanna might well be, I thought; made of the same stuff, though it was molded now very differently. I shut my mouth abruptly, thinking anything I said Raun would take to serve *his* purpose. I could not know if they would be mine.

Raun's face changed, set. When Ajanna reached for me Raun said quickly, "Ajanna, beware! Look. Think. This one comes from Ocean, sent for some purpose of Ocean you might do well not to meddle in."

"What do you say?" Ajanna asked impatiently. He did not wait for any answer. "Was your brain clawed like your leg? Or have you addled it gazing overlong at the sea? Will you say *I* owe reverence to watersprites?"

"You are a fool, Ajanna, for all you are a high chief!" Raun answered with some passion. "I have thought much on this matter since I fell from favor with lords of Sky. You know that the winds that rule our fate come from the sea—"

Ajanna laughed at Raun's vehemence and interrupted him. "Do you think I concern myself with the doings or fancies of housefolk? But I say one thing you shall not do:

you shall not interfere with those whose task it is to serve windriders."

He looked at me, and I looked back as best I could, and a sort of puzzlement came into his eyes and veiled that limitless openness of them. He frowned a little, measuring me, pausing. Then a young female, one of the housebound, slipped slyly under one of Ajanna's arms and pressed herself against him. "Ajanna!" she cried archly. "You won't want to waste your time with the flotsam Raun finds on the beach!"

Ajanna turned his head and glared at her, disposed to be angry. She stood her ground. He looked her up and down, as well he might, for she was very lovely, golden sleek with large, golden-brown eyes set in a delicate, heart-shaped face. She wore a long skirt of very fine, soft leather, nipped tight at the waist to show off the sleekness of her bare torso and the soft plumpness of her breasts and arms. Ajanna put one hand heavily on her shoulder. "Ah, Coory," he said dismissing me, "certainly my time wouldn't be wasted with you."

Cooing, Coory steered him into the large tent that backed an open area to one side of where we stood. Raun dropped my arm finally, and I almost fell—crippled as he was, it had been he who held me upright. I closed my eyes briefly, struggling just to stand, and when I opened them again it was to meet the gaze of a pair of eyes more wild and menacing than anything that had gone before.

The eyes were those of a windrider, a female with gaunt, hawklike features in a sallow face dominated by her enormous dark eyes. Dark, perhaps black, they were; the fathomless darkness they looked on made their own color unimportant. Her figure was as gaunt as her face, arms and legs grotesquely thin in the tight-fitting windrider's dress, looking the more so from the contrast of her body being grossly swollen with child. She walked alone even of windriders, within a cage of her long braids. The lank strands of her lusterless dark hair were slicked close to her skull and gathered at the nape of her neck, from which sprang the more than a dozen thin braids that hung to her knees, snapping snakelike along their length with her movements. She passed me by.

"Wiela!" Raun hissed at her. "What is this new madness?"

The windrider stopped short and fixed Raun with the gaze of her terrible eyes. "Madness?" she said. Softly, with menace, she went on: "I don't see that the frame of either my mind or my body concerns you."

Raun faced her more boldly than I thought I might have done. "You must excuse me!" he said. "I didn't know you could be such a fool as to throw away your rank in this fashion."

Her eyes narrowed. "It's Ajanna's doing, none of mine," she said in a queer, flat voice.

Raun's tone was as flat as hers. "Do you mean to say he did this by force?"

"Houseman, do you doubt my word?" she barked then. Raun shook his head doggedly. I looked from one to the other of them, and felt the air bristle with matters long past and unsaid, eerie and twisted, which raised the hair on the back of my neck. "Bah!" said Wiela, suddenly impatient, turning away. She caught my gaze on her. "And who are you to gawk at a windrider?" she demanded.

"Oa," I said hastily, standing my ground largely from being unable to move.

She stared, seeming taken aback. One of the watching housefolk broke the silence with a nervous snigger. "Oa! Where'd she get a lord's name?"

"A lord of Ocean," another mocked. "It means nothing. You heard Ajanna."

They laughed, low and meanly, wary of Wiela.

"Yes, a lord of Ocean," Raun said hotly. "What she brings may be much—for all of us!"

The other housefolk stared at him, hard-eyed. He would have gone on but Wiela interrupted. "Enough!" The harsh imperiousness of her voice stilled everyone. In the new silence she looked me up and down. "You look like any other housewoman, but for the eyes. It takes more than water-colored eyes to make a lord—even a lord of Ocean." Her gaze swung back to Ruan. "It's just another of your fancies," she concluded in cruel dismissal.

The silence that followed these words no one dared break until Wiela herself said to me, "You can come help me bathe, girl.'' She strode off without looking back to see if I obeyed. I did, limping slowly in her wake even while I thought I could not, that I did not have the strength left.

Wiela led the way through the camp and across an open stretch of grassland that sloped from the camp to a stream choked with stunted willow running down the bottom of the valley. She stopped beside a pool formed by a turn in the stream where the current slowed. She stood for me to undo the lacings that molded her leather riding dress so tightly to her body.

It was not only from arrogance that she had me wait on her: her body had been strained beyond its capacity and the only strength left to her was her will. I doubt even that could have forced her bony, bloodless fingers to this task she set me. Her eyes dulled with weariness overtaking her. The darkness she had seemed to look on so terribly was veiled over. Her weakness, greater than my own, eased my awe. She had been hard driven even before this latest strain of her pregnancy, I thought. I felt even some scorn for her putting herself to the discomfort of the stiff leather clothing. ''Why don't you wear something looser?'' I said. ''Surely you could be more comfortable.''

''Soon enough I'll have to lay aside my riding gear,'' she answered. ''I won't do it any sooner than I must.'' Her tone reminded me of all she was and stopped my further questions.

She sank into the pool of sun-warmed water and let the water take the weight of the body that had grown too heavy for her. I sat down on the bank nearby until she bade me shake the dust from her clothes and hang them in the brush to freshen.

When I came back to the pool a windsteed was also there. It stood in the deepest part of the pool, where the water rose nearly to its belly. The wedge-shaped head, as large as the trunk of my body, stretched on its long neck toward Wiela. A muzzle, which looked very soft, nudged her gently. The fleshy tail sank into the water and twitched, raising waves that lapped against Wiela's body and the banks of the stream, and tangled the long floating strands of her braids with its mane.

The creature raised its head at my approach and met my gaze. I was entranced: its eyes showed me the innermost being of the winds blowing free—wholly free, as I had never yet been. I remembered the beauty of the windsteeds running, the wind taken flesh they truly were. The windsteed took a step closer to me, and I reached out to touch it.

"Don't you dare!" blazed Wiela. "None but a windrider proven may lay hand on a windsteed!"

I snatched back my hand at her tone. "But—"

But nothing. Wiela stared right through me to the bare slope of grass rising behind me. My head sagged. I could not meet her unseeing stare. Finally I could only think as I had not yet that I had given up too much with my Imperial rank—even the heart of myself—and I was nothing.

Wiela stood and shook the water from her and bade me help her into her clothes. She went over all the lacings after I did them up, to pull them tighter. Then she turned her back on me and wound her hands into the long, wet strands of the windsteed's mane. Stepping on the knobby joints of one foreleg, she swung herself up to the windsteed's back, and they splashed across the stream.

I raised my head and followed them with my eyes. I felt in my own flesh an echo of the supple motion of the windsteed's acceleration and a faint taste of the release it must give from the heavy weight of earth. Although the sight only sharpened—painfully—my awareness of all that I lacked, I could not turn my gaze away.

The flying windsteed rose to the crest of the slope and disappeared over the other side.

CHAPTER

4

There seemed nothing for it but to return to camp—if I could manage even that much. I took one step at a time, favoring the one leg that hurt so much more than the other, though it hurt badly. Over that sun-beaten expanse of dry grass I trudged. The grass stalks were broken every which way into a chaotic thatch that was scattered with refuse from the camp: an ugly, careless midden wherever I looked. I lacked the strength to raise my gaze from it altogether.

"Watch where you're going!" came an angry voice.

Then I lifted my head, but the speaker had already gone on. I saw I had come back among the tents. There were many people bustling about excitedly, more so than before, I thought—about what, I could not see. The tents themselves, I saw, were laid out in a pattern. Lesser tents, such as that Raun had sheltered me in, scarcely tall enough for a person to stand erect, nor much wider than that height, ran in rows curved concentrically around a larger tent and a clearing. There were a score or more of such arrangements that I could see, and I could not see the whole of the camp. The lines of tents in the various sections ran against each other like conflicting wave trains, with some confusion at these borders. Each section was a House, I supposed, each with a chief—like Ajanna.

If the tents were ranged in some order, certainly nothing else was. The windsteeds had left the camp to run along the stream in the bottom of the valley. Afoot the windriders were scarcely less impressive than mounted. They stalked about the camp, lean and menacing, long braids flying. Everywhere they went housefolk swirled in their wake. It seemed to me a sort of storm raged through the people, as if the dark cloud of dust that presaged the arrival of the herds had indeed loosed some force to wreak havoc in the camp. And the herds themselves, the seemingly thousands upon thousands of monstrous beasts, circled the rim of the valley unceasingly with a deep rumbling mutter of noise that permeated everything.

I could not rest, hurt and worn as I was. I stumbled here or there in the wake of the others. No one seemed to notice, or care if they did. Anyone could see at once I was a stranger; there were no others of coloring so light as mine. By my stumbling weakness, my restlessness and poor clothing, I might have been one of the very least of the campfolk caste.

And notch by notch the excitement rose, all through the afternoon. Dust from the passage of the herds drifted down through the still air, filling the bowl of the valley with its clouds and the yeasty smell of the beasts. Like the others I coughed and gasped for breath—and like them trailed about, in search of what, I did not know. The excitement only grew.

At sunset there was a lull. Then a full moon rose beyond the ridge and the restless tide of the herdbeasts. Windriders strode with sudden purpose through the camp, as ever trailed by the housefolk. I came last of all.

At the edge of the camp was piled an enormous stack of sticks and dry brush. Lean, dark figures of windriders surrounded it. One came among them larger even than Ajanna: Murrila I heard him called, chief of all the chiefs. He carried a torch, in the light of which the windriders' eyes glittered like jewels. Ajanna himself and a dozen others bulking as large were isolated pillars towering over even windriders. Housefolk wormed between the windriders, who took no notice.

Three windriders brought a bound herdbeast calf to Murrila. Someone took his torch. The bawling calf fell silent at Murrila's touch. He jerked its head back, stretching its throat taut. He made one quick slice with a knife, and blood ran darkly over the woodpile. Deftly windriders skinned and butchered the carcass and laid the pieces about the woodpile.

Murrila took back the torch and swung it so it flared brightly. He thrust it into the woodpile; fire exploded with a roar in the dry fuel and rose in a reddened pillar toward the sky. Murrila cried out. In a wordless keening, his voice rose higher than the fire's roar, and the windriders' voices followed. The windriders stood straight and tall, staring up into the vast starlit sky where they sent their challenge—for challenge it surely was, I felt that clearly through all my exhaustion. The windriders looked twice their former stature. The housefolk slinking around them were no more than troubled shadows. I, a stranger, felt myself also lifted above any personal fate, toward a ritual plane, and I thought at last the strange, driving disturbance of the day moved toward release or resolution.

The first flames dropped down. The fire sighed and snapped into the larger pieces of fuel. Murrila's voice rose again above the noise of the fire: "Let the least among us stand forth!"

I looked about me, wondering who that might be, and was surprised to see a windrider step into the clear space left between the crowd and the bonfire; to the windriders, I supposed then, the campfolk were so much less as to seem nothing at all.

The windrider was young, naked but for painted marks on his face, and his oiled skin glistened. His braided hair was coiled tightly against his skull. He stared around at the crowd unblinking and said in a bold voice, "Braha I am, windrider and beastherder. Do any challenge my right to ride between earth and sky?"

Yes, I thought, they ride "between"—in a place apart, like ritual, like Dance. I shivered with anticipation, as if at the approach of that clear, high certainty of Gandish Dance.

I put it from me, though only slowly, when I remembered I had forsworn the things of Empire.

Half a dozen persons stepped forth, cloaked, male and female, young, hardly adult. Each placed a token in a skin bowl Murrila held. Murrila shook the bowl and, without looking, picked one token, which he held out in his open hand for all to see. The candidates bent forward eagerly. The one whose token it was gave a crow of triumph and threw off her cloak. I saw she too was naked and oiled, hair and skin alike tawny in the firelight. For a brief instant I thought I recognized her as a housebound female I had glimpsed in the afternoon: such fiery coloring of one had caught my eye. But her bearing made it obvious she came of the windriders' caste.

She stalked across the clearing and Braha swung around to meet her. They grappled. The crowd leaned forward as one, intent on their combat. Their slender, oiled limbs moved in a complex pattern, weaving together and tearing loose again, like no fighting I had ever seen in Empire, where it was mostly a matter of trickery and ambush and knives in the back. This *was* like Dance, having about it a sense of ceremony, simple though it was, compared to what I had known. Still, it held me, for I was hungry for some conclusion to the tension that had been building throughout the day.

A cry of triumph sounded. One of the combatants reared up, leaving the other lying motionless on the ground. It was the challenger who stood, the tawny female. She lifted her arms and cried out proudly, "I am Surya, windrider and beastherder!"

Murrila's deep voice sounded. "Surya, ride free. Ride with the wind."

Surya bowed her head to him very slightly and stalked from the ground, her young face hawklike in the fire's glow. I followed her with my eyes until she was lost in the crowd, wondering greatly that I could ever have mistaken her for housebound, so clearly she was a windrider. When I looked back at the open ground, the other was gone without a trace. He was greatly shamed by his loss, it seemed. I heard some housefolk refer to him as "Brah," cutting his name short in their contempt. I did not see them call him so to his face, however.

"Let the next stand forth!" Murrila bellowed.

One after another windriders came out onto the ground to await challenge. Each moved and spoke and fought much in the manner of the first. The very simplicity and rawness of the bouts gained a sort of power in that setting of open air, bonfire, and glittering, intent faces. But each bout ended without ever touching *me*. Restless, I shifted my weight from one foot to the other.

"Lirra!" came a hissed warning at my side. I started and turned and realized the hissing was the name of a windrider moving forward so close to me I had to take a step backward lest she collide with me. Her gaze, set on the bonfire, ran past me unseeing. She seemed afire herself; I could feel a great heat coming off her. She was all of a single color, or seemed so in the dimness, a dusky brown: eyes, skin, coiled braids, the leather cloak tied loosely at her throat. It was a drab color, but there was sparkle and fire enough in her movements. She threw off the cloak and entered upon the ground. I marveled that any came to challenge her, and marveled more when I saw her fight. But her opponent was scarcely less skilled or slower than she. When at last Lirra stood motionless above her beaten opponent, I let my breath out very slowly, more loath than before to be let back down into my own self.

The bouts that followed Lirra's were between partners similarly skilled, and were equally prolonged: the challenges had progressed to more experienced ranks of windriders. Still there was nothing for me. I looked about, dissatisfied, and saw Raun in the crowd, easily recognizable by his height and his silhouette misshapen with his crippling. I edged close to him. "What are they fighting *for*?" I whispered in frustration.

He grunted. "One who'd ride must prove worthy. It's fitting that a windrider's rank must be justified by thorough and repeated trial. Ocean itself couldn't arrange things differently. Ranking is inherent in the differences among people."

Windriders must fight just to prove themselves what they were? I would not have guessed: I had seen none whose rank *I* would have questioned, no more than in Empire, where the Imperial kin ruled by inherent right of race. Blood could be renounced, to be sure—and rank perhaps lost. I wondered then if Raun had not once been a windrider and lost his right to ride when his leg was crippled. "What happens to the losers?" I asked.

I was watching the face of one who had just lost the current bout. As Murrila confirmed his failure, his windrider's arrogance faded; he darted about him sly, nervous glances as he slunk from the ground. He shrank into himself until there was no resemblance at all to the tall windrider who had proudly stridden out upon that ground. "He's lost his windsteed," I breathed.

"Yes," said Raun in a short, bitter growl that I took to confirm my guess that he too had once ridden and then fallen.

"There aren't enough windsteeds for everyone who could ride to live a windrider's life?" I asked Raun.

"Lords of Sky, as I told you, are cruel," he answered with a sly, sidelong glance at me. He went on matter-of-factly however, "They'd have us know what it is to be deprived of their favor. There're only a certain number of windsteeds, and their number doesn't grow, for new births are as rare as deaths."

"Then the windsteeds don't care who rides them?"

"They have their rankings. Anyone can see that. It's a chief's duty to match a windsteed with a rider who's worthy—if he wouldn't shame the windsteed and offend the lords of Sky who favored him with his chief's rank!" Raun broke off and hissed in a sudden intake of breath. I followed his gaze to the Ranking ground.

Wiela stood there. Her misshapen body was grotesque in the distorting light of the fire. The break in the succession of sleekly muscled bodies jarred on everyone. She could not fight in her condition. And her face jarred even more: her expression. Those wild eyes seemed to have looked on much more than other folk ever did. The windriders shifted about uneasily, and housefolk whispered among themselves.

Wiela spoke up proudly, varying the formula. "I, Wiela, have already been bested off this ground—as all can see. Take *his* leavings, who dares!"

"The fool!" Raun hissed. No one heeded him, particularly of the many who crowded onto the ground to cast tokens.

After the lot was decided the disappointed took themselves away muttering, leaving a female I had seen beaten in an earlier bout. She moved toward Wiela, who stood with bent head. The other touched Wiela's shoulder in token of victory. "Hadda I am," she said nervously, not very loudly. And then, to Wiela, "You're welcome in my tent." There would be no fight, I saw. Still I held my breath.

A larger figure strode onto the ground: Ajanna. "As the only parent of rank, I claim the child—and its mother," he called out in his harsh voice. Hadda shrank back from him unprotesting into the crowd. Wiela stood her ground, lifting her head finally, staring at Ajanna with an odd expression, a half smile on her lips. She looked as if she thought she had after all somehow won.

Raun stared at her transfixed. "She's housebound," he exclaimed. "She has no rights against a windrider. Why does she insult Ajanna? He would not fight off the Ranking ground. No one could think this is *his* doing—"

Wiela's strange gaze swung suddenly toward Raun, as if she had heard him, though I did not see how she could have through all the other noise, or seen him out of the light that shone by now only on the Ranking ground, for the fire was burning low. Raun broke off speaking abruptly.

Murrila called for the next bout with unusual intensity, and both Ajanna and Wiela left the ground. After several more bouts, Raun said, "These are chiefs who fight now."

They were not, at first, of Ajanna's rank or stature; when those high ranks were reached, there was in fact less to see. Each took a turn on the empty ground, and spoke the ritual invitation to challenge, but they spoke it in a perfunctory manner, and one after another went unanswered. Housefolk began to talk freely among themselves. I watched the high chiefs. "They all wear riding dress under their cloaks," I exclaimed. "They have no thought of fighting."

Beside me someone snorted. "Even they think twice about fighting the likes of themselves."

"Nonsense," Raun said irritably. "All their lives are

one long combat. They're always watching for a weakening among the others. They fight on the Ranking ground—but only when they're certain it's worth their while."

"Who can wonder, considering what can happen!" said the other out of the darkness.

I asked, "Does Murrila think someone will challenge him?" I had caught a glimpse of oiled skin beneath Murrila's furred cloak.

"Oh, no," said Raun. "There's been none to challenge Murrila for many seasons. But he takes nothing lightly. He would not deign to think he could *not* be challenged."

But it seemed there was a challenge against Murrila. The crowd, which had begun to drift away, surged back with renewed interest.

"What is it?" cried those who could not see through the press. The bonfire had burned so low it gave no light at all. Voice rose out of the darkness on every side of me.

"Someone challenges Murrila!"

"A challenge! A challenge!"

"It's Ajanna!"

"You are hasty, Ajanna," snarled Murrila. His deep voice rumbled through the crowd, lower than any other.

"That we have yet to see," returned Ajanna in a haughty tone.

"See? When do you, Ajanna, ever look to *see* anything, save what you wish to believe?" Murrila returned witheringly.

Ajanna hissed. "I heed nothing that is not real!" He did not seem to be disagreeing with Murrila, who did not answer back again. Others spoke in low voices, wordless murmurs, unheeded. All fixed on the two chiefs standing in moonlight looking even larger and more mysterious than they were: vast beings of shadow, silent now they were closing on each other. In a single mass they rolled across the ground. The crowd hushed. For a timeless interval the only sounds were the sighing of the faint night wind and the rasping breath of the fighters.

Was this then the culmination of the long ritual? It had come almost as an afterthought, with nothing about it of purpose or preparation. And yet I waited, I and the others, housefolk and windriders, to see what would come of it.

The rolling clump came to a stop. It separated into two figures, one rising above the other.

"Who won? Who won?"

I was carried forward in the press over the dark ground. No one could see which was which, those two figures were so like each other.

An arm rose against the sky. Murrila's voice came unevenly and gasping at first, then steadied. He confirmed his rank as chief of all the chiefs. He moved away with windriders and housefolk clustering about him, while Ajanna lay where he had fallen, a motionless lump on the dark, deserted ground. The Ranking ritual was finished. It had come to nothing. I hardly cared; I could take no more. Dazed, I stood to one side of the press streaming away from the Ranking ground.

Raun called out, "Oa! Are you there?" I moved toward the sound of his voice, only because it was familiar, and found he stood beside the last faint embers of the bonfire, over the dark hulk that was Ajanna. "Help me, Oa," Raun said, bending down. "It would be a coward's trick to leave him lying here." His tone stung me so I bent down beside him.

Between us, Raun and I got Ajanna to his feet and walking—we could not carry his weight. Ajanna grunted when I shifted his arm across my shoulder. He leaned on us heavily, caring nothing who we were. Raun guided us through the camp to Ajanna's large chief's tent. We dropped Ajanna onto skins piled for a bed. He groaned and lay still.

Raun disappeared and returned with a torch, driving before him a cluster of slim-hipped girls, Coory and some others, all giggling. They fell silent when they saw Ajanna. "Wash him, and bind his injuries," Raun ordered them. He cuffed one who stood back from the task.

Ajanna spoke softly, "Ah, Coory, my lovely. Send for kwass to drink and sit here beside me." Coory cast a triumphant look at Raun and the others. She handed them the objects she carried and composed herself on the bed. Her bright eyes watched everything.

I shrank into a corner and bumped against a figure

sitting there huddled in the dark. "Oh! Wiela—" I said in
dismay, and broke off at the blank, hard look she gave me.

Raun's voice came from behind me, as hard. "Wiela no
longer, by her own doing." I looked around at him,
puzzled. "The Wind's Sigh," he explained. "The honor-
ific ending of her name is only for windriders, not for
housebound folk like Wiel."

I realized all the names of windriders that I had heard
ended thus in the lilting syllable that was the whole of my
name as we pronounced it in Empire. The Wind's Sigh,
was it? No wonder these people were astonished to hear
my name. I made a wry grimace; I could hardly think
much could come of the chance.

Raun moved aside, answering some demand Ajanna
made, and I caught Coory's eyes measuring both Wiel and
me. I stared back at her grimly, and she finally looked
away, but not before I had caught a flash of spite from her
lovely eyes. I slumped to the ground, borne down by the
thought that the petty, conniving ways of Coory's like
must now also be my fate.

I was not yet to get any peace. A rush of windriders came
into Ajanna's tent, calling out in loud voices, excited,
striding up and down, unable to be still. Like great leather
wings they flung their cloaks back from their naked, oiled
bodies, now also covered with dust and bruises, and they
seemed even wilder and larger than before.

Ajanna pushed himself up on one elbow to face them,
his black eyes glittering. "Ha! Bretta!" he exclaimed.
"Kiia. Is that you, Galta? Housefolk, fetch kwass for
these windriders to drink!"

"Hail, Ajanna!" answered the one Ajanna had called
Bretta, a young, well-formed male who I remembered had
given a good account of himself in the fighting. "You
showed Murrila up! The time'll soon come you'll beat
him, and we'll run his vast herders as *your* herders."

Ajanna scowled at him. "Have you given up your rank
to become housebound? What do windriders care for beasts
and possessions?"

Someone thrust a drinking skin at Ajanna. He drained it
in a single long draft and tossed it to the ground, saying

harshly, "I'll take Murrila, in the end. But not for his House. Only because I *will not* see anyone ride before me." The others fell silent, abashed, as well they might be, by the very tone of Ajanna's voice. Who could doubt he could encompass all he willed?

Ajanna lay back, resting his head against Coory's sleekness. The others looked about awkwardly at each other until one gave a reckless laugh and said, "I'll drink to that!" Then all spoke hastily at once while they passed the skin bags containing fermented herdbeast milk, the drink they called kwass. Under cover of serving the windriders, the housefolk in the tent also sneaked a share of the kwass for themselves.

Lirra came in, leading two others. The bright, flashing vitality she had going onto the Ranking ground was turning strident. Her eyes and her voice were wild. Like all the others she was drinking heavily.

More came, whose names I didn't know, chiefs as well as herders from many Houses. The tent grew crowded, and the air very close. Restless windriders needed a lot of space. In the mood they were in, it seemed to me risky to collect so many in the confinement of a tent. I pushed myself as far out of the way as I could against the wall of the tent.

A windrider lurched drunkenly across the tent and grabbed a young housewoman coming in with more drinking skins. The two fell heavily together amid gurgling skins. I could not see them for the press, but now and then I heard the sounds of their scrabbling lust, as awkward and hasty as that of revelers in the back streets off the Northern Road in the Imperial City on festival nights. I sat stiff with scorn. Any who dared to try to so use me would get a surprise! But I also felt the windriders' heat, and knew I would not be sorry to find a partner for myself this night—that was one way to release. But it must be someone I chose for myself. I looked over the people in the room, both windriders and housefolk, with this new purpose in mind, a purpose for which caste differences had never mattered much in any land.

Behind me a deep voice said with amusement, "Even

those who ride between earth and sky sometimes stand with their feet on the ground—even in the dirt.''

I looked around to find a windrider nearly as large as Ajanna standing in the doorway looking over the scene. He looked nothing like Ajanna but for the size; colored dun and ruddy; large, but quiet as the earth itself. I did not remember him among the chiefs at the Ranking, nor from any of the fighting. He wore no ceremonial trappings; under his plain herdbeastskin cloak his body was naked and oiled. When the other windriders greeted him with easy friendliness, I learned his name was Halassa.

Across the tent, Lirra came to her feet in a single, fluid motion when she saw Halassa. The wildness in her burned low, I saw; it no longer snapped out threateningly. She walked steadily though she was surely drunk. ''Let's leave them to it,'' she said to Halassa, reaching an arm beneath his cloak to clasp him companionably around the waist. Laughing softly, they went out together into the night.

They were as fine and proud as any had been for the ritual fighting, but with the fire in them burned down to embers that could warm the other without danger. Such easy companionship between lovers was something I had never seen in Empire. Watching them out of sight, remembering what Halassa had said on entering the tent, I said aloud, ''Those two don't seem to touch their feet to the ground.'' Hearing me, Wiel gave a snort.

''That's easy enough while lords of Sky hold them up,'' she said in a bitter voice. ''They don't know what lies beneath them.''

To myself I acknowledged there were many things I had done that I might not have dared if I had known what could come of them. If I had known what awaited me here, would I have left Empire—no matter the price of staying? I sighed. I didn't know. I couldn't think. The noise and frenzy of the windriders crowded into the tent beat at me until I could think of nothing but escaping them. Everyone was so drunk, even the housefolk, I thought no one would notice—or care—if I came out from my shadowed hiding place. In Halassa and Lirra I saw just how far yawed the gulf between windrider and housebound. Individuals could fall—witness Wiel—but none could rise.

And it was only the arrangement of Empire. But there I was born to the top. Heavy indeed of heart, I croseed the tent and slipped out into the night.

The moon newly risen at the beginning of the rites was setting. The air was cool with deep night, refreshing after the confinement of Ajanna's tent, the noise of the continuing revels elsewhere in the camp diluted by the vastness of the earth and the night. I was loath to go to my solitary bed in Raun's small tent. Instead I walked away from the camp down toward the stream that ran in the bottom of the valley.

The windsteeds, which had earlier run screaming, were calmed. Their massive forms stood here and there in groups, looking like outcroppings of solid rock, nothing like the embodiment of wind that they were in motion. I could think I had imagined the glamour of the windsteeds and their riders. Such things could not easily be real.

More clearly, I saw in my mind scenes of the Imperial City on the Flod, where my life had been full and significant. I thought of the long hours I spent in practice preparing myself for the High Dance. When I had Danced alone for a long time in the silent, lofty, sparely furnished practice halls behind the palace, my mind would become one with my flesh, and my body would move wholly in accord with my will, and my will would seem a high, sure purpose—in such moments I had forged my ambition to take and hold the dynasty of Gand.

But it came to nothing. I wondered now if Ajanna had felt something similar when he challenged Murrila. I would not have thought it from the fighting, but his proud declaration just now made me think again. I paced hastily some distance with my mind in a whirl from which the patterning of the High Dance slowly emerged. In my muscles I felt the set movements of limbs and body, the difficult discipline of breath and stillness. I felt in my blood the ordering that came of the patterns, and knew thereby how all other, lesser Dancers would have been molded to my will by my performance: fifteen, twenty, thirty Dancers— more, perhaps, I could have pulled from themselves to move at *my* will. If I had stayed in Empire.

I paced that alien plain in the darkness, thinking—

feeling—the Dance I had never *seen* or felt in its fullness. The simple ritual of the windriders' fights came to me again. It had held the people—it had touched me, though it could not satisfy me. How much stronger would be the hold of the High Dance! If I had started upon it, truly I would not have been able to refuse its culmination—in the Dynast's will and in Jily's death. My decision to leave Empire was surely justified. I could not have stayed. I *would* not regret leaving.

But I had lost Jily anyway. And though I was free of Empire, I was nothing.

There came a slight noise, a windsteed perhaps. At the thought of the windsteeds my bitterness increased. I knew I must not think they were not real. Though they could not be mine, they were the center of the life of this plain. I realized I had been pacing back and forth ever more anxiously. No doubt it was I who disturbed the windsteeds so they moved about. I stood still, then, but I could not stop my fingers twisting ceaselessly together, twining uselessly about nothing.

It grew lighter. The windsteeds took on flesh and life and no longer resembled rock. I saw there was a young one, no taller than I was, all legs and neck with a short brush of a tail sticking straight up in the air. The noise I had heard was its play with the very shadows of dawn. Leaping and prancing, it seemed itself to flicker in and out of being; my eyes could scarcely follow it through the uncertain light of the new day. The other windsteeds paid no heed to the foal's antics or to me. Nipping delicately at straws of dead grass, they nickered companionably to each other and slowly moved away.

Full day came. I pushed my way into the brush that grew thick along the stream. I made a bed among the dry leaves and there, at last, I slept.

CHAPTER

5

Sinn stood in my path, sturdy and grizzled, the oldest of Ajanna's housefolk, expecting to be obeyed. "Oa!" she barked. "You may call yourself what you want. But you are no windrider and you shall work if you will eat."

I gazed away over her left shoulder, silent in my sullenness. Had I forsworn Empire to become a slave among Sinn's people? But I had returned to their camp when I had finally slept my fill. And I *was* hungry.

Looking away from Sinn toward the camp, I saw housefolk moving like ghosts through heavy curtains of the smoke from green wood fires. They were smoking the meat of herdbeasts. The smoke made my eyes water. The stench of butchering was everywhere. A group of housefolk knelt over the work of preparing winter sausage that Sinn wanted me also to do. One of their number held my gaze, one who worked among the rest without yet losing anything of her air of difference: Wiel. She wore no tight-fitting windrider's leathers now, but shapeless housefolk garb, and her braids were ragged and slatternly. But if she would do this menial work, I thought, so would I. Without answering Sinn I went, still limping a little, to take the place that was vacant beside Wiel.

There were fresh hides spread on the ground, piled with meat scraps and with berries from the thickets by the stream. Skin bags held fat rendered from herdbeast marrow bones. Wiel hunched over a large bowl formed from the shoulderblade of a herdbeast, wielding a long, round-tipped leg bone of a herdbeast to pound these several ingredients into a paste. As soon as I saw what she was about, I took over the task of adding the bits of meat and other ingredients, leaving her two hands free for the pounding. When Wiel judged the paste ready, we stuffed it into the long tubes of herdbeast intestines. Then I took over the mallet while Wiel mixed another batch of the sausage stuffing.

We were not left long to work in peace. The others worked only by fits and starts and from the outset resented that Wiel and I worked steadily. More and more of them left their places to stand about us and call our industriousness mean-spirited. Wiel kept at her work and truly seemed not even to notice the others. I stared at them disdainfully, the while methodically pounding the paste, and those who chanced to cross my gaze dropped their gaze before mine.

That they could not stare me down made them angrier. In a group they came for me finally, surrounding me on all sides and dragging me roughly to my feet. They scattered the bowl of sausage makings, and then Wiel scolded.

"Stay out of our way," one of them answered back.

They had no awe of her now, it seemed. I could have no awe of *them*, even when they held me powerless. I stood with my head high, disdaining to struggle vainly in their hold. But a houseman thrust his face into mine so suddenly I started.

"Hold still!" he exclaimed. "I want to see these marks I've been hearing so much of." His fingers pulled at my eyelids, none too gently, and rubbed the tattooed skin at my temples. "It doesn't come off," he said.

"Of course not!" another answered him mockingly. "Those are marks of the highest rank Ocean knows. Didn't Raun say so?"

"Oh, she's a great lord!"

They laughed heartily, though they glanced again and again over their shoulders toward the bulk of Ajanna's large chief's tent, where some windriders were.

"Think of her name!" one gasped between bursts of laughter. "Oa!" And they laughed yet harder.

Raun's claims for me, and my own name, had let me in for a joke that it seemed could not pall. But I had had enough of it. Goaded, I hissed, "I am a lord! A higher lord than any of you'll ever see, let alone be!" But it was obvious to me these people understood nothing beyond their own narrow lives. Neither the person they made such sport of my being nor the Imperial heir I truly had been could mean anything to them. They saw only I was no windrider and concluded I was game for their jibes; it was useless to answer them back. I pressed my lips tightly together, determined to give them no more satisfaction. But they had gotten me to speak one time and did not soon give up hope of more sport.

"What's this bickering?" came a lazy voice from the direction of Ajanna's chief's tent.

At once the housefolk let go of me. I looked around to see a windrider come around the side of the tent. It was Lirra. I knew her at once: the one who had so impressed me with her fire in the Ranking fights. She looked impressive also in daylight, lean and muscular, tall as I was, square-shouldered and well-built. Her flat face resembled my own Imperial features. Her skin and eyes were alike brown, her eyes slightly lighter in hue, enhancing thus her appearance of wildness. Her brown hair hung below her knees in six or eight separate braids which started from a line of parting drawn around her head like a crown. With every step she took the braids whipped and coiled about her, so she looked like a dustdevil advancing through the camp. Her gaze flickered over us.

"Housefolk," she said dismissingly.

It was a moment before I remembered that was here no term of honor. Meanwhile the others thrust me in front of them to shield them from Lirra's notice. I stood and stared at Lirra, near as fascinated by her as by the windsteeds. I felt great awe, as for windsteeds running, but no fear. She was dangerous, certainly, but not petty.

Adjanna loomed suddenly behind Lirra, bulking so much larger he made her look fragile, though she was not. He showed no signs now of the beating he had taken so recently from Murrila. He held himself easily, with an air in his very stance of barely restraining himself by even his great strength. Other windriders followed him. Behind them I saw also Raun, his eyes alert in his narrow face. Always, Raun watched me; at least he had left off voicing his demands.

"She says she's a lord!" one of the housefolk, sheltering behind me, suddenly hissed—made nervous by the windriders' interest. Ajanna and the others looked me up and down. He did not remember me, I thought.

"A lord of what?" he asked. Even when he spoke as now in idle curiosity, wildness lurked in his voice. His presence shook me—and drew me. I forgot Lirra. I faced him, the very dangerousness of him drawing me.

"Lord of—" I began boldly, and then I paused, thinking where my careless outburst might lead, thinking I must hoard my store of knowledge until I discovered if I could make any use of it. I dropped my gaze. "I will be a lord among you," I said lamely.

The windriders stared, then laughed with real amusement, and I burned at seeing how unbridgeable was the distance between them and me. It was a stratagem of housefolk to slyly keep quiet when faced with windriders, but I saw no other course open to me. I held my tongue.

Ajanna grunted, already losing interest. "Housefolk! They're all the same. They talk too much and work too little. While you're yet condescending to be housebound, girl, fetch us some kwass to drink." He turned to go back into his tent.

The housefolk spoke up again, maliciously refusing to see me let off so easily, blaming me for the scare they had brought on themselves by their disturbance that attracted the windriders. "Why does she wear marks of rank?" they cried.

"What?" Several windriders turned back from Ajanna's train and came close and peered into my face: Kiia, I think, and Galta. The housefolk shrank away, but I stood my ground and stared levelly into those wild, restless eyes that were more like those of windsteeds than of any humans. Kiia wet a fingertip and rubbed at my temples as the houseman had done, but of course the marks did not rub off. "It can't amount to much," he concluded. "It can't be very high rank. You can hardly see such thin, pale lines."

"It can be no rank at all unless it's ratified on the Ranking ground," Galta said sharply.

"Isn't this the girl the housefolk pulled out of Ocean?" Kiia persisted.

Galta shrugged. "What can it matter where a housewoman comes from?" Together they looked at me a moment longer before they turned to follow their fellows into Ajanna's tent. "Kwass," they called back then over their shoulders.

"Kwass, girl!" the housefolk repeated, mocking me.

"Not for you!" I said. But I pitched my voice low enough that the windriders could not hear. Not from fear, but because I did not want to seem as petty and small-minded as the others. A small distinction, perhaps: if not to myself, to the windriders and housefolk I was housebound. "You forgot to tell them my name!" I added, taunting them.

They looked at me strangely and made no move to recapture me. "There's only so far one goes with windriders," one said soberly.

I snorted with disdain and walked off as boldly as I could, still limping, leaving the work.

I did not go far, and I soon came back, for lack of any alternative.

Ocean was at hand, to be sure. The little creek that watered the valley where the camp lay ran through a narrow gap in the bluff directly out to the sea. I was loath to trust myself again to Ocean, however. In any event I had lost my boat, and the willow scrub along the stream would scarcely suffice to build another. I asked Wiel what lay in other directions.

"The plain," she answered, surprised.

"And then? Beyond the plain?"

"South lie the fens," she said.

"Fens? Swamplands? And a great river perhaps?" She shrugged; I guessed she did not know but would not admit it. I guessed there might be the Flod spreading wide and slow below the cataracts. For Ocean lay to the west, that I could see plainly; so if I remained in the true world at all, I could not have crossed Ocean. Storm and current must have driven me along the coast of a land that must also somewhere border on the river Flod, north or south, and Empire, west of the nameless mountains. "In other directions?" I persisted. "No plain can run forever."

Wiel scowled. "Inland, far, far inland, the land breaks," she acknowledged.

"Mountains, do you mean?" But Wiel could—or would—not explain anymore. She had never seen the Broken Lands, she said. I tried another tack. "What other peoples are there on the plain?"

"There are no other peoples," she said flatly.

"What of me?" I asked, smiling a little.

"You are housebound." Her voice held a windrider's careless scorn. "There's nothing 'other' about you." And with that, she made clear, I had to be content.

And truly even if the plain was not endless, it doubtless ran farther than I could walk even when I recovered fully from the journey that had brought me here. And there was one more, very telling, argument: if this land was only bordered by Empire, that was where I had no mind to return, even now. This land was, I supposed, the Land of the West of the legend of Gandda—my chosen destination. Now I had reached it, I could not see I had any benefit of it. But I could not either believe *I* would come to nothing. For now, however, I could only bide my time, though it galled me, for I was not accustomed to any such restraint.

I kept much to Wiel's company. I think her distaste for me was less than for the others without rank, because I was as much a stranger to housebound life as she was. Perhaps I did not remind her so strongly of what she had lost. I don't know if her former companions among the windriders would have continued friendly to her; she gave them no chance. In fact, if Wiel noticed anyone at all, it was Raun. He and she and I soon fell into a closeness that might have arisen more from scorn and suspicion and self-seeking than from liking, but was none the less enduring. And in that, perhaps, we were only like all housefolk.

Some days after the Ranking fights the weather changed. The sea winds grew chill and brought ragged clouds over the camp, though as yet no rain fell. Frost withered the dry grass and leached the color from it, so the ground looked even barer than before. I knew this weather: the season of the Sere Wind we called it in Empire. Winter would follow it closely. There came to be a sense of urgency in the camp, increased by the bellowing of the herdbeasts, which were getting short of food and hungry.

One morning the windriders of the high chief Osia, whose House camped next to us, all rode out together and did not return. Those of another House followed, and another. The herds circling the rim of the valley shrank.

A few days later Ajanna strode from his tent just as I was passing. He bore himself tautly, so even his great mass and weight seemed too slight to contain his spirit, and his gaze passed through me without a flicker. Involuntarily, I shivered and stepped back, lest he notice me and turn that awful gaze on me in earnest.

I need not have bothered. He was watching some windsteeds coming toward him, utterly silent, over the open ground. Their footsteps made no sound on the soft ground, nor did their tossing heads or waving manes. The very sight of them stopped the breath in my body. The grueling, petty life of this camp became insubstantial as an unpleasant dream beside the higher reality of windsteeds, even for me who could not enter into that other life.

The windriders of Ajanna's House strode from their tents swinging their long cloaks across their shoulders: Lirra, Halassa, Surya, Kiia, and all of the others. They sprang upon their windsteeds and locked their feet in the hollows of the windsteeds' throats. Without a word of farewell or a backward glance they were gone, taking the last of the herdbeasts from the ridge.

The camp seemed abandoned with only housefolk left. But we were also to leave, I learned, on a long trek to the fenlands in the south Wiel had spoken of, to escape the fury of winter storms in this open land. Desultorily the housefolk turned to taking down the tents and loading the

gear on the aged herdbeasts left by the chiefs of the
Houses. We set off a day or two later, on foot, in a long,
untidy column. We could make no brave show such as the
windriders had done.

There was no road marked on the plain for us to follow.
Once we topped the ridge and left the track made by the
herds, we entered on a vast, rolling land bounded only by
the horizon, where the waving grasses dissolved without
hindrance into sky. It was a land large and empty enough
to dwarf all individual creatures, as Wiel had intimated. I
felt it and, though no one forced me and I was near
recovered from the battering and bruises I had got on my
journey upon the Flod and Ocean, I stayed with the others.

By the third day of the trek Coory fancied she was with
child. Raun said she always did so on the long treks
between summer and winter camps and the truth was that
she was lazy and feared the exercise of walking would blur
her delicate lines. But to spare the rest of us her ill temper,
she got her way, and rode in a litter dragged behind a
herdbeast.

Wiel would have none of riding in a litter pulled by
wretched herdbeasts. Gaunt as she was, her time looked
far nearer than she said it was. She walked, and kept the
pace. Slow as that pace was, Raun could not keep up.
Every day he fell behind and did not drag his withered leg
into camp until long after dark. That, too, became routine
as we moved day after day across the plain, guided by sun
and stars, the routine broken only by the river canyons that
we came upon without warning, as if the plain had only
then gaped open.

Climbing down the steep wall to the narrow ribbon of a
stream in the bottom of a canyon and up the other side was
usually an entire day's task. The descent into these depths
of the earth, shadowed even at midday, made the housefolk
uneasy. They refilled the water containers and scrambled
with rare haste and energy to regain the plain.

One night after we had spent the day crossing a canyon,
Raun did not come into camp before the rest of us had
gone to bed. The nights had grown chill enough that I lay
snuggled under sleeping skins with even my head covered,

but still I heard Wiel's restless tossing, and I slept poorly. Toward dawn she woke me again. "What ails you?" I called to her.

"Nothing," she said crossly. "Go to sleep." But I poked my head out, and beyond her I saw the dark pile of Raun's sleeping skins still folded, unused.

"Why, Raun's not come in yet!" I exclaimed.

"I know!" Wiel said. Her face was a pale blur, her expression hidden by the darkness. Her voice was full of foreboding. I sat up in alarm.

"What is it? You think something has happened to him?"

"The fool has gone up the river we crossed today," Wiel said in a strained voice. "He couldn't be satisfied with his leg ruined, my rank lost—"

I remembered tales Sinn and the other elders whispered nights around the fire, of catbeasts nearly the size of grown windsteeds who lived in the depths of canyons as far from the sky as they could get, creatures of darkness and destruction, who shunned daylight. Because they were there, windriders hunted them. Ajanna and some of the others, mostly the high chiefs, wore necklaces of rivercat claws and cloaks of fine furred skins.

"That's how Raun ruined his leg!" I exclaimed. "In a rivercat hunt. He *was* a windrider!" I had half guessed it, but could not really imagine Raun, sour, grizzled, and misshapen as he now was, to have been a free-striding windrider.

"Yes, he was a windrider," Wiel murmured in a low, mourning voice. "A windrider such as few have been. I've seen many grow to their strength, but never was one so openly favored by lords of Sky. Rauna was as strong and fearless as Ajanna and sharper-witted by far. Rauna laughed at hindrance and danger, as any windrider does, but he saw them clearly and was the greater for it. Not Ajanna but Rauna should have won this House in which we are bound. He should have ridden first, before all." Her voice grew venomous and so low I had to listen carefully to hear what she said. Even then I could not understand her well.

"I curse you, Ajanna!" Wiel hissed. "For all you've

taken from me together with the sight of Rauna riding to meet me. I thought I finally had you. You tricked me but I shall yet get you!''

''But how did Ajanna cause Raun's injury?'' I exclaimed, confused. ''You said a rivercat—?''

''Everyone knows the two brothers went hunting a rivercat,'' Wiel answered disdainfully. ''When they returned Ajanna carried Rauna, bleeding and fevered from poisoned wounds, before him on his windsteed, and a fresh catskin strapped on behind. It's the skin and claws of that cat that Ajanna wears. Ajanna said the rivercat, slightly wounded, had ambushed them and clawed Rauna but he, Ajanna, had tracked it to its lair and killed it single-handedly. Rauna never said differently. But I know, as surely as if I had seen it, that Rauna would have gone first for the cat. And he would have had it but for some treachery of Ajanna's, whereby Rauna was wounded. Ajanna took care to wait until the wounds grew poisoned past proper healing. Only then did he bring Rauna out of the canyon and offer to share the catskin with him—''

Wiel broke off speaking and paused for so long I thought she did not mean to say more. ''And then what?'' I cried.

''Then?'' she asked. ''Well, then, at the next Ranking, Ajanna took a chief's place—killed their father to get it—while Rauna lay still barely alive, his own rank gone by lot, undefended.''

I had hung on her words, breathless with wonder and horror to think of what Rauna had risked so lightly and lost so irretrievably, caught up as surely as if it were my own fate Wiel told—and it was akin to the intrigues and treacheries of the Imperial kin, except that it happened on such a stark, barbaric scale, and it ended so conclusively. Just as lightly had I thrown away my rank in Empire. I could not yet think my life ended thereby.

Wiel's voice throbbed with passion. ''I had Ajanna trapped this time, I was sure of it: I drove him wild with rage until I was certain he would kill me. I meant to bind him with blood guilt—with my blood if he won't acknowledge Raun's. But he escaped me. I don't know how. He threw away the knife I myself held for him. He turned a foul trick on me and left me thus. . . . But I will yet turn it to his disadvantage.''

I could not understand what it was Wiel had done—how the matter of begetting a child could amount to so much—or what could have driven her to such a twisted course of hatred that she would destroy even herself to gain vengeance. It was madness, and yet she spoke with such conviction as to near convince me. ''And your lords of Sky permit all this?'' I cried—meaning what she had done as much as anything of Ajanna's or Raun's doing.

Wiel did not waver from her one point. ''Lords of Sky care nothing what goes on in the depths of canyons, I think! Only I dare tax Ajanna with his perfidy, for I knew his wickedness devised the whole, but he mocks me to my face. And he mocks Raun, endlessly, so now Raun has gone back into a canyon thinking he'll hunt down a rivercat. But crippled as he is, it's the cats that'll hunt him. Anyway, what good would it do now? It won't restore his leg. He won't wear the catskin Ajanna shared with him. No, Raun will die, and I'll have to add that to Ajanna's account.''

So caught up I was in Wiel that I did not hear the sound of Raun's dragging footsteps. From a thin light dawn had cast before it, Raun thrust suddenly between us, like a rivercat himself, his face vicious. He must have heard at least part of what Wiel told me.

''None of this is any concern of yours, fool Wiel!'' he hissed. ''You babble and gossip like the housewomen you have made of yourself. You bind yourself with your madness—Ajanna has no need to do it.''

Wiel sat up, enraged. ''Yes, I am bound, and like any petty housewoman I'll seek revenge against Ajanna for what he's done to me. And for what he did to you, since you won't stand up to him.''

Here she went too far, for I had myself seen Raun stand unflinching before Ajanna's temper.

In a cold, tight voice, Raun said, ''Ajanna did me no ill, except that he saved my life when it had become worthless to me.''

''Never will I believe that,'' Wiel cried passionately.

''You may do as you please, but you shall not believe

that I have so embraced my rankless condition that I hide from the truth like housefolk.''

Thus I saw their defeat, how suddenly it had come, and with what finality. Strong windriders' passions, once turned toward each other, were now twisted and bitter. Their pride was no less than that of any windrider, but balked of expression it ravaged each of them from within. Their silence now was terrible. I settled myself in my sleeping skins, but I lay long awake, thinking how fiercely these people lived—and how immediately and precariously. Raun and Wiel were silent, but I did not think they slept either.

Riding life haunted Raun and Wiel, certainly, but the other housefolk not much less. All their thoughts and doings centered on the windriders. At times during the trek the herds were not far from us, foraging in small groups on the scant dry grass. From high places on the plain I often glimpsed herdbeasts, slow-moving lumps dark against the pale plain. More rarely I caught the soaring flight of a windsteed.

Now and then a windrider came to visit a favorite among the housefolk or fetch gear from the stores we carried. Walking separately from the slow train of housefolk, one morning Wiel and I disturbed Coory and a windrider rising from a tousled bed on the ground. Coory stretched lazily and licked her lips. The windrider dismissed us with a glance and pulled on his leathers. We stayed to watch him run into the rising sun, heading back to the herds.

I marveled again at the effortless grace of a windsteed running. I had just seen the mass and ungainliness of this one standing still, but she moved as if she had no more substance than a cloud scudding before the wind. "Look how she *likes* to run!" I exclaimed.

"Of course!" Wiel said.

Beside the windsteed ran the foal I had seen before; there was only the one just now in all the Houses. The young thing ran like the wind, like its dam, all long limbs that seemed to flicker in and out of material reality. It was a fey thing.

"I wonder if this one will come back," Wiel said softly.

I looked at her, startled. "Come back? The foal? It will leave? Where will it go?"

Wiel shrugged, her eyes still fixed on the running windsteeds. "They all leave, once they're weaned. No one knows where they go. Most return after a few seasons. The ones who don't—" She shrugged again and added, "As you said, they like to run. And with a rider, it seems."

I could not contain my wistfulness. The words burst from me: "If only I could ride—"

"Go ahead, then!" Wiel said, turning on me, irritated. "You can compete for rank like anyone else, can't you?"

The world seemed to stand still. Wordlessly I stared into Wiel's eyes, doubting her. Her eyes held so much that was inexplicable. But to ride . . . "I—" I stammered. "Any-one—?"

"Of course!"

I had not known. I had so clearly marked the distinction between windrider and housebound, I had assumed it to be caste fixed in the blood, no matter of choice or changing—as in Empire. I claimed to have forsworn Empire, but still I had seen all I looked on with Imperial eyes. Now I looked anew. I had seen windriders could fail: Raun, Wiel herself, the youth Brah whom I had seen on this trek among Murrila's housefolk looking utterly the slave. It had not surprised me that windriders could fall. Now I also remembered Surya, in whom briefly I had thought I had recognized a housewoman. I had. I had never guessed that housefolk could rise, but what Surya had done, I would also do.

My spirits soared. I laughed aloud as my fancy winged past the fighting to an image of Murrila confirming me in rank and leading forward a windsteed for me to mount. Impulsively I reached out my hand to grasp Wiel's arm. "We'll ride together," I cried. "You'll take back your rank."

Wiel shrugged my hand away. "No. This one" —she looked down at her swollen body with loathing—"will never leave me the strength to regain my old rank or to hold it long if I did." She cut off my protests. "Oh, I daresay I can get a foothold, but never the fine windsteed

that I had. I'll only get some decrepit nag that has changed
hands at every Ranking and scarcely knows any longer
who it is—and I'll have to fight off children to keep even
that.''

I refused to be drawn into her hopelessness. I spread my
arms expansively, seeing what the plain spread so far for.
It *was* too large for a person alone, but how could I have
failed to see that the great purpose of this enormous sky
was to carry windsteeds? In my exaltation I seemed to feel
the touch of lords of Sky. That majesty we lacked in
Empire.

Coory said suddenly, ''Aren't you the lordly one!''
There was mockery in her tone and in the way she looked
me up and down. I stared beyond her, refusing to be
drawn into the bickering of housefolk. I felt my body grow
lean and taut with purpose, anticipating a windrider's
carriage. The mockery left Coory's voice. ''Indeed, you
are,'' she said.

Wiel made some slight noise. I glanced at her and saw
her uncanny gaze fixed on me measuringly, like Coory's.
Wiel muttered, ''You might just be. . . . And to some
purpose—''

''What?'' I demanded, suddenly wary. Did she see
some avenue to using me in her mad schemes? Some one
thing of my difference?—of Empire? Cold fingers of dread
reached into my spirit. I was glad suddenly that I had yet
said nothing of Empire, not now in hope of any gain from
my private knowledge, but for fear it could interfere between me and this new ambition.

Watching me, Wiel's eyes grew harder still; her gaze
was no longer that of Coory or of other petty housefolk
seeking mean advantage. It was like nothing so much as
my Imperial kin assessing changes of high rank. She did
not answer my question, and I found I was reluctant to
repeat it.

''Let's go,'' she said curtly. I nodded.

I followed Wiel, but I looked back at Coory. She stood
smiling after me, no scorn for the moment but only invitation in her smile. My steps dragged a little. She was very
lovely. I thought I might like what she had to offer.

* * *

Buoyed by the ambition to ride—once I thought of it at all,
I thought of nothing else—I felt little of the increasing
rigors of the trek. The weather grew colder, and the land-
scape became flatter and seemed more desolate without the
variety given by the earlier slight roll to the terrain. The
streams we crossed now were sluggish and lay on the
surface of the land instead of cutting deep canyons into it.
They widened into marshes where our passage spattered us
with foul, half-frozen mud; the Lesser Fens, the housefolk
called them.

Finally we reached a swamp that had no farther side
visible: this was the Long Fen. On islands and reefs of true
ground rising from dank, muddy pools, scrubby trees grew,
mostly bare of leaves but carrying half-rotted fruits that
looked like diseased swellings in the bark, for they were
the same drab color. In the spare shelter of these trees we
pitched the tents. We had reached the winter camp. When
I protested the unpleasantness of it, Wiel said coldly, "We
can't go deeper, to the true forest, if we want the windriders
to come after us. These trees are better than no shelter at
all. You wouldn't want to be out on the open plain when
winter comes in earnest."

But obviously *she* wanted to. And like her I looked only
to the plain now. I cared nothing now whether or not the
fens backed onto the Flod where it came out of Empire.

The first night a hard frost came, and in the morning the
worst of the mud and evil smell was gone. We slaughtered
the herdbeasts that had carried the gear on the long trek
and roasted the meat in large chunks stuffed with the
fentree fruits. The cloying sweetness of the fruits gave a
strange and somehow compelling taste to the stringy meat
of the overaged beasts. And it was a change from the
journey fare of pounded sausage and dried meat. When
this was gone we would have no more fresh meat, save
what small wild creatures we snared ourselves, until the
windriders came for the Ranking at midwinter—the Ranking in which I intended to compete.

For the rest, camp life was the same as before: hard
work, made worse by the cold. I had scorned comfort
already in Empire, and I thought I could do no less here
though I was tried so much harder. I didn't complain, but

the hard realities of the life dragged at my spirit ever more, until I could no longer be very sure I would prevail when the test finally came . . . or ever ride. Knowing how the housefolk would mock, I had not spoken my ambition aloud since that once with Wiel. Goaded finally by fears and doubts that kept pace with desire, I determined that I must speak.

It was too cold to sit long over evening fires. All crawled early among sleeping skins. I huddled close to Raun and Wiel in the tent we three shared. I took a deep breath one night and said in a rush, "Tell me what I must know to compete in the Ranking." Wiel answered me at once, as if she had been waiting for my questions.

"The Ranking is open to anyone who enters a token in the lottery, except that it's pointless—and shameful—for someone of higher rank to challenge a lesser windrider. The winner takes the place and holdings of the higher rank, leaving the loser the lower, or none, if the challenger is without any rank. The fighting allows use of all resources of the body, but nothing else—"

Raun broke in with unusual heat. "What nonsense is this you prattle, Wiel? You talk as if the Ranking were a menial chore for housefolk!" His voice turned proud. "Fighting for rank is an offering of oneself to the lords of Sky. It's an ordeal that purifies and makes one fit to rise above earth and approach the sky."

In these words I caught a glimpse of the windrider Raun had been. Like Ajanna, as Wiel had said, but finer. His words added a dimension of spirit to the wonders I already anticipated from riding—and made obtaining them seem more difficult still. "Yes, I want to ride," I whispered.

Raun ignored me. "What have you done, Wiel, to put such thoughts in Oa's head? I suppose you think this is a way to revenge yourself on Ajanna, but how can you think that she'll be able to do him any harm?"

Wiel's defensiveness showed Raun had hit the mark. "You haven't watched her as closely as I have! Oa could hold a House—more—"

"So? She won't come close to the high chiefs. No female ever has. They're not heavy or strong enough. Ajanna'll care nothing for a minor chief. You're the one who can't see, Wiel. Oa is something different from us, windriders or housefolk. She might bring out of Ocean a new breadth to our lives, which have been too narrowly confined to wind and sky. You'd do better to let her make her own way in her own fashion than to channel her into a windrider's life."

Raun's talk of Ocean always infuriated Wiel. She raged at him: "I see as well as you do that she's something different. But I won't waste my time on the fantasies you weave about her! I've seen no sign of Ocean's interest in us, if lords of Ocean exist at all! You're crazy. And even if these tidings from Ocean that you make so much of truly exist, how do you know they'll get you anything?"

Raun would not or could not answer her. He said instead, "You're in no condition to train Oa."

"No, but I can tell her what she can expect from the windriders she might fight, and you can show her their tricks and the counters to them."

"No."

"Raun!" Wiel bit off his name, its contraction as painfully obvious as that of his withered leg, which had caused it.

"Very well," he muttered.

Perversely, Wiel's temper flared at his yielding to her. "Oh! Ajanna won't let her ride anyway. He'll bind her just as he did me."

"Wiel, you know that's not true," Raun said doggedly, but with no expectation of convincing her. "If Oa can fight, she'll ride."

So it seemed I got my way, but not without tying myself even closer into the twisted, housebound lives of Wiel and Raun. But I did not stop to count the cost of that.

As midwinter approached the windriders trickled into the camp in the Long Fen, House by House, driving their herdbeasts in among the fen trees where they could forage protected from storms. The storms came hard on the windriders' heels, strong winds that piled drifts of snow deep over the camp, worse than any winter storms I had known in Empire. While a storm raged, we huddled in the tents, near senseless from the noise and the fury, wholly at their mercy. And yet the others assured me we were better off than we could be elsewhere.

Ajanna, drunk and raging, was one of the last to ride in with his herds and herders. He had lost a number of herdbeasts when a storm came up so suddenly he had not had time to gather the herd together. Rumor speculated about what could have distracted him from the storm warnings, but no one dared ask him; Ajanna was something apart from even the other high chiefs among the windriders. He stalked about the camp with an angry word for anyone in his path. When I heard his voice I could not but think of Wiel's tale, and of the dark doings she hinted at in Ajanna's past. She had seemed to think he was hardly a windrider at all.

Ajanna happened upon the clearing where Raun and I wrestled upon our spread cloaks, stripped of our clumsy tunics. I was unaccountably awkward; my limbs wanted to Dance. "What's that?" Wiel cried from the side. "Oa! What're you doing? Raun, show her again." Grimly I drove my muscles to the unfamiliar patterns while Wiel shouted encouragement indiscriminately to both Raun and me. Wiel saw Ajanna first. Raun and I fell apart and looked only to see the cause of her abrupt silence. I stared back at Ajanna as boldly as I could. I had forgotten the size of him and his aura of wildness barely controlled.

"And what do you think you're about?" he asked unpleasantly. So dark he was, hair and eyes utterly black—impossibly so.

Raun answered him. "I believe either of us"—he nodded at me—"may compete in the Ranking without *your* leave."

Ajanna snorted. Perhaps it was a laugh. "Go ahead, if you're fool enough to try after the last thrashing you got from a stripling of no rank." Standing close to me, Raun's tension was palpable. He said nothing.

"As for you"—Ajanna turned to me—"you look sturdy enough to be useful. I've no mind to lose a good housewench. I'd just get stuck with another useless mouth to feed, like Wiel here, who's hardly fit to carry a child to term after playing windrider for a few seasons."

Wiel snarled at his slighting reference to her many

years' standing of more than respectable rank for male or female. Ajanna raised his eyebrows at her. "Ah, you're still a little saucy," he remarked. "You'll soon learn for yourself that your fighting days are over."

He turned back to me. "You, I remember. You want taming, I think, and I want some diversion." He lunged, and his massive hands snapped about my arms. He was quick, despite his size. He pushed me along ahead of him, half carrying me. I managed to scoop up my cloak from the ground and pull it about me. It was far too cold to walk around naked.

We came to Ajanna's large chief's tent. The housefolk who were there shrank into the corners. Ajanna shoved me, so I stumbled and fell to the floor. He took up a full drinking skin and drained it in one draft. Everything about him was on a large scale.

I straightened my cloak about me and sat, cross-legged, on the skins of the floor, which were soft with the long winter hair of herdbeasts. The tent I shared with Raun and Wiel was furnished with worn castoffs. I lifted my head, determined to face Ajanna. I had not thought he would remember me.

Ajanna put aside the empty drinking skin and belched. The tent seemed to shrink in size when he moved about it. He said mildly, "Why do you housefolk want to ride? I make no great demands on you. You get food and shelter. Look at Coory: she's content with her lot, and she takes some pains to be pleasant to the windriders. Why can't you follow Coory's example?" He looked me over meaningfully. "You're young and well-formed. Why don't you make something of yourself in the House?"

My breath came hissing, sullen with the impotent rage of the enslaved, as I thought of Wiel's fate. Once I would have relied on the Dancer's tricks of control, that always served me well enough; I had since learned to doubt myself. And Ajanna knew nothing of housebound life if he thought anyone could share Coory's easy life without the protection of his favor. Anyway, I did not want to: Coory was confined as narrowly as any of us.

"I want nothing from you," I said evenly, though he stood over me with an arrogant look of dominance. I forced myself to meet his gaze. "I want to ride. I shall enter the midwinter Ranking. Meanwhile I'll run no risk of getting a child to keep me from it. I won't lie with you or any male."

From corners of the tent, the housefolk gasped. Ajanna laughed shortly. "Even a watersprite can't be so stupid as not to know the remedy for that—I would have thought!"

Coory came in then and stopped short, eyes narrowing when she saw me, or rather saw Ajanna occupied with me. She would take no interest in me when he was about, I saw, whatever she thought I might amount to in the long run. I glanced at her and said to Ajanna, "Why can't you be content with Coory? What do you want with me?"

He shrugged. "A passing fancy, you may be sure. It's not worth your making it any harder on yourself." Though he made this effort to persuade me, I saw he expected me rather to bow to his windrider's will.

But I had always been stubborn; no one had ever been able to talk me into anything. I said, "It's you who make it hard on yourself. I will have my way."

Ajanna stood silent. He must have thought I was bluffing; perhaps he was so unused to housefolk standing up to him that it gave him pause. He took a pull on another drinking skin. "What's the matter with you?" he burst out irritably. "It's cold, miserable, hard work riding herd, which is what a windrider does most of the time. Why can't you be satisfied with a life of ease and plenty?"

I snorted, thinking of the Imperial ease I had already thrown off. With new belligerence I said, "Would you be?"

"That's nothing to the point. I am a high chief. Whoever takes my rank will take my life with it. Your fate is less certain. Females' ranks hardly seem more than no rank at all."

I thought how I had thrown away my rank in Empire, which could have been reckoned as high as his—and lived. In that I was more than him. I said grandly, "I'll try all your ranks and then tell you the difference."

He growled impatiently. He had paced the tent while we were talking, but now he crouched suddenly down behind me and caught my hair to force me back. My hair had not yet grown out from the short-cropped style then fashionable in the Imperial City, so he found no firm grip. I understood there was no more to be gained with words. I rolled away from him, pulling his knife from its sheath along the outside of his calf, the hilt at his knee, facing me. I stood up holding the knife ready.

"I've killed before," I said, "and I'll do it again if I must. If you won't give me your windrider's word that I will be free to enter the Ranking."

Ajanna's eyes widened and he did not move. The murmur of housefolk stilled. Ajanna said coolly, "You have the sniveling spirit of a housewoman, to think of such tactics. You'll never be a windrider. You fool! Don't you know neither winds nor windsteeds will lift up those who kill without leave of lords of Sky?" He snorted and continued, "But it's all of a piece with the sly ways of housefolk—lies and bloodthreats."

I blustered on, "If I use a knife it does but even your advantage of size so we can fight fairly." But I was shaken by his words, for I had learned enough about windriders to know Ajanna would not deign to alter the truth, and what he said also made some of Wiel's mad words comprehensible.

Ajanna stood up so quickly I had no time to act. He towered over me and bellowed, "Fights belong on the Ranking ground in the sight of the assembled lords of Sky. I don't fight the likes of you even there—nor will I lie with you. Get out!"

I scrambled to my feet. To give the lie to the trembling in my knees I paused to toss the knife to the ground at Ajanna's feet. I managed to walk from the tent with a semblance of dignity. The cold ground burned my bare feet, but that was as nothing compared to the searing of Ajanna's words in my mind. I tried to tell myself the deaths at my hand or by my order in Empire could make no difference here. But I could not be sure.

In our own tent, Raun and Wiel looked me over curiously. They said nothing, but I daresay even Raun expected my body to be marked by Ajanna's anger if not by his passion. The mark he had put on me—of doubt—did not show.

And I *had* gotten my way, even if it was by housebound slyness and trickery. I knew I would do worse if I had to.

The next day I was back at work doggedly practicing, determined to root out all distracting instincts of Dance and Empire. Again I sensed I was watched. I swung about to find Murrila, chief of all the chiefs, standing under the trees that ringed the clearing. He looked even larger than Ajanna in his enveloping fur cloak, which was the same soft color as his grizzled, shaggy head. His presence seemed less than Ajanna's, quiet and self-contained. His gaze disturbed me more, so unwavering as it was. I turned my head away sharply. When I looked again, he was gone. But I remembered his gaze.

Later, pondering it, I wondered if what disturbed me was not a similarity to the Dynast of Empire, who had searched so deeply into me. But, for Murrila, to what purpose? I didn't like to think. Compared to such determination Ajanna's will seemed merely heedless—not unlike my own.

CHAPTER

6

An eerie, gusting wind blew through the camp midwinter night. Between scudding clouds the moon shone intermittently. On ground cleared of snow and brush for the rites, the bonfire was lit. In its light the bare trees of the Long Fen seemed to writhe with desperate pain. When the windriders called out to their lords of Sky I stood silent with the housefolk; as yet I was nothing in the sight of lords of Sky.

Sparks flew from the bonfire to ignite a living tree. It blazed up at once and burned, a twin torch to the bonfire, until it died as suddenly as it had started. The crowd murmured uneasily. I tried to find a good omen in the occurrence: that a new fire should blaze up beside the windriders' traditional bonfire meant I should win rank.

But I could not be certain and, naked under a thin cloak, I shivered. I envied the high chiefs the catskins they wore with the soft fur turned against their flesh, but it was not only from the cold I shivered. Though Ajanna had yet done nothing to prevent my entering this Ranking, I could not forget what he said. Nor could I forget Murilla's inspection, and I had to wonder if this night might test more than anyone suspected.

The Rankings began. I held back from the first bouts, as Wiel had advised me, saying they were hard to hold and hardly worth it. Surya held the rank I had seen her win in the last Ranking. Braha took the rank above that he had then lost to Surya. The third place fell to a housewoman who had been a windrider in earlier years. The eyes of her half-grown children gleamed with pride, but even I could see she had but few seasons left. It might be one of her own children that would soon take away her rank for good. A windrider's life could be short and nearly as bitter as lives of housefolk. I remembered the sight of windsteeds running, and I thought it would be worth any price to ride.

The ground was taken by an inexperienced boy who had gotten the rank from an injured windrider he could not otherwise have beaten. I glanced at Wiel. She nodded. I, with others, stepped forward to place a token in Murrila's bowl. He drew the token of another. I retrieved my own and returned to the crowd.

Four times I entered the lottery and still my token was not chosen. I saw Ajanna watching me from his place across the empty ground. I would not turn aside, I vowed. I raged at every restraint that had been set on me. Let the lords of Sky do what they would: I would not submit any longer to the petty round of a housewoman's life!

Wiel grew uneasy. She whispered, "It's unlucky to lose so many chances in the lottery, and it's coming to the ranks of experienced fighters. Perhaps you'd better wait for the spring Ranking."

For answer I walked onto the ground once more to cast my token. This time it was drawn. Wiel came to take my cloak. "Watch his feet," she whispered. "Wunna's the kind who'll try to trick you." She scorned him, though she thought he could be a match for me. I would not consider that possibility. I only nodded and dismissed Wiel from my thoughts. I no longer felt the cold. The world shrank to the small circle of bare ground, its flickering light, and Wunna, my opponent.

He sprang at me but his hands slid harmlessly along my

flank, unable to grip its oiled surface. I reached, grabbed, and swung, locking and twisting his arm, as Wiel and Raun had schooled me. Wunna spun away, slippery also, and too heavy for me to hold.

He turned and crouched. I stepped into his trap, prepared, and swung him off balance, but again he twisted free of me. He kept his feet and came back at me. With the attacks and defenses Wiel and Raun had taught me, I countered his every move, but awkwardly—too slow; the moves came to me only with careful, conscious effort. As I tired and my control slipped, Dancer's steps that were near instinct to my muscles tripped me up as often as Wunna did. I had to fight myself as well as Wunna. Grimly I kept at it. I had no choice.

Then I was down, so quickly I did not know how it had happened, the breath knocked out of me. Wunna bent over me. Dazed, I watched him and thought I could not move. But somehow I squirmed aside. Gasping for air, I struggled to my knees. Wunna's face, set in triumph, swam before my eyes. . . . I could not rise.

So, I thought: I was no match even for Wunna, whom Wiel held in scorn. The training Raun and Wiel gave me was too little and too late. My thoughts clouded with despair, with the dreary round of House chores, the tedium of camp life, and the disdainful looks from windriders—when they saw me at all. Was that to remain my lot?

In desperation I shoved Wunna off and staggered to my feet. He came for me, grinning, still sure of victory. Nor could I doubt it.

But I eluded his grasp. He lunged at me again, more wildly, and missed, and his face grew puzzled. I was myself puzzled, but only for the merest instant while I was caught between Wiel and Raun's recent training and another discipline much more deeply ingrained in me. Then I slipped over completely into that role I had once so coveted, and I Danced.

The High Dance quickly grew strong in me. Wunna began to move in response to it in what space I left him, forced unknowing into his role by the commanding nature of mine. He almost tripped over his own feet. The Dance was leaching his strength away and pouring it into me: that was the power of a Dance of more than one.

Time seemed to stop. Wunna's movements grew awkward, then slow, almost disappearing from my awareness that was so dominated by the Dance. All my being moved in the discipline of it, treading out the patterns of power. Trapped, Wunna Danced also, danced a counterpoint to my steps. And Danced where I could not get at him.

I shook my head angrily and near broke the pattern I had built. Hastily I restored it. I knew I was being thwarted but I did not know why. Soon I saw, however, that I would never get him.

Oh, I could keep dancing—hours. But with only the two of us in the patterns, we were too surely balanced. Without more Dancers in the victims' roles, I could not fulfill mine. Angrily I reached out with my mind and my will, demanding.

And I found what I could feed on: Ajanna, his will enough to fuel a hundred Dances; Halassa, steady as the earth and as invincible; wild Lirra; Braha; Surya; and all the other windriders; and the housefolk with their own drives and hungers. The rites of the Ranking had caught them up and left them open to my demand. They did not need to Dance; it was not so in Empire, but here their concentration and participation were complete without that aid.

I took what I needed and Danced on. My awareness sank to details of muscle and nerve. The Dance, in which my body was so long schooled, came alive in my flesh.

Yes, place one foot there. Raise a hand, so. Turn. Snap. Of course: my hands closed where they came to rest, as they had done once before, under Kastra's tutelage in a practice hall in distant Empire, upon the neck of a slave.

Wunna's eyes, close to mine as I bent over him, bulged in sudden shock. He began to fall.

The Dance was taking him, the High Dance, that killed.

I was not so lost in the Dance that I was not aware, if dimly, of the Ranking ground, of the assembled windriders and the incorporeal lords of Sky—and of the prize for which I Danced. Ajanna's presence was particularly sharp:

I heard him saying that the winds and the windsteeds would not take up one weighted with death. I thought, if Wunna dies I will lose the very prize I fight him for.

I fought myself then, and the generations of Imperial kin come alive with the Dance in my flesh. . . . But I Danced on. . . . I could not stop. The Dance held me and would not be appeased short of a death. I must Dance until Wunna died.

No! I raged, and I tried to think. The Dynast had intimated he could manipulate the High Dance. On that very account, believing he could arrange that Jily would Dance into my hands at the critical moment, I had forsworn Empire. Now I grasped eagerly at that evidence that the High Dance could be controlled, even a large Dance.

My will surged through my flesh. If the Dance could be controlled, *I* would control it! My hold on Wunna did indeed slacken, though all the world seemed to go horribly awry at the break in the smooth unfolding of the pattern so near completed, and my mind seemed to dim, and I could not hold my limbs.

I would Dance awkwardly, from gawkiness of youth, Kastra had promised; but I had strength and sureness and they would tell. Oh-h-h! Desperately I wrenched myself away from Wunna, who fell to the ground in a crumpled heap, still breathing, but barely. His puzzled face stared up at me. I looked away, shaky on my feet. I was scarcely less bewildered than he.

"Oa! The Wind's Sigh!" the crowd breathed as one.

I felt their voice as a horrible assault, but it brought me nearer my senses. The attention of every person in the crowd had been fixed on me, I knew, feeding my will. Had they noticed anything out of the ordinary? Would they remember? For now I knew only their attention was breaking up and falling away. I stumbled as I walked across the ground and saw how I had spent myself

And I was not quite done. I forced my head up. "I am Oa!" I cried. "Windrider—" I stared at Murrila. He looked back at me with his clear, level gaze. Slowly, I thought reluctantly, he spoke the words I required, confirming my claim. I nodded and finally moved off the ground.

The cold wind stung my bare flesh where the skin was scraped raw by ice and rock. At my back Murrila called for the next bout. I fell into the crowd. Everywhere my body felt bruised and strained. Wiel slid my cloak around my shoulders, but I could not stop trembling.

The Ranking proceded: windrider by windrider, all the scores of them; the several dozens of lesser chiefs; and finally the high chiefs. Ajanna entered the ground. He was not stripped for fighting. His eyes swept the crowd lazily, daring anyone to call his bluff. I thought his gaze lingered on me. I squared my shoulders and stared back, perhaps more defiantly than need be. He grinned, mocking me, as if to say I was now a little more than I had been rankless, but so very little he need take no account of it. I shrugged. Not for him but for myself I had fought.

No one came to challenge Ajanna, nor did he challenge any of that handful who ranked above him. I thought how Murrila had beaten him in that last Ranking. That must rankle with someone like Ajanna. Flushed with my victory, I thought if I were he I could not have let such a challenge rest incomplete. But Murrila calmly confirmed his own rank, and the rites ended.

The feasting began. Housefolk who earlier had mocked me now meekly served me skins of kwass. Windriders spoke to me pleasantly. Wiel had warned me their purpose would be to probe what chances I might have for rising in rank and what chances they might have in fighting me. Let them see, I thought, savoring my triumph, thinking I could face anyone.

With some others still clad only in cloaks I entered the shelter of Murrila's tent. "In whose House will you ride?" the others pressed me. So long as I was not a chief myself I must ride as herder in some chief's House.

High chiefs, Ajanna and Murrila among them, stood nearby. Prompted by a taste for danger that had never yet been quenched, I spoke out so they would hear: "I'll ride in Ajanna's House."

Murrila swung around to see who spoke, and frowned when he saw it was I. "Do you swear the oath?" he asked me.

"I do," I said.

"Ajanna! You must accept her oath!"

"Let me see if the windsteeds accept the result of this Ranking before I act on it," Ajanna said. Surely it was not like Ajanna to stickle for forms, even if he was within traditional rights. Murrila raised her brows, then shrugged.

I felt a chill more profound than that of winter cold. Had Ajanna seen in my fighting something that should not be? Or remembered the conversation that had passed between us and the bloodthreat I had made in the carelessness of anger? I felt, as I had not before, how very much I may have yielded to Empire to gain my purpose just now. From the outset of my ambition to ride I had sensed a threat in things of Empire, but without Gandish Dance I could not have won windrider's rank. Now I had incorporated what conflict there might be between Empire and windrider into my own being, beyond any easy untangling. I dared not ask what test still awaited me. And even if I could turn from it, I would not.

I spent the night in celebration with the others, but it was only sham now Ajanna had soured my triumph, and the hours of darkness passed with agonizing slowness.

Dawn was still and dim, no presage of day. My body felt unfamiliar to me from the close-fitting riding gear Wiel had helped me don, from exhaustion and worry, and from an excess of kwass. I stood with the others newly ranked and waited for Murrila to bring windsteeds. Finally I felt neither excitement nor fear. It was as if I stood by as a spectator in the dream of some other person.

Windriders jogged along the fringe of the fen woods, driving loose windsteeds before them. Some windriders sped in front to bring the windsteeds to a halt in front of us. Murrila spoke from his great height windsteedback: "Braha, take Morningstar; Lanna, Nightwind; Oa, Madder—"

I did not heed the rest. Somehow I knew Madder by his name. I reached for his muzzle and stroked it. It was even softer than I had thought. He lowered his head and butted me gently. I laughed. The sky brightened. The unfamiliar-

ity was gone: I knew I would ride Madder. I wound my
hands in the heavy hair of his mane and pulled myself onto
his back higher than my head, scorning the aid to footing
of his knobby leg joints. My legs slid around his neck as if
from old habit and locked into place in the hollow of his
throat. The warm aura of him enfolded me. He twitched
his tail and danced a little to one side. I thought he was
pleased with me.

The others mounted. The circling windriders pulled their
windsteeds back. Madder saw an opening before I did and
was off in a great leap that nearly unseated me. I grabbed
at his mane flowing back around me. My heart soared.

Madder ran with a high, easy gait that left the plain a
blur far behind us. The wind of our passage blew through
my mind and body. I was one with the sky that spread not
only above but all around us. On and on we ran and
always the plain stretched before us without end.

The memory of that first ride will run forever in my
blood. I can close my eyes and feel again that escape from
earth into speed and space, like Dance except it was not
interior to me, not mental at all, but *real*. "Between,"
windriders called where we rode: between earth and sky. It
cannot be described to those who do not know it. It is
worth any price.

Gradually I became aware of other windriders on the
plain. There were not only the others on trial but dozens
sweeping forward in a broad swath, separated from each
other by distances too great to recognize faces. I nodded to
myself, understanding that a windrider rode alone.

Though I never noticed turning, fen trees appeared in
front of us, and I knew we must have run a circling
course. The windsteeds ran nearer each other, snorting and
tossing their heads, not at all winded. In the massing pack
I had a better measure of my flying speed, and of my own
puny size compared to Madder's bulk. Awareness of my
fragility only added to my exhilaration. I threw back my
head and laughed aloud.

My head came down, and I saw Lirra, laughing also,
rode beside me on a milk-white windsteed. She tossed me
a drinking skin. I caught it, perhaps a little awkwardly,

and raised it in salute to her before drinking. The sour fermented milk ran through my body like fire. I tossed the skin back to Lirra, grinning. She saluted me, and I understood that I was one of the company of windriders. Windriders did not always ride alone.

The ride ended abruptly at the edge of the swamp. Murrila, towering higher than any other even mounted, called to those of us on trial. He looked us over. There was no need for such ceremony as had accompanied the fighting: our survival attested to the decision of the windsteeds. When he came to me Murrila said, "Ajanna, you may give oath now."

I stared boldly at Ajanna, daring him to set further hindrance in my way. With apparent indifference he recited the words that bound me formally into his House and the fellowship of herders.

I repeated the words of the oath, acknowledging my rank below that of Ajanna and the lords of Sky. I thought Ajanna's look was mocking. I tossed my head. I had given my word; if he and the unseen lords of Sky indeed outranked me, I yielded to them.

For me the great thing was the riding itself, but Wiel's triumph was that I became a herder in Ajanna's House.

"Now he'll fall into your power, Oa," she gloated. "Ah, Raun, I have wrought well this tool of our revenge."

I almost told them their training had failed me, and only my Imperial past has enabled me to win rank. I checked the hasty words that came to me. I was a windrider, and therefore cut off from the past when I had been something else. I was not supposed even to remember my past among the housebound. But I did remember—much—and it occurred to me I should keep it for myself, so I said nothing.

Raun and Wiel, caught up in their usual argument, did not notice my silence. Raun said sharply to Wiel, "I seek no revenge. Nor can I understand you. Ajanna is sworn to protect Oa's honor and her herdbeasts, and he won't break his word. Truly that binds him. But that gives neither Oa nor you any control over him."

"Wait, just wait," Wiel hissed at him.

"Hush!" I ordered them. I did not care what they saw

in me or wanted from me. I was above it all: housefolk pettiness, Ajanna's disdain, crazy Raun's imaginary lords of Ocean—above even Dance and Empire, for had not Madder carried me into the sky?

But I learned the elements still claimed some power over me when, after the midwinter lull in the weather, winter closed in around us more fiercely even than before, with such storms as there could be no riding in.

CHAPTER

7

On a pile of herdbeast skins, I lay, in a tent, drowzing, my
head pillowed on Lirra's knee, a full skin of kwass wedged
against my side—against the cold. The wind had dropped;
it was quiet and bitterly cold. Even inside the tent full of
windriders I wore my riding leathers fully laced and a
cloak besides.

Lirra would not be still—could never be still. Lounging
on her side, her head propped up on one elbow, she talked
to Halassa. Her voice flowed like a stream in spate, quick
and sharp and restless. I was too drowzy to make out her
words or the slower, even tones of Halassa's answers, but
I could not quite drop off to sleep while she kept moving
so restlessly. Usually she amused me—her restless, easy
companionship, her never more than half attending to
anyone, and the give and take of her casual shy pleasure
when I lay with her. She neither gave nor took very much;
that was fine with me. But just now I wished she would
have the consideration to be still.

We were in one of the large tents set aside for windriders.
From the far corner, where Surya and Braha and some
others sat at a game played with counters of bone and

pebble, loud words rang with sudden dispute over the rhythmic clacking of the play. With a grunt of irritation I sat up and pulled the drinking skin to me, worrying at the stopper. Still speaking, Lirra twisted around to see what I was doing, her lithe body dark and sinuous in the half-light filtering through seams and cracks in the tent. I pulled the stopper free and lifted the gurgling skin to my mouth.

Abruptly Lirra broke off speaking. A swath of strong light fell across me, dazzling me so I could not see. But I knew, by the way the others all quieted, who stood there in the entrance to the tent.

"There's no meat for the housefolk to cook. There's no more milk to make kwass. The housefolk complain to *me*. Am I to fetch herdbeasts at the bidding of housefolk while the lot of you lounge at your ease?"

Windriders long confined in camp were always on the verge of exploding into violence. Only the thought of riding kept them peaceable; sometimes the thought became too remote. I sat very still, keeping an eye on Ajanna standing in the entrance and the other eye on the windriders already in the tent. They also watched Ajanna, and each other—and me. As always, there was something different in the eyes of more than a few of them when they watched me.

Unlike housefolk, windriders would not speak a word about it; there was no more talk of watersprites or even of lords of Ocean, among windriders, after the Ranking. I knew they also kept alive the notion I was different. I dropped my gaze from theirs, scowling. I didn't want to be different. I wanted to be a windrider. When Madder first took me up, I thought all my past had fallen away from me.

Ajanna said, "It's the task of junior herders to fetch herdbeasts out of the fen. Braha. Oa. See to it." And he left.

Still the others watched me. But there had been nothing out of the ordinary in the way Ajanna treated me. There never was—quite. I rose to my feet, settling my cloak around me.

"Well, Braha," I said. "Are you coming?" I spoke coldly, not liking him much or his company. I would have preferred Lirra for company at work—as at all else just then.

Braha muttered assent but he paused to settle something about the gaming. Disgruntled by the outcome, Surya called after him when he came, spitefully, "Ride well. With the wind." We neither of us answered. We would ride. We could not hope it would be very well in the fen.

The light was strong outside; the sky was a cold, cold white, glittering like a snowfield. It was too cold for snow, so cold even the wind seemed stopped and all the earth and air held motionless. The deep snow already fallen was heavily crusted with ice.

We found our windsteeds just beyond the camp, with the others of Ajanna's House. Dun Madder and Braha's blue Morningstar came out at once from the pack of them, head stretching toward us, snuffling a welcome.

Windsteeds had a strange intelligence, only partially touching ours. They knew their own riders, certainly. They came when wanted, usually without being called, and snuffled, and nuzzled us, as now, with every sign of pleasure. Yet they did not mind exchanging their riders if chiefs reassigned them. A few, it was true, such as Ajanna's Scudder, settled on some one person and refused all others; others occasionally took a dislike to particular riders, and would not allow them to mount. The chiefs always acceded to the windsteeds' preferences. They could hardly do otherwise: no one could force a windsteed against its will.

Madder lifted one foreleg and curled it in a friendly fashion so I could more easily reach the knobby joints to climb to his back. I was stiff enough from the long cold I took his aid. I slid my feet into the hollow under his throat and burrowed my hands in his long mane, against the wonderful heat of his body. In the coldest weather, windsteeds moved in an aura of warmth. At a nudge of my knees, Madder turned to go deeper into the Long Fen.

Windsteeds responded to the slightest touch of knee or voice; with familiarity they came to move seemingly at a rider's unspoken wish, particularly when running on open plain. Then, the others told me—and I had already briefly felt it for myself—windsteed and rider became truly one,

wholly sharing the senses of their bodies and the percep-
tions of their minds. For this experience the riders lived;
and also the windsteeds, it seemed, putting up even with
the likes of that day's errand delving into the fen. What
constrained me to the task was the herder's oath I had
sworn; like any windrider I stood by my word, so as not to
denigrate any least thing about myself.

Madder walked disdainfully through a thickening growth
of the stubby fen trees, occasionally nipping a twig that
still bore a dry leaf, and eating it. The tree canopy rose to
the height of a windsteed's head, and that of the rider on a
windsteed. I wrapped myself as best I could in my leather
cloak and Madder's mane, but the prickling branches were
everywhere and more than once got through my guard. I
didn't much care. I was glad to be riding even in the fen.

For a time Madder's every footstep broke through the
crust on the ice and dropped into the softer snow underneath;
up and down we scraped against one tree after another.
Then we came on a path herdbeasts had packed, and the
footing became easier. The windsteeds picked up speed.
The branches whipped at our faces the more, but it was
worth it.

The path soon widened into a clearing, where the snow
had been pawed over repeatedly by herdbeasts seeking the
thin dry grass beneath it. Madder ran full out and my
spirits rose. Behind me, Braha gave a yell, of sheer joy to
be riding, I thought until Madder spun to an uneasy halt
and I saw several cows with young calves sheltering in a
thicket at the far end of the clearing. Braha came up beside
me.

"We should milk these cows, now we've found them,"
he said.

"You do it," I answered impatiently. "I'll go on to
look for a yearling for butchering."

Braha did not disagree; I hardly gave him time before I
was off, alone, deeper into the Long Fen, where the trees
grew thick but also taller, so Madder could move more
freely underneath them.

Madder crashed through brakes of underbrush, playing
like a young foal. Laughing, I urged him on, and he ran,

exhilarated as I was. Suddenly, snorting, he pulled up, too late.

A lead of water, running somehow with enough current to keep from freezing, opened within a dense thicket. Madder plunged through a broken bank, chest-deep into black water, which was thick with mud and congealing ice. "Madder!" I cried in dismay. But I could only leave him his head. He leaped and plunged across the water and scrambled finally up a slippery bank. His efforts covered both of us with gobs of freezing mud, which smeared my leathers and stuck in his long winter hair. He swung away from the water with an air of disgust, throwing back his great, wedge-shaped head.

I laughed at him then, and he was off again, as before, with great heedless leaps, and I forgot my errand completely until a cow ran out in our track.

She looked to be heavy with milk—to have lost her calf. I searched awhile for it, but could not find any sign of it, and so went on, marking the way so I could return and drive the cow back to camp. We would have kwass without work for a time.

I kept my mind more closely on my work, and presently I came upon a group of several score beasts that looked to be Ajanna's. It did not really matter: during winter each House took what it needed from what its herders could find in the fen. Later, on the plain, we would separate the herds again. I cut two yearling bulls from the others and turned back with them toward camp. Herding one beast through fen thickets was work; three were near impossible, I found when I collected also the milk cow. Soon I was in a rage, and Madder was loping in circles just to keep the three in sight, and we made no forward progress at all.

Braha rode up, having doubtless heard the commotion I was making from a long way off. A dozen full skins of milk bounced against the gear strap cinched around his windsteed's barrel, and he drove a yearling, running close on its heels to control it.

One of my yearlings twisted away suddenly, and Madder nearly unseated me turning after it. Despite the warmth coming from my windsteed, I was cold clear through. I would not have felt it, wet though I was with icy water and mud, if I had only been riding freely. The frustration of herding through trees brought also all other discomforts home to me.

"Are you going to help or not?" I snapped at Braha.

His riding leathers were perfectly ordered and spotless, fit sleekly over his slim, youth's figure. He looked at his ease. But for the bulging skins on Morningstar's gear strap and the trotting yearling, evidence that I could hardly gainsay, he looked as if he had not been put to any trouble. Of course I scorned him for it. He was only half-grown, I thought, both younger and lower ranked than I was, a child almost, but too controlled and careful for such, by far. "At least I have had a run to show for my trouble," I said haughtily.

Braha liked me no better than I did him, likely for no better reason than that we were in something of the same position, newly ranked; and that windriders shared nothing easily, not even rivalry. His dark eyes flashed at my words. "A run, yes," he said. "Do you mean to run your windsteed to break his legs? He'll do it, you know."

Those words stung me as no others could have done. Tight-lipped, I said, "Let's get these miserable beasts into camp." Seeing my face, Braha must have decided he had said enough. Without a word he swung Morningstar out to one side to head off the second of my yearlings.

With two of us at the task we could work the herdbeasts closely and keep them moving steadily, if slowly, in the direction we chose. It was drudgery, but Braha refrained from quarreling further with me, though since I kept watch more on Madder's footing than on the herdbeasts, I could not have seemed to be doing anything like a fair share of the work. I felt much more cordial toward Braha by the time we saw the first tents of Ajanna's House and could call out housefolk to take the herdbeasts off our hands. I slid down from Madder's back regretfully and rubbed his face a little before I let him go. Then I reached to take some of the filled drinking skins Braha carried, and we went together into the camp.

On foot, once again we had nothing to say to each other. We dropped the milk skins among some housefolk gathered around a cooking fire. Raun was among them, watching me; I looked right through him. "Bring me clean leathers," I ordered another houseman, and waited a moment to see him turn away to do my bidding. Wun it was, I saw only then, first glimpsing the sullen face that had been turned from me. He had been high enough ranked not to have thought to be bested by one with no rank at all; no doubt housebound status came hard to him.

It had come hard to me as well, I thought, dismissing him from my mind as I ducked into the nearest of the large riders' tents behind Braha. It was empty but for us two, and a little warmer than the outdoors. I slumped to the floor, fully feeling my tiredness. Braha looked around, with surprise that I had followed him. I had meant nothing by it, but seeing what he thought I had in mind, evoked it; and I smiled a little as I pulled myself up and untied the lacings of my muddy leathers. I pulled the shirt off over my head.

Braha came toward me very slowly, eyes wide, as if he were unable to tear his gaze from the clear blue-white of my bare skin. It was a color no windrider had ever had, but it was my natural color. For I was no longer at all cold: Braha's strangely intent look aroused my blood as quickly as the exhilaration of riding had done. Braha came to stand over me kneeling on the floor. He put a hand to my pale hair, still too short to braid, near transparent, a silken cloud around my head.

It was fear he felt for me, I realized. I tasted it like a heady drink and, for all I did not like him, I wanted him and thought I would have him. I no longer feared for my Dancer's control by then—or for anything.

Braha hesitated. Frowning, he touched my temples, putting one finger gingerly to the thin blue marks there of my Imperial rank. I tugged impatiently at the laces of his clothes. Despite himself, he shifted his position so I could reach to peel off his tight-fitting leathers.

His boy's lean grace and delicate skin put me in mind of dark-skinned Southern youths I had found across the river in the Imperial City—and found much pleasure in. I did not lack the skill to make sure Braha also pleased me, despite his strange fearfulness—indeed, he was perhaps in the end the more eager because of it, as I was. Our bodies closed on each other finally with a greedy, unquestioning hunger that swallowed us up together.

I hardly noticed when sullen Wun came in with an armful of fresh clothes: we had no thought at that moment, either Braha or I, for clothes.

Later Ajanna came in, and Braha drew away from me at once. I scowled, thinking he need not leave me on Ajanna's account: that was one direction toward which I had no inclination. Nor could Ajanna have any liking for me, I thought, the way he hounded me to the worst chores of winter herding more than any other newly ranked windrider.

"Oa," Ajanna said now, indifferently, "hail. And Braha. There's another storm blowing up." As some other windriders came in, Ajanna offered Braha the drinking skin he carried. The younger windrider took it with a deferential air.

I sat up, feeling acutely my different appearance from all others with my pale coloring and pale eyes, feeling apart from them, as I did not want to be—and scorning on that very account to dress with undue haste.

"Give me some kwass!" I said imperiously, holding out my hand to Ajanna for the drinking skin Braha had returned to him.

He gave it to me with a careless gesture and a mocking glance—even in so little the great power of him was obvious. Unused and restless, his power drew me. I had to acknowledge it, for I scorned to deny the truth of anything. It was the very risk and danger of him I hungered for, I thought: something different from any easy, physical pleasure. Or perhaps it was only the brewing storm I felt. . . . Abruptly I lifted the skin and drank deeply, not wanting to feel anything outside me.

The storm came, and others after it, and I found no answers in any of them; but finally there was an end to winter.

CHAPTER

8

Under a soft blue sky the plain looked to stretch forever, inviting, pale green with the first shoots of new grass. Some herdbeasts who had come out of the fen on their own had gone far enough out on the plain to be small dun dots that in no way interfered with the emptiness of the view. I stood tall where long, soft spring winds purled around me. I was surely the first impediment they had met in their long sweep. I quivered with eagerness to ride *far*, as I had not yet done. It was time to be gone.

But I turned my back on the plain and walked into the Long Fen once more, where rains had melted nearly all the snow, and melted also the mud, which was everywhere. The spring equinox had come. It was time for the Ranking. Then we would ride—those of us who could still claim rank as windriders.

When my turn came, I strode out onto the trampled mud of the Ranking ground like every other windrider, to proclaim my rank and await challenge. Of course challenges came: my rank was high for one so little tested, and whatever difference the others perceived in me, they could not accept that it assured my rank.

It was Surya, lean and tawny, who won the lottery and walked out to meet me. She had already fought once to hold her own rank and again to take a higher one before she came against me, but she walked still with a light step, seemingly untired. And seemingly tireless: I soon realized I had accomplished nothing in beating Wunna and must truly prove myself anew. I saw my Dancer's training and discipline and the hardships I had endured since I left Empire were hardly more than the normal life and upbringing of windriders. In myself I was nothing out of the ordinary among them. Only Gandish Dance gave me an advantage, but at a cost I did not yet know.

I delayed using the Dance until I saw Surya would surely take me. That I could not endure. I let the High Dance take me then, and soon we moved together, Surya and I, in that tightening pattern, and presently she slumped in my hands.

Then I had to fight free of the Dance to keep from killing her. I had waited so long before I called on it to aid me, I had little strength left to fight it. I had controlled it once, with difficulty. This second time was more difficult still, but I did it. When at last I stood motionless over Surya, I felt strained and grim. She lay on the muddy ground and laughed at me.

"Anyway, I have the rank just below yours, Oa," she said. "I may get you another time." Bearing me no ill will, she got to her feet and brushed the mud of the fen from her oiled limbs.

I walked away beside her while Murrila confirmed my rank. From relief I laughed a little, shakily. "That was close," I said. "I almost killed you."

She glanced at me, a frown on her narrow, tanned face. "You'd kill for these low ranks? Well, you need not boast of it!"

I stopped short. "Boast? You think I'm boasting? I don't want your death to bind me to earth so I can't ride!"

"Lords of Sky wouldn't hold it against you," she said dryly. "What happens on the Ranking ground is their will."

I stood so long, Surya went on ahead of me. I had not understood Ajanna correctly. I need not have worried, after all, when the High Dance would have made me kill. Yet I was glad that I had fought off the Dance, that I had subdued it to my will and not let it run free. It seemed to me still to be necessary, even if it was not the lords of Sky who required it.

People called out that I blocked their view. I moved on into the crowd, thinking this night I could celebrate to the full: there could be no more doubt that I was a windrider.

But I did not try for higher rank, not that night. Nor did the other windriders take much interest in the fighting, eager as I was to get these rites behind us, that we might ride out onto the plain. Of them all, only Braha fought to his limit. He would be a chief, I saw, in a few more years, when he reached his full growth. He was growing quickly. Just since midwinter he had grown a handspan taller than me. And he was determined. I lost count of the bouts he fought; he took the rank higher than mine, and then some. Nor did I lie with him that night; he could hardly crawl from the Ranking ground after his last bout—though he had won it.

In the morning I did not remember who I had lain with, though I did not think I had been alone all the night. I was only grateful to find myself in a tent. A sudden shower in the night had made a morass of the last few bits of solid ground, and more than a few windriders had slept where they fell, drunk, in the stinking mud that was everywhere. It was time indeed to be gone!

With other junior herders I made a sweep through the fen after those ornery beasts that had escaped us before. We drove them into the camp to carry gear for the housefolk on their long trek to the summer camp. Raun waited with the other housefolk to take the herdbeasts and bid us farewell, staring at me with the same hungry gaze as always. Seeing it, I sat up taller on Madder's back, stiff with irritation.

"Where is Wiel?" I called out to him. "I would speak with her." Raun's gaze did not change and I felt shamed. But what did he expect of me? I asked myself resentfully. I was a windrider now. Even if I had once been what he thought, I would have put it behind me now to ride.

"She's over there," he said with quiet dignity and a

slight gesture of his head. I slid down from Madder's back and went where Raun indicated—for shame, I suppose; to deny to myself that I felt it.

Wiel was in a grove of trees a little way outside of camp. The spindly fen trees had budded out with small, pale leaves and fleshy blossoms. The air was heavy with the fetid odor of the blossoms, growing stronger even and more unpleasant than the rank smell of the mud. Wiel's baby swung in a leather sling from a tree branch, mewling unheeded. Stripped of her ungainly tunic, Wiel exercised madly to regain her lost strength and agility. Her face was fixed in bitter determination.

"How goes it with you, Wiel?" I blurted, to make my presence known.

She came around to face me. She peered at me as if she did not recognize me. "Ah, Oa. Hail," she said then, mockingly. "I didn't hear you. You're as quiet as your name: the Wind's Sigh. With your rank, you yet deign to spend time with a housewoman?"

What could I answer? There were but few reasons why windriders sought out housefolk, and for none of those reasons had I come in search of her. Indeed, I wished I had not come. Her air of madness made me uneasy. Silently, chewing my lip in indecision, I watched her.

"I won't be housebound for long," she continued. "After the midsummer Ranking, I'll ride."

"But the child won't be weaned—"

Wiel looked at it with contempt. "Let some broodwoman take it on. If I wait on its convenience, Ajanna will see to it I'm with child again, and I'll never escape him."

I glanced at the child myself, frowning. I could understand Wiel's feeling, ugly and noisily demanding as the creature was. I said coldly, "You know you need bear no child you don't choose." I knew by then of the lovers' plant, which grew everywhere on the plain, and most female windriders as well as many housewomen always carried a supply of its dried roots. It was a poison, and one sickened from eating it; but the sickness was short and prevented the longer disability of pregnancy.

"Ajanna—" Wiel began.

"No." I cut her off with conviction. "Ajanna cares for

nothing but himself. He won't take a step out of his way for anyone, either to harm or help. He's probably forgotten you.''

"He shall learn to remember!" she declared with passion. "You're going to see to that for me, Oa. You shall carry out my revenge."

I hissed with anger and refused to answer back to her madness. For madness it was, simply that, I thought with greater certainty than ever before. The child was a symptom of her madness, that I would never make sense of, for it made no sense—from the outset it had injured only her, never Ajanna. Earlier, housebound myself, I had been impressed by the very fire of her madness and thought there lay some great mystery behind it. Now I thought it was nothing so much, just the bitterness of failure eating at her spirit so it was grown as brittle as her flesh. Her windrider's arrogance was become a housewoman's obsession—and nothing I, a windrider, need heed.

Then my gaze crossed hers: I saw again her strange dark eyes, dominating her face more than ever as her flesh wasted, looking on what still I doubted I would dare to look, windrider though I was, and again I wondered.

"Get about your business!" Wiel hissed at me. "I'll be better company when I'm a windrider myself. Go away!" She began again to stretch and flex her limbs.

Rather offended, I went away as she bade me. I had been willing to be friends with her, in acknowledgment of the aid she had given me; it did not occur to me that my very generosity could only emphasize the gap between us, that it was partly from kindness that windriders did not acknowledge housefolk but looked right through them.

Madder came to me, and I swung up upon his back. He leaped away and the wind of passage blew from my mind all thoughts of Wiel and of the camp of the housefolk as the fen fell behind me. I rode out over the plain after the herds.

Where the herds had passed a rank smell lingered in the air. The ground was but churned mud, the grass eaten, and the flowers trampled. A low muttering I felt first in my bones grew to a roar long before I saw the beasts that caused it. Finally, from one horizon to the other, the joined herds of all the Houses stretched before me, herdbeasts in their thousands, a living, dun-colored plain. The herders going among them on their windsteeds to divide the holdings of the separate Houses looked like rare rock outcroppings jutting above this plain: for all we herders looked down on the herdbeasts from windsteedback, they were enormous in their own right, great, shaggy creatures all the colors of the earth, ungainly heads and shoulders near a third of their bulk, small-eyed and small-witted, hard to get moving or once in motion, stopped.

I came to the edge of the herds, and my senses filled with the roaring restless mass. Currents of excitement ran through the massed flesh, sparking by the very crowding, so one beast or another lurched into a clumsy run and slammed its enormous weight against others and set them off as well. I grew dizzy trying to see everywhere at once—dizzy and strangely exhilarated. I hardly knew myself. I could not be still. Thrusting myself up to fill my lungs so my voice would carry over the noise of the beasts, I hailed the distant riders. Several heads turned toward me. "Hail, rider!" someone called back to me, the voice coming very faintly through the trampling of the herds.

The rumble changed its pitch. An eddy of excitement snaked toward me through the herds. Madder shivered at the touch of it and drove his way into the mass of beasts. All through my body I felt a heat and a breathlessness so swiftly swelling that they could find release only in great danger.

Without another thought I swung one leg high over Madder's neck and slid with my back against his shoulder down until my two feet touched the hairy back of a herdbeast. I set my weight full on my feet. The herdbeast bucked and lunged in terror but was hemmed in closely by the others around him; his back was broad and my footing secure. I let go my hold on Madder.

Another herdbeast matched the pace of the one I bestrode. I took a few running steps along the back of the first beast and leaped to the other. Glancing down between them, I caught a narrow glimpse of trampled ground, the new spring grass beaten to nothingness by those that had already passed.

I yelled a challenge to the herds. My voice was lost in the noise of the herds. All around me the beasts ran full out, roaring and pounding: a force that could not be stopped or resisted, which I rode. I knew it was senseless: the utter frivolity of the danger I courted was itself intoxicating. My arms and legs twirled of themselves with an excess of life.

I danced across the herd, leaping from one beast to the next, twisting and whirling and jumping high—no Gandish Dance now, but one that arose from the herds' patternless frenzy. I felt all-powerful, as a lord of Sky might.

Then my foot caught in a tangle of the herdbeast's unshed winter hair. I stumbled and slipped along its sloping withers. The roar of the galloping hooves grew louder as I fell. My sliding fingers scrabbled, then caught in the rough coat, and I pulled myself to safety. On all fours I clung to the herdbeast's back, shaking, my breath heaving. Before my closed eyes the death by trampling I had narrowly missed was vivid.

I got slowly to my feet and looked out over the herd. The ridged, hairy backs, moving fast, rose and fell with the inexorable rhythm of storm waves. Without a windsteed I was nothing, a mote in a frenzied sea, which could dash me into oblivion at any instant and never notice it. Far off across the endless ranks of herdbeasts, my windsteed ran riderless, himself caught in something like my intoxication, perhaps; for once not coming to my command.

The herdbeasts around me, still running hard, were running free of the rest of the herd. Spaces opened between them, and I saw the true danger of my mad impulse. Who could say how long it would be before the massed herds behind me thinned and slowed enough that I could safely drop to the ground? Long before that I would lose my uneasy hold on the beast I rode and fall back to the earth to be trampled.

I must get back to my windsteed at once—or lose the chance forever.

Crouching, I measured with my eyes the distance to the nearest herdbeast. The earth flowing by beneath the beasts was close and real. I took a deep breath and leaped across that churned ground. My feet landed neatly on the shoulders of a herdbeast and made a dance to his bucking protest. My blood ran faster with the taste of such high danger, I felt myself again a being of account. I crouched again to leap, a great distance, laughing softly in triumph.

A shadow fell upon me. I looked up in surprise. Scudder ranged alongside, mincing her steps to slow to the herdbeast's pace, tossing her head with impatience. Above her loomed Ajanna. Without bothering to put his command into words, he held out his hand to me.

I hesitated, and glanced across the thinning herd toward my windsteed. I saw I really had no choice but to accept Ajanna's help. I leaned out and grasped his wrist. He steadied me, and I stepped on his bent knee and swung up behind him on Scudder's back.

Scudder leapt away across the plain, nipping the herdbeasts in her path so they jumped aside squealing. I gripped hard with my knees, not wanting to hold on to Ajanna, his broad back so solid and erect, motionless before me; thinking of the oath I had sworn to him, wondering what he would do to punish my foolishness. For I saw very clearly how foolish I had been. I was hard put to keep from trembling, seeing the danger I had run now it was over. The thought that Ajanna would know my fear stiffened me.

When we came even with my own windsteed, I knew I must lean out over the rushing ground to grab Madder's trailing mane and pull myself across to his back without giving Ajanna the trouble of stopping. My pride demanded it, and somehow I did it. Madder lengthened his stride to match Scudder's but he could not keep her pace. Ajanna drew away without a word or a glance.

Sulking, I rode on, letting Madder choose his pace. I feared Ajanna could prohibit me from riding and, more than ever, riding was what I wanted—all I wanted. I hung my head and huddled over Madder's neck and worried. The herds passed ahead of me into the night, calming as they spread out, and quieting.

Still sulking, I ignored the windrider who came alongside me in the dark. I heard a low chuckle and sensed more than saw something held out toward me. There came the slosh of liquid in a drinking skin. I took the skin and a deep drink and passed the skin back. Looking sidelong, I saw it was Halassa who rode beside me. Our windsteeds ran easily together; smoothly; silently rocking. "What are you laughing at?" I asked.

Halassa stoppered the skin and reached around to fasten it to a gear strap. He leaned toward me confidentially. "I don't know that I'd think much of any windrider who could see the herds for the first time and not try to ride them—and not get carried away with it. I myself rescued Ajanna once."

I turned to him with interest. "Did you now?" I said.

"Mmmmm. But Ajanna's good. You should ask him to show you his technique if you want to do this again."

I growled, thinking how Ajanna had humiliated me. And I did not know what else was in his power to do, now I had given him my oath as herder. I said indignantly, "How can he punish me for something he's done himself?"

"Punish you? Who said anything of punishment? Punish a *windrider?*" The notion seemed beyond Halassa's experience. He dismissed it. He said, "I doubt if Ajanna ever danced so far over a spreading herd as you did today."

"Indeed?" I said, feeling ever more cordial toward him. I remembered the exhilaration of leaping through that raging flood of herdbeasts, and I felt myself invincible. I need not heed Ajanna! But I could not pass up the temptation of measuring myself against him. "The weight and size of him may be a drawback for some things," I said judiciously. I heard Halassa laughing again softly, and I laughed myself.

But I stopped laughing and scowled, remembering how often Ajanna had singled me out to fetch herdbeasts from the fen for milk or butchering, in the worst winter weather, and how he had refused at first to acknowledge me windrider at all.

"Ajanna means me ill," I said angrily. Halassa only grunted—disagreeing, I thought. "He does," I insisted.

"And you call yourself a windrider?" Halassa asked then, in the same easy voice he always had, but it silenced me.

While I rode nothing else should matter, not Ajanna or anything—and it did not. While Madder swept on through the night, Halassa and his Starwind became only a shadow in darkness. The hollow sound of hooves on trampled ground gave way to the sleek sibilance of grass when we came where the herds had not been. The sound caressed me sweetly. Truly, riding was all.

Halassa leaned across the open ground sweeping by unseen and tugged at the short braids my hair had grown out to, which spilled from a crest running from my forehead to the nape of my neck. "Your hair glows in the dark," he said in an altered voice, and I knew he had been more aware of me than I of him. I bethought myself how from the first I had been drawn to the quiet, sturdy bulk of him, and wondered how with one thing or another I had hardly come to know him in the winter. I turned to look through the darkness for him. "In the darkest night I could find you," he said. The catch in his voice called up a different heat in me from what the herds had done, and a similar recklessness.

"I will dance upon the night!" I cried. I got my feet under me and stood free on Madder's broad, rocking back, and leaped to Halassa's Starwind, or rather into the darkness where I sensed her to be.

Halassa caught me and held me close against him, so I felt his quickening, laughing breath. I wrapped my arms around him tightly, feeling his bulk that was as solid as a windsteed's, liking this companionship that was as easy and sure as riding itself.

Halassa ran his hands over my body, and my own breath came as ragged as his. I reached inside the stiff folds of his riding leathers, to the sleeker hardness of his body.

Starwind slowed. Holding on to each other, Halassa and I slipped to the dark ground.

CHAPTER

9

When I woke the earth was still dark but the huge sky was clear, pale and empty save for one small cloud near the horizon, which glittered with the fiery colors of the unrisen sun. Halassa called to our windsteeds. I lay on the ground a moment looking up at him large and solid, pleasingly so. . . . I thought how he had pleased me in the night just past; I felt desire stir—no, now I would ride. I jumped to my feet and laced my leathers with a better will even than I had stripped them off. I mounted Madder and ran ahead, while the day lightened the earth, across a plain that seemed never to have been touched. Nor did I touch it: I rode "between."

Later I let Halassa catch up to me, and we came to the herds spreading across the plain for grazing, separating into the holdings of the individual Houses. We rode more slowly then, with the others, working north behind Ajanna's beasts.

Herding was work, as Ajanna had promised me. The herdbeasts' great size was matched by great stupidity and a stubbornness that amounted to madness and often seemed to border on the unnatural—perhaps supernatural—as windsteeds in their very different way also did. Herdbeasts could not live without us. Alone, they would graze down one part of the plain to desert they could not then escape; or they would wander so far from water they would die for the lack of it; and if they did scent water they were likely to run themselves over a cliff to reach it if they were not held back. Once they must have been otherwise; by long herding they had become beasts that must be herded—even as by long running and riding windsteeds riders became beings that must run and ride.

The herds tied us to the earth by a bond that we heeded, for upon them our lives and livelihoods depended; but it was a bond so fragile that we were not held except that we willed it—because only so could we live riding.

There was a rhythm to our work, over the long run, which also held us: the long drives north and south across vast distances of plain. Marking the changes of season and direction were the four meetings for the Ranking rites: brief interruptions in the long drives, intervals of confinement that built up to the great flash of release in the actual fighting.

Season by season I fought and won and rose steadily in rank, learning ever better how to use Gandish Dance—if never so completely as to stifle my distrust of intruding it into this windriding life. I acquired a reputation for wildness that grew with my rank and derived finally only partly from my different origin. There was nothing I did that was not what windriders did, and that I was a windrider none could dispute unless they beat me on the Ranking ground, and none did. But the difference remained, as stubbornly real as my different appearance. I felt it myself, and felt goaded by it to want always . . . what, I did not know; mostly I was goaded to wildness. And mostly I thought whatever more I wanted was only what came to windriders.

The second winter was mild, more rain than snow, but not much of either. We did not know at first what change this weather portended—then, at the beginning, it was merely an inconvenience, keeping the fens from ever freezing solid, so the mud and stink of them dogged us through our stay there. We cut it short.

The following summer the grass on the plain was thin, and after the autumn Ranking we in Ajanna's House ran far inland, seeking new pasture for forage before winter came on. It was late in the season—already cold but still dry—before we finally turned south across a region that was not what we were used to, cut with unusually deep, treacherous canyons. They delayed us yet longer. However, they grew shallower and more open with each we passed heading south.

But always one more canyon yawed! I peered into the morning mist rising through the autumnal stillness from the canyon ahead. The mist thinned as the sun rose, so shapes of windsteeds and riders gradually became distinct from the shadowy mass of the herd. The angry mutterings of the herd seemed to grow louder, as if the mist had been containing the noise but, weakening, could do so no longer. The beasts were restless from being run all night in a circle. They sensed the nearness of the canyon, which we had waited for daylight to cross; they felt our edginess about it, and perhaps something on their own account. I kept moving, as I had all night, to keep them together.

Halassa and Surya jogged toward me. "I'm going into the herd to fill my drinking skins," I called. They glanced at the muttering herd but said nothing. They might not have gone into it, but I would. I turned Cloud to run along the edge of the herd while I searched for a cow with only one calf, who would have milk to spare. There: the piebald. Cloud pushed into the herd readily for once, surprising me.

I was Cloud's first rider, and I had ridden her only a season. When Ajanna assigned me a rare new windsteed, I had taken it as an acknowledgment of my proven ability. Cloud's skittishness had since made me doubt it. More likely Ajanna gave her to me to pay me back for the inconvenience some wildness or carelessless of mine had caused him. He was not likely to have thought whatever I had done was most often at *his* lead.

I thought Cloud beautiful, truly like cloud or mist, her sleek storm-gray hide blotched toward the hindquarters with paler grays. In some light she looked to have no material substance at all. But she was always very surely herself. Her very willfulness and unreliability enhanced this impression of individuality. But this once she moved into the herd just as she ought to.

I leaned down to pound the hilt of my knife against a stubborn herdbeast that would not move to let us pass. It jumped. Cloud shied, but steadied and went on. Coming up on the piebald cow from behind, I sheathed my knife and dropped a rawhide noose over her head before she became aware of me. She stood stock still, snorting. Cloud took the rope in her teeth and lifted her great, wedge-shaped head to pull it taut. I slid to the ground. Cloud swung out just as she should to clear a space for me. I reached under the piebald to milk her. Her single calf peered at me under her belly. It was a fine, young beast, born early in the season.

My bucket full, I crawled into the larger space under Cloud's belly to empty the bucket into several small-mouthed drinking skins. The dregs left in the skins would inoculate the fresh milk. In two days' time it would be fermented to the thick, sour liquid that would warm me against the cold. Winter was coming on, and we had a long way to go.

Cloud allowed the herd to pack about her tightly, confining me in a dark cave under her belly. The smell of the herd was strong in the enclosed space, and intensified by the mist dampening the hairy hides. I wormed between Cloud's forelegs and stood under her head with my back to her chest. I reached out to free the piebald herdbeast from the rope.

I felt Cloud trembling at this close confinement by the herd. "Easy, easy," I crooned. She reached her head past me to nip the herdbeasts pressing against her, and they kicked out in alarm. I heard the plunk of a stray kick nicking the bony hardness of Cloud's long legs. Aroused, she struck back. The herd began to move.

Above the scuffling noise of the herdbeasts I heard the thin shouts of herders working to keep the herd under control. I cursed myself for a fool to trust myself on foot in a herd alone with the inexperienced Cloud. I had been herding long enough to know how unreliable a herd was in changing weather—especially so near a canyon. I knew; I would not see I had come just *because* of the danger.

Mouths gaped wide all around me, all teeth and tongue, dripping slime. Beasts bellowed deafeningly. Their eyes rolled, showing the whites like maddened creatures. Shaggy winter hair made them look even larger and more ferocious than they were. Though I looked down on the herdbeasts from windsteedback, they were imposing indeed seen from where I stood on the ground. My head was on a height with an enormous head jutting directly from mountainous shoulders.

The raw power of the herd seemed to raise me up on its crest, like a soaring windsteed lifting me into a storm, exhilarating; but I knew that if I did not soon gain the safety of Cloud's back I would not come out of the herd alive.

I pulled my knife from its sheath in my leggings. I pounded with the hilt on the forehead of a lumbering beast caught by an eddy of the herd and shoved under Cloud's neck against me. Slowly the beast gave way. I laughed aloud. Cloud tossed her head and tried to back away from the beast—or from me. Abruptly the lumbering beast burst into rapid motion and smashed into the herd, which reacted at once with heightened movement. Soon I would be swept into the maelstrom of heaving bodies and ground into the dark earth beneath their feet. My blood ran hard and fast. Never had I been so keenly aware of how sweet it was to live and how full of life I was. I lifted my chin, breathing deeply of the herd's excitement and the danger.

A herdbeast ranged alongside Cloud and stopped, facing into the current of the herd, which split briefly to go around the three of us. I saw my chance; I was not so drunk on the danger I did not still want to live.

I stepped forward under the herdbeast's head and sliced my knife across its throat. "Give me your life, lord of Earth, that I might live to ride," I murmured hastily, so as not to omit the butcher's rites altogether. I stepped back from the spurting blood: I must not slip on it.

The beast crumpled and silently fell in the middle of the crazed herd. Smelling death, Cloud froze. I stepped lightly to the shoulder of the falling herdbeast and flung one leg over Cloud's back, at the same time whipping my hands among the long strands of her mane. The knife I held in one hand dripped hot blood on her neck.

Cloud whirled in terror, smashing against the herdbeasts, exciting them still more. All existence seemed comprised of plunging herdbeasts. I yelled in challenge and gripped hard with hands and knees. It took all my strength to keep my seat while Cloud fought her way through the herd. Then I could have known it was for that intoxicating ride I had come into the herd, not for the lesser intoxication from kwass. But just then I did not know anything, so caught up I was in the moment.

Cloud burst free of the herd and ran upon open plain. She ran frenzied, faster than ever before, and when she would have slowed, I urged her on. It was a long while before I thought of anything but running, and when I did, what I thought of was how the oath that bound me to herder's duties chafed me more and more.

But I turned back.

A stiff breeze had blown away all but the last tatters of mist, so that from a distance I could see the windriders of Ajanna's House gathered around Ajanna sitting on his huge dun-colored Scudder. The herd was still restless, but the threat of stampede seemed to have passed.

Cloud pranced as she approached the others, expressing my own high spirits from our heady ride. The others grinned at me in greeting. They might not have wanted to share this particular exploit, but they understood it, being windriders.

Ajanna, alone ignoring me, said sententiously, "This may be the last canyon we'll have to cross for a while. And so the last water we'll find. Don't rush the beasts. Make sure they drink well. Let them graze. Canyon greens'll put some weight on them for winter. There's been little enough grass on the plain to do it."

While he spoke, Ajanna's eyes roved over the lot of us, near two score. He divided us into squads for the work. "Clear the beasts out of side canyons," he ordered those with whom he grouped me. "The rest of you be ready to drive them up the far wall and keep them on the plain when they get there. I'll go upstream ahead of you to turn the leaders of the herd back. Everybody out of the canyon by sundown, unless you plan to hunt rivercats—or to be hunted by rivercats. Lost beasts'll be deduced from your personal holdings.'' He looked over my head at some imaginary object on the empty plain behind me. "Including the one you just butchered for no reason, Oa.''

I scowled, but I knew Ajanna was within his rights to take from my holdings. I cared more about the humiliating manner in which he did it. Without a word I rode after the others to drive the herd over the edge of the canyon.

We followed the herdbeasts down a steep, crumbling slope into the depths of the earth. The wind on the plain had been chill, harbinger of winter, but in the canyon was a wholly different season, calm and balmy, at least for a few midday hours. While we slowly worked the herd upriver, the sun rose until it stood straight overhead and lit the canyon brightly. Summery air filled with dust from the herd's passage. I flung back my cloak and tugged at the tight lacings of my shirt at my neck. I cursed Ajanna for making us all so uncomfortable by this sudden start of his at considering the welfare of the herd so closely.

I turned Cloud into another narrow side canyon. Its walls were oppressively close and the herdbeasts amazingly sly about working their way unseen into its farthest reaches. I let Cloud go after three cows who passed us and then stopped to nibble the brush. She rushed them, but one lingered for a last mouthful. Cloud stretched her neck to nip the cow's rump. The cow squealed and jogged away, leaving clumps of her hair on the ends of branches as she passed.

The patches of hair looked just like the detritus still hanging in the trees from spring flooding. I tried to visualize water filling the canyon to such a height, mud-colored, angrily swirling, but the dry stillness made it impossible to imagine such a quantity of water—and this last spring, anyway, there probably had not been.

The air was better when I came to the main canyon, where an afternoon breeze sprang up over the river. I raised my arm to signal to Halassa. He would drive the beasts across the river, where still others waited to herd them up the other wall of the canyon.

Cloud's hoof clanged upon rock. In front of me the river and its canyon swung in a wide curve to the left. There were no more canyons opening on this side, so I signaled back to Halassa to cross the river. I was the last herder, at the very end of the herd. Cloud tossed her head in distaste at the thick brush, as high as her shoulder, which clogged the bank all the way to the canyon wall—another indication there had been little in the way of flood this spring. Cloud picked her way, setting each foot with exaggerated care, and I scanned the brush for any movement that might betray hidden beasts.

The sun dropped behind the rim of the canyon. Shadow reached across the river to me. Cloud flushed a yearling herdbeast, and I watched its passage, marked by violently waving branches, through brush taller than it was. The canyon floor steepened, and the brush stopped at a pile of boulders higher than Cloud's head. The first yearling and another I had not seen burst from the brush and scrambled up the rock. Cloud clattered after them, sure-footed now she could see the ground.

The river was dammed by the rocks into a large pool. Ajanna's Scudder stood knee-deep in the water, floating her tail over the waterfall of the overflow of the pool. I did not see Ajanna, but I heard his voice raised in anger. I followed the noise through the brush that again choked the canyon into a clearing already crowded by Ajanna and the two yearlings. Ajanna succeeded in driving them into the water, and Scudder, well trained, pushed them to the other side of the river.

Ajanna had obviously been lying on the bank after bathing, to dry in the short hours of warm sun. His naked body was now covered with dust, and hair shed by the yearlings, who seemed to have trampled his clothes into the mud at the river's edge. I laughed. Ajanna swung his clothes against the brush to clean them, ignoring me. I clucked to Cloud to go on to the shallower water at the head of the pool to cross the river. Dusk was near. It was time to get out of the canyon.

Ajanna jumped me when my back was turned. The two

of us were carried over Cloud's back into the water. I gasped at the cold and could not breathe for a long instant. I kicked and scratched myself free and sat up in the shallow water. Ajanna stood over me, laughing. His body, mud-streaked and massive, was so perfectly muscled that it looked graceful. A last sunbeam lit up the water in his long, black hair, so it glistened like the glitter in his black eyes. His eyes were as open and vast as a windsteed's. I stared long into them before I could wrench my gaze away.

I looked to search out a thrashing noise on the opposite bank. Cloud, who had been skittish about the canyon all day, had taken advantage of the commotion to make a break for the plain. Up a steep slope she bounded, cloud-like indeed, her gray hide gleaming through the shadows with blotches of silvery blue. She was lovely to watch, but she was leaving me stranded. Angrily I turned to Ajanna—and bit off my hot words unsaid. He, too, was watching Cloud, and I saw an opportunity to get my own back.

Slowly, ignoring the pain of the cold water by an effort of will, I gathered my feet under me and jumped. I struck Ajanna with all my weight on the side of his leg below the knee. He took an involuntary step back and lost his footing on the slippery streambed.

As Ajanna fell I continued on toward Scudder, who was watching us with such interest that she forgot to chew the branch she held in her mouth. Before I lost my momentum I grasped her trailing mane and pulled myself onto her neck. I urged her toward the other bank: let Ajanna be the one who must climb on foot the steep, dusty wall of the canyon.

Glancing back, I saw Ajanna get to his feet and shake the water from his head. He gestured to Scudder, who obediently dropped to her knees and rolled in the water, forcing me to swim free.

I swam on across the pool, resigned to climbing to the plain on foot. I could see it was still daylight above the rim, but in the depths along the river it was already dusk. And it was cold. The summery warmth was disappearing even faster than the daylight.

"Why do you hurry, Oa?" Ajanna called after me. "Do

you think I can't protect you from the rivercats?" His harsh voice echoed from the canyon walls, mocking me again and again.

"I can take care of myself," I called back haughtily, trying not to shiver and destroy the effect I was trying for.

"Then stay and hunt with me tonight." His recklessness was contagious. At once I craved the danger.

"Very well," I said with a show of indifference. I sat on my heels on the cobbled bank. I felt about for a flat stone and pulled my knife from its sheath in my leggings and set to honing the gleaming white blade of hard windsteed rib bone.

Ajanna dropped lightly beside me and slapped Scudder's rump so she kept going. I marveled again at the ungainliness of a slowly moving windsteed. The spindly, contorted legs seemed in the way of each other and too rickety by far to hold up the massive body. Windsteed bones were very light, the long bones hollow tubes of incredible strength. Our tools made from sharpened ribs and shoulder blades were light and delicately shaped but very strong.

The sound of Scudder's crashing progress through the brush died away. She climbed the canyon wall to the plain, driving a last few herdbeasts before her. Everyone else must be gone. The rumbling of the river swelled to replace the daytime noises that faded with the light.

Ajanna brushed the mud from his riding leathers. He was so much larger than me that his body seemed of utterly alien proportions. If he had been a rivercat he could hardly have been more different from me than he was.

He put on his clothes and crouched down beside me. "See the opening in the brush there? It's a trail wild beasts made to get to the river. No doubt a rivercat will come by sometime in the night to see what might be here. We'll wait here for it."

I nodded.

The darkness increased until I could see nothing. The high canyon walls cut off even the starlight that kept the plain from utter darkness when there was no moon. The river was a flowing shadow, seemingly independent of its all-pervasive noise.

The hours passed slowly. Ajanna sat so still that I had

little awareness of him except for the steady warmth of his huge body, against which I huddled in my wet clothes. Indeed, in the darkness filled with the river noise I soon lost all sense of myself. Doubtless I sat as still as Ajanna could have wished.

Something brought me alert. I flexed my fingers on the hilt of my knife to make sure they were not stiff. I became aware that Ajanna was tensed and listening. From upstream came a rumble such as a river makes when the water rises for an instant.

Something moved between me and the river, something large, flowing like the river. Even as I perceived it, Ajanna exploded into motion. I leaped with him, raising my knife to strike.

I collided with something solid. My knife smashed into it and scraped against bone. Close to my ear I heard the rush of Ajanna's breath expelled in effort. I jerked my knife back and struck again.

Fire streaked across my shoulder and chest, and remained, burning. Something, or someone—was it I?—cried out. I could see nothing and, after the single cry, the struggle seemed utterly silent, any noise drowned out by the river.

Suddenly it was over. My knife hung in empty air, and I lost my balance and fell forward upon the cobbled riverbank. Ajanna's voice rose above the noise of the river, cursing.

"Oa? Where are you? Are you going to cower like some frightened little beast just waiting to be killed? It's we who hunt the cat, not the other way around."

His scorn goaded me. I staggered to my feet and moved toward the sound of his voice. My outstretched hand encountered his body, as hard and massive as the cat's.

"Don't put your knife into *me!* I think the cat's gone upriver. Follow close so I know where you are."

I swung my knife aside; I had been about to stab him. I grabbed a fold of his leathers and stumbled after him. My head swam and my shoulder throbbed. The roar of the river had turned threatening. Ajanna took longer steps than I could, and every so often I had to jog a few extra steps to keep up with him. This difficult uneven pace absorbed all my attention. I let everything else go. Even shivering was an intolerable effort.

We came into more of the dense brush. I lost hold of Ajanna, and now the brush kept me from walking at my own pace. I pushed it aside awkwardly, for I held a knife in my right hand and my left was strangely numb. The long knife caught in the brush. I yanked it free as I went on—that was somehow easier than stopping.

A thrashing sounded somewhere ahead. Ajanna's voice cried a challenge. A raging snarl drowned him out. Wildness swelled in me to match the rage I heard. I shouted and broke into a run. The brush seemed now to part before me of its own accord.

My hands encountered something warm and furred, and solid as rock: the rivercat had waited for us. Muscles rippled and twisted under my hands. Suddenly green eyes thrust in my face and held me in their gaze. The cat's gaze screamed rage and bloodlust. Fascinated, I watched the preparation in the cat's mind, the coiling back, the sleek play of perfect muscle, and I came near accepting that I was its fit prey.

Dimly I felt another presence, one that sprang forward past me and lunged against the cat, which turned its gaze to look. I heard Ajanna grunt once, sounding surprised.

The rivercat swung its gaze back toward me; but the interruption had freed me and taught me not to meet its eyes if I would survive. Keeping my eyes averted, I swung my knife in the direction of the green glow. The knife went deep into something, but the glow grew stronger and closer. I felt a hot, stinking breath in my face, and thought I must be lost. Doggedly I flung my weight upon the knife and twisted it deeper.

Slowly the cat sank beneath me, and the green glow faded until the darkness was again complete. I could do no more. I slumped over the enormous, still body. The noise of the river rose to cover me.

Day came with light and the reeking of blood. I gagged on the smell, so strong it seemed to fill my mouth. I tried to sit up, but pain rushed through me with such force I gasped for breath and could not move. I lay back and became aware of a curious sleekness under my hands. The rivercat—the hunt . . . but then what—?

Fighting back pain and nausea, I sat up, staring about me. I lay across the cat, whose rich pelt was stained and matted. Fresh blood trickled onto it, which I traced to its origin in a jagged tear in the shoulder of my shirt. The torn leather was mixed with my own raw, bleeding flesh. I stared at that.

There came a groan. The cat did not move. Its head was turned to me, so I saw one eye. It was open, but opaque, so I could see nothing in it. Beyond the cat, Ajanna stirred. I crawled to him, thinking it too much trouble to stand and walk, when I would have to kneel again when I reached him. There was a lot of blood on his clothes, but I could not tell if it was his or the cat's. He opened his eyes.

"Lie still," I said.

Sense came into his dark eyes. "The cat," he whispered. "Oa, did you kill it?"

"I don't know. It's dead."

"Ah." He smiled grimly and tried to move. His face paled, and he bit his lip. His eyes fixed on my torn shoulder. He whispered, "We'll soon be dead, too, from the poison that comes in cat wounds. See if you can find poultice leaves." He closed his eyes.

I stood up, swaying, faint. Wiel had once pointed out the poultice plants to me. It grew beside water. I moved toward the river.

Hooves clattered on rock. Windsteeds broke through the brush and surrounded me: half a dozen of them with Scudder and Cloud riderless in their midst. Halassa slid down beside me and glanced around, taking in the situation. "Someone fetch poultice leaves," he said, and picked me up bodily and carried me to the river.

Halassa cut away my shirt and held me in the river so its current washed the wound. The chill of the water dulled the pain. I noticed the river ran away red. "Have you other wounds?" Halassa asked.

"I don't know," I gasped.

His hands slid over my body and legs. "None of this blood seems to be yours," he said.

Lirra came up behind Halassa with an armful of the large, fleshy poultice leaves. She folded up her long legs to squat down beside me. She packed a great wad of leaves against my shoulder and bound it in place with shirt lacings.

I said weakly, "How deft you are. And gentle."

Halassa snorted. "Why must you always follow Ajanna's example, Oa? You know very well windriders may know ease and affection." His head was bent, intent on his work, so I could not see his expression. But I thought, as perhaps he intended, of the times the two of us had been together, by ourselves or with Lirra.

It was true there was much to a windrider's life besides harshness and danger. But the high, swift feeling of danger, like that of riding, was one I could not resist. Always I left Halassa, and Lirra, and the others for whom I had affection—to follow such as Ajanna, for whom I had none, but who drew me all the same. "I can ride," I said.

"Good." Halassa tied the last knot. He put his hand against my face. Briefly I leaned the weight of my head against it. My head seemed too heavy. "No fever—yet," he said. He stood up.

Lirra said, "I don't think Ajanna will ride."

I looked at her with surprise. "Why not?"

She stared back at me, then laughed shortly. "Why not!" she repeated. "And that's just what he'll say, too. Because he's dying from cat wounds is why not, Oa!"

I could not imagine Ajanna yielding his life to anything, even a rivercat. Even I had not done that. I thought I must be misunderstanding what Lirra was saying.

"He must ride," Halassa said grimly. Lirra nodded. They walked away from me, and their voices flowed into the sound of the river, so I could not make out their words.

The water splashed, and the brush trembled in the morning breeze. For all that I had said I could ride, I did not seem to be quite ready to move.

Ajanna's deep voice rumbled behind me. "Just bind it against the poison. I'll be all right. And somebody skin that rivercat before the pelt is ruined by the blood."

I grinned to myself. I, Oa, had taken—or at least helped to take—a rivercat.

Halassa came back to me with a drinking skin. He made me drink a good half of its contents and then lifted me onto Cloud's back, ignoring my protestations, that I could mount by myself. My shoulder—my whole left side—was numb and useless. I twisted my right hand through Cloud's mane. The yellowing light of day and the great, solid mass of Cloud's body were reassuringly familiar. Of course I could ride.

Lirra rolled up the catskin. "Whose is it?" she asked. She looked at me.

I looked at Ajanna. He was sitting on the ground while the others bound his shirt over poultices. His face was a peculiar gray color. His eyes met mine. "We'll share the skin half and half. Scudder, come here! Lift me to her back!"

The others looked at each other in silence. Scudder lowered her head to sniff at Ajanna's poultices. "Do as I say!" Ajanna snapped.

Scudder knelt, and together the others hoisted Ajanna onto her back and steadied him while she stood up. He collapsed against her neck and would have fallen had not the others been holding him. They tied him to Scudder's neck and to the gear straps cinched around her middle.

Ajanna watched with an angry expression, but he did not object. When the others were done, he looked over at me and said in a tight voice, "Oa. If I am crippled so I can't ride or fight, I curse you for finishing off that rivercat before it killed me." His eyes raged at me just as the cat's had done, but he almost fainted from the exertion.

I stared back at him without speaking, mostly because I could not speak. It was all I could do to keep my seat on Cloud. But I was content: the rivercat I had hunted was dead, and as yet I was not.

Halassa said, "Ajanna, you can't expect a windrider to hold back on a cat hunt or anywhere else. You would have done what Oa did."

The others nodded.

We rode off.

CHAPTER

10

We rode forever, it seemed to me. White snow of winter storms swirled about us. And yet I was so hot I threw off my cloak and loosened the lacing at the neck of my shirt. I knew it was strange; everything was strange to me, fevered with poisoned wounds.

There was not really very much snow—it was just that the wind swirled it around and around. Or perhaps we rode around and around within it. . . . I tried to puzzle out the difference. A windsteed approached, looming into substance out of the whirling snow, distracting me from my calculations. Halassa leaned near where I lay on Cloud's neck, pillowed on her mane.

"Oa, can you keep riding?"

The herds waited for no one. Those who could not ride were left behind—to die. I was on Cloud's back. I was riding. Yet I knew I rode only so long as I could prove myself to lords of Sky and to my windsteed—only so long as I willed. "I ride!" I said aloud.

I heard for myself how weak my voice was. Halassa was silent, his expression grim, not even trying to reassure me. I forced myself upright on Cloud's back, into that terrible white blur of the storm, which made my head spin. "I ride!" I cried defiantly. Icy particles stung my unprotected, heated face. The wind mocked my arrogant claim. But arrogance was all I had left, so I held fast to it. I locked my feet under Cloud's throat. She tossed her head and lengthened her stride, eager to go. She ran full out, and I sat erect against the storm. The confusion of fever and the pain in my shoulder gave way before my will. I rode.

Of her own accord Cloud dropped into an easier pace. I did not object once I had proved my point. I burrowed under her mane and slept. Later my shoulder again hurt unspeakably, and I rode close to the others and drank large quantities of kwass to dull the pain. Windriders might do these things so long as they could also ride alone.

I kept riding.

"There are trees ahead," someone called out. "The camp can't be far.

I looked up blankly. Trees and then housefolk appeared as if from nowhere. The tents, drab-colored like the ground, covered only patchily with snow, were invisible. Knowing, as housefolk always did, that something was afoot, they crowded close, probing with calculating eyes. Some windriders from other Houses, come to the camp in the Long Fen long before us, showed up as well. This was no time to show weakness.

Ajanna jumped down from Scudder unaided. He passed close by me, and I saw his face had grown thin and deeply lined. More than ever his black eyes dominated his face. His gaze crossed mine. I drew my breath in sharply. In the long, fevered ride from the canyon where we had hunted the rivercat I had found only pain and confusion. Ajanna looked to have come through these to some truly new state; I shrank from even the reflection of it in his eyes.

The other windriders of Ajanna's House busied themselves with their windsteeds or their gear, carefully ignoring Ajanna—and me. Ajanna stooped to enter his tent and was gone. Now I must alight.

I took a deep breath and steeled myself. I threw one leg over Cloud's neck. Turning, I glimpsed Halassa's hands gripping Starwind's gear straps. He gripped so hard that his knuckles stood out white against his ruddy skin. But he would not look at me or come to me. Windriders did not belittle their companions by helping them to do things they could not do alone.

I leaned toward him. "Halassa—" Dizziness took my voice away.

The housefolk were upon me at once, sensing in me a source of whatever was amiss, their faces hungry to see a windrider's misfortune. The sight so angered me I threw up my head and slid hastily to the ground with my back along Cloud's shoulder.

I seemed to slide in a stream of hot agony into a burning, bottomless pool of fire. Cloud shifted her weight restlessly, disturbed by the housefolk crowding close. I almost fell over, for my feet could not find solid ground.

I fought grimly for some awareness other than pain. I fought myself harder than I had ever fought an opponent. I moved not a muscle, but my breath came as quickly as if from strenuous exertion. Partly, doubtless, from fear. I had thought the wound must be healing—almost healed. Why, then, this sudden increase in pain?

My unseeing eyes stared into the crowd of housefolk. I became aware of a hard, black-eyed gaze staring back at me: Ajanna's eyes, blazing with anger. For killing the rivercat before it killed him? I shook my head, bewildered, for I had seen Ajanna go into his tent. Then I realized it was Raun I saw now. I almost laughed. I suppose he was angry that I risked my life—before giving him his precious, foolish message from Ocean.

"Houseman!" I called out harshly, cruelly. "Fetch me down my drinking skin!" Raun came forward haltingly. Gingerly—well knowing he was housebound and must not touch a windsteed—he took a skin of kwass from Cloud's gear strap and handed it to me. I gulped the sour liquid. Someone else came up behind Raun: Wiela—no, Wiel; she was not wearing riding dress, so she must be housebound again.

"You're already drunk," Wiel said loudly. "You don't need any more!"

I scowled, seeing she meant to cover my disability. At my scowl, Raun dropped his angry gaze. He was not like

Ajanna after all, I thought, at least not any longer. He could be cowed. As for Wiel, she would help me only to further her mad, housewoman's schemes against Ajanna. Was I, a windrider, to be caught between Raun and Wiel? It was unthinkable. I lifted my head higher, refusing to think it.

Wiel took the drinking skin from my hand and stoppered it. She put one arm under my good shoulder.

"Let's go in," she said. "It's cold."

I shrugged off her hand and walked carefully ahead of her, keeping my attention on the kwass burning in my stomach in order to ignore the other burning in my shoulder. I made it into a tent, but then I collapsed. I let Wiel—I could not stop her—rip off my clothes and bandages. I thought myself my wounds had somehow reopened. But whole skin, new, pink, and delicate, filled the four parallel slashes the rivercat's claws had torn.

"Cat wounds," Wiel whispered. "Poison. How long was it before you got poultice leaves on it?"

"A few hours . . . half the night," I said weakly.

"The wounds healed up and sealed the poison inside."

"What now?"

Wiel shrugged. "You won't die of it now you've lived this long." She did not look very concerned about the fact that I would have to live with it, I thought angrily. Then the pain washed higher, cresting in a flood that swept me away.

I roused, hearing a soft voice call my name insistently. Eagerly I turned toward the sound of Jily's voice. The years of windriding were gone in a flash. Jily!

Fire seared my consciousness, wiping out my delight, and leaving me confused.

"Oa!"

I stared long, as if I had never seen the rough, leather tent where I lay or the golden lovely female who knelt over me. It was Coory. Yes, of course. Jily and Empire were long behind me. Years before I had put them behind me. I had not thought of them for I could not remember how long. Why now? I wondered.

Then I screamed in anger at a sudden thrust of pain and forgot everything else.

Hastily Coory took her hand from my shoulder. "Ajanna wants you, she said tartly. She was not used to such a reception from housefolk or high chiefs or anyone in between. I managed a grin when the pain receded a bit. I got to my feet and followed her.

Ajanna lay sprawled upon piled skins in his enormous chief's tent. It seemed empty without him striding about. It *was* empty, I realized: when he had sent Coory out, we two were alone. I sat down stiffly, nursing my shoulder.

Ajanna spoke with unusual circumspection, in an unusually low voice. I knew his wounds were far worse than mine; I supposed even he must feel them. He said, "I know, Oa, that you weren't born on this plain—"

I looked up swiftly, but remained silent.

"—that you came here over Ocean—"

"I am a windrider!"

"Yes, yes. And though it is often said that windriders don't remember their previous lives, you might have more to remember than others do. . . ."

I grunted. At least he had acknowledged that I was a windrider.

He persisted. "You fight better than one of your youth should know to do—as if you well knew what the Rankings were before you came to them. I think that may come of such memories as I spoke of. I don't care about that. But perhaps you have other knowledge we generally lack . . . a knowledge of healing."

Still I said nothing, more wary than pleased that Ajanna, who seemed never to notice others, had seen something in my fighting.

Ajanna's voice hardened. "If I can't ride or fight to hold my rank, I'll kill you. I have sworn it."

"Bloodthreats!" I hissed, angered beyond caution. "Will you tell me now such words are fit for windriders? Once you thought differently!"

He shrugged, or tried to. It was more like a wince. His black eyes gleamed with a wicked light. Too late I realized he had gotten me to acknowledge remembering something from a time before I became a windrider: the conversation when I threatened him with his own knife if he did not agree to leave me free to compete in the Ranking.

As I had done that other day, he now would stop at nothing to gain his end. This wounding was the first check he had come upon, I realized. I saw he would spend his honor, his pride, his life, to pass this hinder, to hold his rank and ride. He would even beg aid of me. That I was reluctant to see. He was, after all, a high chief, a windrider honed and proven as few could be. And he was Ajanna, always something apart from all others. But he asked much. . . .

"Your wounds don't heal?" I asked, delaying.

He said, "The flesh heals, as well as may be expected anyway, but the muscles aren't growing straight."

He must be thinking, as I was, of Raun's ruined leg, which kept him from fighting even the merest stripling among the lowest ranks.

"Is there poison in your wounds?" I asked.

Ajanna shrugged again, this time without wincing. "That I can bear."

I considered how much worse his pain must be than mine, and I began to think him greater in this resistance to betrayal by his own body than he had been in the earlier perfection of his strength.

I sat silent, considering—but I was delaying needlessly. I thought I could help him; I knew I had already decided to try. No one need ever know where I had got the knowledge, I thought. Empire's name would still not be spoken on this plain. Truly I could not *see* there was any risk, I only felt that old, instinctive dread.

I said cautiously, "Of wounds and their healing I know no more than you do. But I know it's possible to manipulate and stretch the muscles while they're healing. It's painful when the wounds are deep, but it can restore the function of the muscles."

As a child in the Imperial palace I had learned the structure and care of muscles and tendons. The High Dance was strenuous and demanding, as it had to be to test the many spawn of a Great House. In my deep delving into Dance, I had also found the knowledge to survive such exigencies of the Dance. The Dynast had had to fashion other tests for me, which he *had* done—with something like vengeance. I thought again of Jily and of my love for her.

Ajanna recalled me impatiently to the present. "Do what you must," he said.

I stood up, still caught somewhere between his tent and Empire. I pushed away what was not real or before me, saying, "I'll fetch housefolk and show them what to do."

"No! They might talk. The high chiefs must not learn how badly I am hurt. You must do it yourself."

"Ah."

The careful balance among the high chiefs must already be upset by the rumors that would have come of our late arrival. The cat hunt could not be kept secret, but certain knowledge of the nature and extent of Ajanna's injuries would let the others think they had some advantage over him—and that in itself would *be* an advantage.

"But—Raun?" I asked. "You can trust him."

"Raun least of all!"

Then I thought what Wiel charged was true: Ajanna had betrayed Raun.

Ajanna scowled at me. "The wrong I did to Raun was to give him life when he had lost the use of it. As you may have done to me."

"If you think Raun seeks a houseman's revenge, you don't know him!"

"He's housebound!"

"He didn't lose his honor with his rank!"

"He's housebound," Ajanna repeated. For him that was an end to the matter. Ajanna could not comprehend the existence of someone who did not ride.

I shrugged and noticed that I as well as Ajanna could make this gesture without visibly wincing.

"Do your work!" Ajanna ordered. He threw off the skins that covered him and pulled loose the lacings of his clothes.

I gasped. Healthy tissue grew now across the surface, but the torn muscles twisted and knotted beneath the skin gave evidence of the severity of the wounds that covered most of his body; trunk, arms, legs. That the wounds were poisoned I knew by the way he stiffened at my lightest touch. "I don't know—"

"Do your work!" Ajanna repeated.

I grasped one of his ankles with both of my hands and told him to pull against me. As he did so, I gritted my teeth against the pain of my own wounds. If he could bear it, I could, I said to myself.

It seemed a lifetime, those days I spent in that cavernous, gloomy tent, stripped to the waist from the heat of my exertions, my senses often reeling from pain, my whole being bound up in Ajanna's broken body. I pulled and probed and twisted and stretched, and I thought I made no progress.

"Don't stop," Ajanna said evenly.

He never made a sound of pain. Very rarely, if I touched him in some way he had not anticipated, I felt him stiffen for an instant. He always made his body relax at once.

"I must rest," I gasped. I rocked back on my heels and sat, eyes closed, breathing deeply, willing away my weakness.

Ajanna said, "Even when you close your eyes, those blue lines on the lids make it look as if they were open. What do you see with your strange eyes, Oa?"

"What any windrider sees!" I said sharply, opening my eyes at once.

Each line and mark of the tattooing around my eyes told of a rite performed or a test completed, a record of my achievement in the Imperial House. The lines were closely drawn and numerous: as many as some dynasts had. I might have become a dynast.

· I shook my head to shake these thoughts from me. It was the Imperial arts I was using on Ajanna that made me think so often of Empire. I did not like it. But I would not turn aside from the task I had taken on. I had never turned aside from anything . . . save that one time when I turned my back on Empire itself, to come here.

I leaned forward and put my hands on Ajanna's leg. "Twist your foot the other way!" I ordered. "And massage my shoulder as I showed you. I, too, must fight."

Ajanna did as I told him, but he did not leave off

talking. "So you think, Oa, that you and I are windriders like all the others?"

"Yes!"

"And does Halassa think that? Or Lirra? Or Surya?"

I pressed my lips tight together and refused to answer. I knew very well what the others thought: that Ajanna finally went too far in his recklessness and that I followed his example too closely. But of course they did not say so outright.

"They ride where the winds blow," Ajanna said musingly. "But I—I seem to think the wind could blow where I will that it should." He laughed.

"Turn over," I said, continuing with the task at hand.

"Now that I must lie here, I can't do much except think, and I begin to think you're like me, Oa. You care nothing what lords of Sky will: you ride where you will."

"I'm a windrider among windriders, neither more nor less," I said sturdily. "Turn back toward me."

My fingers dug deep into his muscle and must have hurt him. He grunted softly and put his hand over mine, gently. I stopped in surprise, staring at his hand, large enough to cover mine completely. Almost alone of his body his hands were unmarred, strong and healthy, the fingers so long in proportion to the bulk, they looked graceful. I raised my gaze slowly to his face and saw his black eyes, opaque and wide, fixed on me with a look that made my blood pound strangely. I forced a shaky laugh: I could not speak but I needed to exert myself, lest I be lost in him.

"No," he said quite simply. "You are something more than a windrider, as I am. Not, perhaps, the same."

I sat back, pulling my hand from his hold. He let me go. There was nothing of the flesh between us, neither of affection or desire—in a single flash we had already gone far beyond that, but where, I did not know.

"Oa—"

I only shook my head, almost frightened to think what I saw in his eyes, what drew me ever so restless and reck-less after him, was only what *he* saw in *me*.

"Oa—" he said again, in an altered voice.

The moment was gone. What was left was more commonplace: the intimacy of the single small pool of a grease light in the enclosure of the tent, our naked, laboring bodies which had learned so well to know each other. There was one further intimacy not yet consummated between us. Ajanna held out a hand to me anew, smiling a little.

But even sex seemed now something vast and risky between us, and again I delayed answering.

Outside the tent a voice shouted: "The fire stands fueled, awaiting the spark. Lords of Sky approach. Windriders, stand forth!"

It was the call to the Ranking. All else must wait. Slowly I stood up, pulling back my gaze from Ajanna to myself, beginning to untie the lacings of my leggings.

Housefolk came in, Wiel at their head, her gaze going first to Ajanna, hot and eager. But when I called her, she came to me at once. Sharply I bade her attend me. She coiled my braids deftly and fastened them close against my head in a row of spiral knots on either side of the parting that ran from my forehead to the nape of my neck. That task was soon done. Wiel and others scooped grease in handfuls from skin bags to smooth over my naked body. They painted my face with bold black markings that covered over my Imperial tattoos. These preparations, grown so familiar to me through the seasons, walled away any other past. Ready, feeling easy, I looked around for Ajanna.

Coory and the others had their work cut out for them to deal with the tangle of his hair, which he had not borne having touched since his wounding, a thick, black mat that fell below his waist. Patiently they combed out the snarls and rebraided his hair in lapped rows of ropes as big around as my wrist. These they began to weave into a helmet around his skull, so tightly no adversary could get purchase in it. This Ranking there could be no question but what Ajanna would have to fight.

All the while he sat silent and looked at me. I had chosen freely to aid him with Imperial arts. I meant only to restore a little his body's own strength. Now I had to wonder what more I might have done unwittingly. For that Wiel, too, was still going about with a small, satisfied smile on her face made me think more than ever something had happened.

I stood a moment, looking from Ajanna to Wiel and back, biting my lip. Then I shrugged, deciding there could hardly be more than there had been before. I had kept it from touching me already no short time. I took up my cloak and went out into the early midwinter dusk, where windriders stalked toward the Ranking ground, lean and silent, swathed in their cloaks and their pride.

I could think neither myself nor Ajanna ready, but time was not ours for the asking. We must suffice as we were— whatever we were or had become. And when I lifted my voice with the others in the ritual challenge to lords of Sky, I stood very tall and refused to doubt that *I* would suffice.

CHAPTER

11

Certainly I no longer knew anything of the desperation with which housefolk approached the low ranks of the opening rounds of the Ranking fights. Of the housefolk there were but few like Coory who found their lot contented them. The others scrabbled for what they could get, some of them riding a season now or then, the lot of them kept in hope long after it should have been obvious they would never truly become windriders. In the end most turned to explanations of treachery or witchery to justify their failure.

Not far from me that night the old housewoman Sinn stood watching windriders with hungry eyes. Mother of many who rode, she still looked only on her own account, I thought. She, too, had once thought of riding and still dreamt of it. And she was not really so very old, though she looked worn and grizzled. Neither windriders nor housefolk lived many years past their prime; even for those who only looked on, this life was one of a short moment.

Wiel entered the ground among a group of children, casting her token with theirs. Again and again she was chosen by the lottery, and she fought, and one after another threw her and pinned her. She did not give up, though her gaunt, stringy body was blackened with bruises. She was likely near as old as Sinn, I thought; but she was made of something different from what formed housefolk. She fought until her experience and desperation told against a youth who was only arrogant and careless. Wiela would ride—at least until the next Ranking.

Others fought. My own turn came. When I threw off my catskin cloak, I knew the wide, parallel scars running from my throat across my shoulder and down to my left armpit stood out an angry red from my oiled skin. I bore them with pride: they were the mark of my great will and endurance, that which no windrider could claim more. Yet they were barely healed and tender.

Thrown off by a stiffness in my injured shoulder, I won more narrowly than I was used to doing. While I waited for Murrila to confirm my rank I saw measuring eyes remarking on my weaknesses. Determination ran cold in my veins. I walked from the ground only to return to cast my token in challenge. It was not a match I would have chosen had I thought about it, but I did not think: I fought as I must, and I won as I must, for I was not ready to be beaten.

Murrila confirmed my new, higher rank. Now no one met my eyes. I nodded in satisfaction and left the ground. Pulling my catskin cloak around my shoulders, I went to join Lirra and Halassa. I stood proudly and tall, refusing to acknowledge the pain I felt, though I knew it would increase tenfold by morning.

Lirra gestured at the two fighting on the Ranking ground. "Jora has done that trick once too often. He's going to have to learn more finesse if he thinks to rank any higher."

I considered the two males fighting, and I thought Jora's opponent bore himself with something of the style that was my own, that derived from the High Dance of House Gand in Empire. I tried to think it a fancy come of my recent preoccupation with Imperial arts, but I could not truly deny that in the last seasons many of the windriders had adopted similar tactics. The dread I had thrown off for the rites returned, and grew. Grimly I concentrated on the particular fighters. "Tanana's got Jora now," I said, and he did.

"It's my turn," Lirra said. She threw off her cloak and went out onto the empty ground.

These middle ranks were very close. In another season or two I would have to challenge Lirra or someone who had beaten her, or acknowledge I had reached my limits. I measured Lirra as a potential opponent. Though her hair was coiled tightly against her skull, her loose, long-limbed stride gave something of the same impression as her long braids swirling. She spoke the ritual words and crouched down, seeming to pull the length of her arms and legs into herself, to coil them up in order to unleash them against her challenger.

Little indeed of the lover I had known her to be, did she now show to him. He had no chance. The match was over almost at once, having only whetted Lirra's appetite for fighting. She stood by impatiently, her eyes glittering, while the next came out upon the ground. One after another she challenged and beat. That night a strong wind took her up and for a time she became invincible.

"Now me," Halassa said softly. He had been silent, rapt as I was in the spectacle of Lirra's prowess.

I started, realizing Lirra would also challenge Halassa. He handed me his plain herdbeastskin cloak. I laid it over my arm on top of Lirra's, which I had picked up from the half-frozen ground where she had dropped it.

Halassa walked out lightly, large though he was, nearly as large as Ajanna. His skin was sleek and unmarred. He was older than Ajanna, and beginning to thicken with age. He had hardly passed his prime, and there was no softening of his body, but it had lost the leanness of youth.

Halassa's rank was the highest that did not include a chiefdom and a House. So far as I knew, he had never lost a fight. Neither, in all the time I had known him, had he ever offered a challenge. More than once I had heard him say he held the highest rank of all, for chiefs' ranks were less free than his. Once I had pointed out to him that Ajanna rode free of any fettering responsibilities, though he held a large House. Halassa answered that I had always been dazzled by Ajanna and could not see him for what he was. I had shrugged off his words with a laugh, and we went on as before, or seemed to; but I gradually realized we had come to some limit or barrier between us that we could neither of us pass. I had shrugged that off also, thinking thus must matters always be between two windriders, each alone and content, while riding, to be so.

Halassa, alone, stood on the empty ground and spoke the ritual words. Lirra, stepping out hastily to toss her token to Murrila, seemed not to recognize Halassa. Some others came out as well, youths who hoped one day to be high chiefs and wanted the experience they could get from fighting Halassa without running the risks of challenging a touchy high chief. Braha was among these. But of course it was Lirra's token that came out on Murrila's palm. She had been certain it would be and was already advancing on Halassa.

Lirra outreached Halassa slightly, but he outweighed her so substantially her advantage counted for nothing. And now exhaustion lay heavily on her, dimming the wild excitement in her eyes. She had had an amazing run, the stuff of which legends are made. She alone did not know it was over.

Halassa did not belittle Lirra'a accomplishment by failing to fight his best, and the match between them was short. On the cold ground, Lirra lay on her back. Halassa bent over her.

Lirra got slowly to her feet. She shook her head as if to clear it of confusion and walked from the ground. By the time she reached me she was grinning.

"Not bad, eh?" she said.

All within hearing laughed.

"Did you think you had a chance against Halassa?" I cried.

She laughed. "You know, I really did think so! What a feeling that was!"

Every windrider dreamt of being taken up thus by a strong wind. One must ride it while one could, and not ask where it might lead. It was a gift from lords of Sky—like riding also.

I settled Lirra's cloak around her shoulders. Heat poured off her body into the winter cold. The wildness about her was like a windsteed's aura. She shifted impatiently under the restraint of the stiff leather of her cloak.

Halassa approached. He had not stayed to fight again. I opened my mouth to ask him if he even carried a token to cast in lottery but, meeting his eyes, I realized that was an impertinence he would not accept, whatever his affection still for me. He had all of a windrider's pride if not a full measure of arrogance. I shut my mouth without speaking and concentrated my attention on tying the laces of Lirra's cloak, which was difficult, because she would not stand still.

The lesser chiefs fought for minute adjustments of their ranks. So closely were they matched, the distinctions between them were visible only to them. These males—and a few females—were good enough to win Houses that were independent of any high chief, though their herds were too small to attract many herders. Few of these chiefs would ever rise to hold a great House, one whose vast herds supported ostentatious numbers of housefolk and attracted most of the herders. Indeed, few of these chiefs could stand against Halassa or Lirra or some of the others of us crowding the ranks just below them. Braha threw in his token for one after another of these bouts, and finally got one. We turned to watch.

"I'll wager a new knifeblade on Braha," Halassa said.

Lirra leaned forward, her thin, flat-featured face intent on the fight. "I'll take you up on that bet, Halassa," she said. "I can't like Braha."

"He's careful," I said with scorn. Braha had always been very careful of me, from the very beginning when we rode together in the fens, newly ranked and most junior of Ajanna's herders.

"Too careful—with no sense of when wisely not to be," Lirra said.

Halassa grunted noncommittally. Challenging him, I said, "You wouldn't ride with Braha if he took a House." Halassa looked around at me in surprise.

"No, I would not."

For years Halassa had ridden in Ajanna's House—not merely from the habit of having ridden with Ajanna's father before him. He was drawn to Ajanna. And he was drawn to me. Words Ajanna had spoken to me came back to me, and I considered them anew with less anger and more interest and a stirring of the old chafing against restraint and limit: *was there yet more?*

Halassa did not wonder on such things. I could see that in the way he turned on Lirra, the match ending more quickly than any of us thought it would, Braha winning. Lirra was already arguing that Braha won so narrowly that she should not lose an entire blade but only the use of one for a time. Laughing, Halassa declared he would hold her to her windrider's word.

They stood close, laughing and joking. They had forgotten that one of them might easily have killed the other a few minutes before. I had forgotten companionship could be so comfortable, in the time I had spent with Ajanna, who was never easy.

My gaze passed over the crowd around the Ranking ground and I found Ajanna at once. Earlier I had thought the aura of power around Lirra was strong, but Ajanna had an air of wildness so intense and unquenchable all the others seemed tame housefolk by comparison. Yet he stood quite still and relaxed. I stared long at him, trying to see what it was that he was, or how I was like him.

Everyone fell silent as the Ranking reached the high chiefs. For once almost all of them were prepared to fight. Rumors of Ajanna's condition had introduced uncertainty into their rankings even below Ajanna's rank. In a lifetime one might not see so many high chiefs fight as did that night.

Ajanna limped forward in his turn. He well knew many would challenge him, thinking him half beaten by the rivercat. The temptation was obvious. The newly healed wounds slashed every plane of his body, distorting the long lines and mass of his muscles. He limped onto the Ranking ground—but there he stood with his head high, ignoring the wreck of his body, and spoke the ritual words inviting challenge.

An opponent came to him: Lamma, who ranked not far below Ajanna. They closed on each other. We leaned forward, hushed, expectant, then puzzled. Ajanna fought awkwardly and hesitantly, like a youth come to the Ranking ground for the first time. Lamma's blows seemed to confuse Ajanna. Soon none of us could doubt the outcome, least of all Lamma, who danced over the ground in mockery.

But Ajanna endured. He endured so long that Lamma tired. The fight got slower and slower, but neither fell, neither yielded. The firelight glinted on Ajanna's scars: some of his wounds were bleeding now. Lamma limped as badly as Ajanna, and his head slumped.

And still they went on. An eternity passed before, slowly, so interminably slowly that I thought Lamma must escape, Ajanna pressed Lamma down to the cold earth.

Murrila raised an arm to mark the conclusion of the fight. Ajanna swayed from side to side uncontrollably, but his glittering eyes were steady, vast, and great as the night sky above the limitless plain. Ajanna's strength was spent. He was probably closer to death than he had been the night he and I fought the rivercat and his blood flowed unchecked from countless terrible wounds. His will grew only stronger and more determined. He stared at the crowd, challenging all of us, and we dropped our gaze before his.

Lamma did not move again. For his effrontery Ajanna had broken his neck.

Someone brought Ajanna his cloak and draped it around his shoulders. With the addition of another half of a catskin the cloak trailed the ground behind him large as he was. On the hood he had mounted the head of the cat we had killed together. The hood lay now folded back upon his neck, the cat face—daubed with dried blood that could be his or mine or the cat's—staring up into the sky. Though I could not see it now, I knew it had but one eye. My knife had pierced the other.

Ajanna moved slowly off the Ranking ground, and the rest of the Ranking wound down to an end that seemed no conclusion. Even while Murrila was confirming, without challenge, his own highest rank, the housefolk brought us drinking skins. I took deep drafts, seeking release.

Halassa raised a skin in salute to Ajanna and bowed with a flourish. "Hail, Lord Ajanna!" Halassa cried, giving him the title of what passed on the plain for gods. "A high wind in the flesh!"

Ajanna reached for the drinking skin Halassa held, seeing

only that. Halassa's words were surely trivial, perhaps meaningless, to Ajanna as he now was. If I had not interfered, Lamma would have beaten him. But it was not mortal windriders, but death itself Ajanna had beaten this night. I shivered at the thought that with Imperial arts I had had a part in making Ajanna whatever he now was.

Wiela thrust herself among us, naked still from the fighting, her gaunt, oiled limbs glinting when the firelight flashed on her jerking movements. "I come to congratulate you, hard Ajanna, proud Ajanna, and to offer myself as herder in your House again. I, Wiela, give my oath!" Her voice was high-pitched, barely controlled.

"I swear the oath," Ajanna said carelessly. He seemed not to know who she was. He was very used to having a great train of herders, many of whom he hardly knew; he never turned away anyone who wished to swear him the oath. He would scorn to, as more careful chiefs did not.

Wiela was not done. Her body twitched its nervous dance. Her dark skin seemed to fit too loosely over the tense bundle of bone and sinew that was all there was to her. She darted at me glances full of meaning.

"You swear hastily, Ajanna! You should know I carry my vengeance with me still. Indeed, I sent a token of it on before me in the person of Oa." She lowered her voice slyly. "I think Oa has already begun to implement it."

Ajanna frowned. "What are you talking about?"

Wiela leaned toward him confidentially, opening her mouth to speak.

"No!" I interrupted in a sudden rush of anger. "Will you call yourself a windrider, Wiela, and carry on still this mad, housebound nonsense!"

Wiela turned on me, distracted from her object. Her eyes gleamed with cunning. "You haven't renewed your oath, Oa, though Ajanna has again won his House. Don't you dare to ride between Ajanna and me? Surely you who are the Wind's Sigh must ride after the one Halassa calls the Wind Embodied!" Her scorn inflamed by blood, which was already hot from the fighting and from the strong liquor I was drinking.

"I fear nothing!" I said fiercely.

"The oath!" Wiela insisted.

I hesitated. I would not swear at her bidding! But I had never thought not to renew my oath, and there seemed to be nothing for it but to give Wiela the semblance of prevailing. I looked at Halassa and Lirra and spoke lightly, as if I could make a jest of it. "Shall we ride again with Ajanna?"

Halassa mumbled something I did not catch. I grew hot at his tone. Lirra looked puzzled. But they both said with me: "I swear the oath."

Wiela's shrill cry of triumph grated on me with such physical discomfort that I moved away. Suddenly I was sore and tired and cold and quite sober. I stumbled through the camp into my tent—though I was not sure it was my tent—and fell upon a bed of skins.

At the approach of an unfamiliar footstep I came half awake thinking after all I had mistaken the tent.

"Oa?"

Jily! That whispering, silken voice my very flesh remembered, caressed me with a foretaste and the promise of beauty and delight. Wordlessly, unquestioningly, I reached to hold her. I pulled her close, murmuring endearments, and touched my fingertips gently to the perfect curves of her flower face.

Something was wrong. I came alert, feeling wary. My hands explored her sleek, soft body uncertainly, questioning now. She was everything I remembered. It was not she who was wrong, but I. My skin, which should have been as smooth as hers, was rough with grit and oil. Against her sweet softness my body felt lean and hard.

I was not the young near-heir of the Imperial House tumbling her cousin in a secret corner of the palace gardens. I was a windrider—changed far more than mere time could account for.

"Coory?" I said aloud. She laughed softly. I knew it as much by the quiver I felt in her slender throat under my hand as by the sound I heard. Both her presence and her voice pleased me. Though I knew my mistake I did not let go of her. She had called me by name: *she* had made no mistake. "Ajanna?" I asked.

"Asleep. He won't want either you or me tonight."

"He sent you to me?" I asked, startled. Ajanna certainly had cause to feel gratitude toward me, but it was not at all like him to think to reward me.

Coory laughed so low that this time I did not hear her at all, but only felt the ripple of motion faintly through her body where it touched mine. She said archly, "I've no mind to be the prize of the first drunken rider who realizes Ajanna lies alone tonight. . . ."

"You came to me for protection?"

"I came to please you."

I grunted. It seemed Coory had no intention of telling me anything that made sense. But I liked the feel of her in my arms and asked no more questions. She touched me gently, so I felt no pain from poisoned wounds or Ranking injuries. Indeed, I forgot all such.

"So sweet—" I mumbled. As sweet she was, surely, as—no, I would not think of Jily.

Coory murmured softly, wordlessly, and enfolded me in the aura of her presence. She brought me to a high, clear delight, free of pain and confusion. There seemed to be no end to her intoxicating sweetness. I forgot Jily. I felt something akin to riding, such sweet, soaring heights did I reach.

I discovered why Ajanna showed Coory such favor and put up with her temper. I would not again mistake her for Jily, not now I knew what she was in herself. I sighed with contentment, and Coory lulled me to sleep in her arms.

A hard voice exclaimed, "Get out of here, you slut! This is one place you won't work your tricks!"

A sly voice answered, "You're wrong there, Raun. I already have. Be quiet, or you'll wake her. You know what a windrider is like, waking the morning after a Ranking!"

Raun hissed, "Morning is a long way off. You just get along out, Coory. Now."

"Be still!" I shouted, sitting up and crying out furiously. The poison burned fiercely in my shoulder, and the rest of my body ached unspeakably.

"See?" Coory said to Raun.

She touched me with her knowing hands, trying to soothe me. I would not be appeased. I was realizing *why* she reminded me so strongly of my Gandish cousin: it was not only the sweet sensuousness of her but also in the slyness of trickery and betrayal that Coory resembled Jily.

Coory was a housewoman bound to the service of windriders. She knew nothing herself of riding. It could only have been my fancy that she shared the high soaring delight I had found with her. She could think no farther than her own petty advantage. She would betray me just as soon as please me.

Just like Jily. Who had betrayed me. I felt it with all the painful force of my initial discovery so long ago. "No!" I shouted, partly at Coory and Raun for disturbing me, partly at the rivercat whose poisoned wound maddened and confused me, but mostly at the past unraveling so vividly in my mind.

I stood before the Dynast, he who held all the world, or very nearly, and I met the gaze of his pale blue eyes so like my own. He narrowed his eyes slightly, and the fine, blue lines over his eyelids seemed to shimmer and dance through his ancient, translucent skin. "If you will . . . ," he whispered in his rasping voice.

All that I wanted he offered me! At a price: with my own hands I must give him the death of her I most loved. And levelly, head high, I said to the Dynast, "I will," because I could not, in that minute, forswear all ambition. But I did not yield in my heart. In fact, I never made any decision at all. For in the end I found I could not wait even to learn what I might decide. That Jily might live, I turned my back and fled. Though she betrayed me, I did not harm her. For I had loved her. I loved her still. At the thought of her my limbs loosened. . . . It was intolerable! "No!" I shouted. I started up from where I lay, feeling no pain now of cat wound or Ranking bruises, feeling only that old, inner, enraging goad.

Raun and Coory fell back before my rage, familiar with the rages of windriders. I did not see them. I swept up my catskin cloak, still warm and sweetly perfumed from Coory's body—or was it, after all, Jily's? I had no time to think or to search for other clothes. I could only flee—as I had fled Empire long ago.

I strode out into the bitter cold night, biting my lip until the blood ran in an attempt to keep from crying out at the pain each step cost me, welcoming the pain because it distracted me from the agony in my mind.

Dark figures lurched about the camp. The celebration had dwindled, but it was not over. "Oa!" someone cried out to me drunkenly. I went on.

"Oa?" Halassa's bulky figure moved out from a knot of windriders, but when I did not answer, he turned back.

I walked more quickly when my bare feet felt the awful cold of the half-frozen mud of the fen. Clouds were breaking up to reveal dark patches of starry sky. The bare skeletons of iced trees glittered in the starlight. A large, dark mass moved without a sound between me and the trees, and blocked their glitter from my sight. My windsteed, Cloud, came to me. I climbed to her back. She swung around and headed for the open plain, lengthening her stride. Though the footing was treacherous, I urged her on.

When Cloud ran full out on the unobstructed plain, I grew calmer. I relaxed my fingers, which clutched her mane, and stretched my cramped legs. Her warm windsteed's aura enfolded me, body and spirit.

"Faster, faster," I whispered to Cloud, bending my head low over hers, smiling into the dark night. She stretched her stride still more. The wind of our passage took the words from my lips. The earth blurred beneath us and fell behind. I was myself the wild winter wind that rushed unseen along Cloud's swift passage through darkness and a long, long night.

CHAPTER

12

Only when the scant winter day had struggled free of the night did I signal to Cloud to return to the camp in the Long Fen. I was again Oa, the Wind's Sigh, careless, free, a windrider—nothing else, or so I pretended, even to myself. I rode, herded, fought, drank, loved, dared. I felt always against my face the winds of the plain, which were real, and refused to acknowledge the cruelly tormenting winds of memory.

But the winds on the plain were themselves changing. That winter never came to much; after midwinter there was no real storm. The thaw came early, and by the time the spring Ranking was done the plain was as brown and sere as it should not be until autumn. We ranged far across the plain that year, seeking forage for the herds, farther north than ever before, well beyond the wide valley of the River-that-ever-changes, which was usually our most northerly reach. That valley was drying also and not so pleasant as it had been wont to be—which pleasantness had accounted for our giving it a name, as we seldom did with any natural feature, and for making it a goal and meeting place. We ran far east also, to the very end of the plain where badlands of rock rose to higher country.

The following year we ventured even there, four of us, climbing with our windsteeds through the Broken Lands. We rode in a tight pack—Ajanna, Halassa, Braha, and I—to discover whether there was forage. Things had come to such a pass that we could think lords of Sky might grant us pasture there on the High Plain, in their own special place. It was Ajanna's idea. That in itself was not remarkable, not as he had become since the rivercat's wounding him. That any others went with him was a better measure of the situation.

For my part, I had been resting at a waycamp by a spring in a grove of plainwillow trees, where Ajanna's House and two or three others, that of Braha among them, had paused on a long sweep east after the midsummer Ranking. Ajanna, large and grinning, came by where I sat with Halassa and Lirra to propose the expedition. He wanted Halassa, as anyone would, going into something uncertain and possibly difficult. Halassa gave a grunt of assent without questioning the foray. Lirra turned her head as if to avoid hearing if Ajanna asked her also. I did not notice whether he did, leaping up wild to go. Perhaps because of my dancing at his heels like a skittish windsteed foal, Ajanna marked the sobriety of Braha, who was full of the cares of holding his small House, and challenged him also to come. Braha was enough the windrider he could not stand aside.

And so we came here, we four, for such chance reasons, and we found only desert more barren than our own withered plain, no grass to speak of, only parched shrubs in a pavement of wind-packed gravel: the High Plain, where no windriders had come in so many years we had not known for sure what we could find.

As we ran steadily east across the High Plain, I grew ever more uneasy, for it struck me Empire must lie this way. Mountains loomed in the far distance, gray shadows like the nameless western mountains, viewed from the Imperial City. They might be those very mountains. Or perhaps many ranges intervened. Or perhaps there was no meeting with Empire in any continuous reality. I did not

know, either, not really, how I had come to the windriders'
range.

"There's nothing for us here!" Braha said suddenly,
loudly. "Why do we go on?"

Uneasy as I was myself, I hissed in scorn of his
fearfulness. In fact, I would not have been sorry to turn
back, but neither Ajanna nor Halassa said anything, and so
we rode on as before.

The sky seemed to thicken and lower. Soon I could no
longer see even the outlines of the distant mountains.
Indeed, the sky hung so low and heavily that I could
hardly hold my head and shoulders upright against it. Its
color was a strange yellow that hurt my eyes. Cloud tossed
her head and ran raggedly. I tightened the grip of my
knees on her massive neck and leaned forward, speaking
softly and soothingly until she ran more easily. I glanced
at my companions.

Beside me, Halassa rode stiffly upright, his expression
grim and set, but unwavering. On my other side Ajanna
rode, tense, too. His eyes were open wide to the strange
sky. His lips parted as if he meant to gulp it into his lungs
in great drafts. Beyond him I saw Braha's face was pale.
His gaze darted here and there, and his fingers twisted and
twisted in the long strands of his windsteed's mane.

"Listen!" he hissed.

The yellowness of the sky took on form and mass.
Bizarre shapes coalesced, dissolved, and reformed. The
light was dull, for there was no sun. Braha hissed again. I
heard a strange, low moaning that came from nowhere in
particular but was all about us. Otherwise the air was very
still.

"What is it?" I asked.

Halassa's voice was grimmer than I had ever heard it.
"It's a mad wind. A storm of the High Plain. They say it
can blow the mind out of windrider and windsteed, so they
wander senseless until they die."

"You know it's true!" exclaimed Braha.

"It's said some of those who ventured to the High Plain
never returned," Halassa said sturdily.

The sky, which had hung at the height of our shoulders,
sank toward the ground and confined us in a small area of

yellowed earth set with the sparse shrubs of this inhospitable plain.

"What should we do?" I asked.

Halassa shrugged. "Ride." He glanced at me. His mouth smiled, but his eyes did not. Starwind flung her head about in distress. Halassa bent forward to calm his windsteed and did not look at me again.

The wind started to blow in gusts that bound the yellow sky tighter about us. Veils of yellow separated the others from me. I caught a last glimpse of Braha's face. His eyes were wide and glazing over. His bloodless skin reflected the yellow of the sky. I felt a chill in my gut. Braha's windsteed bucked and fought, and Braha only bounced limply on his back. The sky closed about him, and I saw him no more.

Cloud ran full out, but it seemed she moved in place. Always off her right shoulder was the same bush and a small clump of rocks with a few straws of grass growing through it. I supposed the rocks kept what moisture there was from evaporating, and so nourished the plants.

Bush, rocks, and all, we flashed by Scudder and Ajanna. Ajanna's eyes flamed fiery out of the flat yellowness that veiled the rest of him. He leaned eagerly forward into the wind, no more aware of me than Braha had been. His lips were spread in a wide grin. *He is mad*, I thought, aghast.

The yellow flowed thicker, and he was gone like the others. Cloud's steps faltered. No more than I, could she see the ground. Her head swiveled, questing. Everywhere there was only yellow. Its texture varied, but neither earth nor sky was distinguishable. The wind blew in crazy gusts and swirls, not physically overpowering, but confusing, so I could not tell its source or where to point Cloud's head. Nor could I distinguish up from down. I grew dizzy. Cloud's steps slowed unevenly. The wind seemed to lift her and toss her about. I knew it was mere seeming; physically the wind did not have such strength. But Cloud screamed.

I felt tendrils of confusion reach into my gut and my mind. I pushed away panic, knowing it led where I could never return from. I must not give in! That was all I could think of while my mind clogged with images of the wind, particular patterns it made of the yellow—complex, shifting patterns that caught my gaze and drew me in and shifted again to bar my escape.

It was a natural phenomenon, perhaps, compounded of dust and air, heat and altitude; but at the very edge of the supernatural. In that it was akin to the High Dance of the Imperial House, except that I was given in it not the commanding role I was used to, but that of the victim, to be seduced and tricked and bled, perhaps of life itself.

This mad wind was such a Dance, or could be understood as one, which could kill me.

But while I now moved at the storm's bidding, trapped in the victim's part, I was still also a windrider. Distorted as her gray-blotched mass was by the roiling yellow wind, Cloud's great warm living bulk remained solid under my hands and legs. She was caught just as I was, perhaps *because* I was, and stopped and started in panics that several times nearly unseated me. Yet, through it all, the ties that bound us to one another endured. And we lived.

Gradually I understood that I need not die. While I knew myself, I yet lived. While I willed it, I could know myself. So long as will remained, I would fight. Many times I had fought off the High Dance to save the lives of windriders when I had taken their rank. Now I must fight for my own life against a Dance that was greater still. I must bend it to my will.

In my mind I drew a bush. I placed it at Cloud's right shoulder, and below it stones and straws of grass. I gathered my will to impress the image upon the wavering substance of the storm. For a time it remained only what was in my mind. Even so it gave me a focus for my thoughts, so panic could not enter so easily. And after a time Cloud seemed to run more easily, perhaps reassured by my calmness, manufactured though it was.

After a longer time I thought the yellow thinned. Was not that a glimpse of solid ground? My assurance grew that ground lay beneath us, and I could almost make out the shadowy form of a bush—a real one, not quite the same as the one I imagined. I relaxed my concentration, and the yellow thickened again at once. Cloud stumbled and barely recovered.

Hurriedly I recalled the image of bush and stone and grass. The image showly grew stronger and clearer. I understood it was not quite real, as reality had once been; that it was much a matter of will—of pretense. It was also necessary. Though I was very tired, grimly I held on, and little by little the simple image took on truly objective reality—or near enough.

The yellow drew back for a windsteed's length all around us. Then two lenghts. I placed another bush in the space, and another, and another. I managed an outcropping of rock. Another followed of its own accord. The yellow thinned above me, and the sun shone through it weakly.

I was too tired: I could do no more. But still the area free of the mad wind expanded in every direction. Whether by my will or some other cause, the storm was weakening. Leaving behind at last the little bush with its stones and grasses, Cloud ran on after all the yellow was gone until I could not feel the slightest taint of madness in the air. We ran still upon the arid plateau of the High Plain, but where in that vast area, I could not tell. There were no landmarks, but I knew the windriders' range lay in the direction of the sun, which was setting in front of us.

Through the night we flew above the desert plain. A great array of stars wheeled slowly across the sky above us. Beneath us the dark ground unrolled, silent and empty, as if in a time when the earth and its creatures had not yet come to life. I was not surprised to see no sign of my erstwhile companions on this expedition.

I dozed fitfully until, near dawn, a break in Cloud's stride brought me fully awake. We were riding in a mist through which loomed strange things. They seemed to approach us, but then flee my gaze before I could discern what they were—if they truly were. It was some time before I recognized the Broken Lands, that jumble of rock and chasm at the edge of the High Plain, through which we must descend to reach our range.

Cloud walked slowly, picking her footing carefully. If she broke a leg in this treacherous place, I would be stranded without hope. Her footsteps striking the bare rock boomed through the mist with a hollow noise that seemed to come back at us from all directions, as if it emanated from the veiled, shifting forms that surrounded us. They could be anything, I thought: rocks or the things of earth inchoate, struggling toward birth.

Cloud stopped abruptly and put her head to the ground, whiffling through her nostrils. I leaned forward, puzzled: now the ground itself was mist.

"It's water!"

And I started at the sound of my own startled voice.

Cloud drank noisily. I slipped from her back and knelt in the crust of mud extending above the water's edge. I drank from my cupped hands. The water tasted cool and sweet. I splashed it over my face and neck, scrubbing with my hands to wash away the clammy sweat of fear left by the mad wind. That was proof, I thought wryly, that I was not new-made, but had ridden through the windstorm.

A hollow booming was added to the splashing noises. I looked up to see a large shape looming through the mist. This time it was something real and living. Cloud nickered her greeting to windsteeds. Scudder drew up beside her and drank greedily from the pond with simple, common-place noises. Ajanna sat motionless on her back.

"Ajanna?" I said doubtfully; he sat so still, in an aura of otherliness.

His head turned toward the sound of my voice. "Ah, Oa," he said. He crossed one leg over Scudder's neck and leaned his arms on it. "So. We two survive." I nodded, for so I supposed.

Ajanna looked around. The mist confined us on every side, free of anything like madness but impenetrable to the sight all the same.

"We can't ride through this," he said in disgust. He shifted his weight and came sliding to the ground. His great bulk standing beside me was very solid. "Oa, do you have any kwass?" I turned to Cloud and tugged at her gear strap. My fingers were cold and awkward.

Ajanna loomed over me impatiently. He pushed me aside and loosened the damp rawhide ties that fastened a drinking skin to the gear strap cinched across the barrel of Cloud's body. He drank deeply and handed me the skin. When I had had enough he took the skin from me and finished it. I watched him, thinking how very large and solid he was. I took a step toward him, and the heat and scent of him became stronger than the damp, dank emptiness of the mist.

Ajanna set aside the empty drinking skin and looked at me speculatively. His strong fingers fastened the lacings of my clothes as deftly as they had undone the drinking skin. My own fingers, reaching to his leathers, were as clumsy as before, but they accomplished their task.

I averted my eyes from his scarred, misshapen body. I did not want to know that he was any particular person, especially not that he was Ajanna, who had once been brought low enough that but for me he would not have survived. All I wanted was the close, animal comfort of his hot, solid body. I did not care what he wanted. We coupled on the ground like a pair of beasts.

I found the animal comfort that I wanted, but it was not in the nature of such things that it could last long. Soon I shivered in the dank cold. I sat up and reached for my clothes. The leather was stiff and clammy, but the exertion of dressing warmed me somewhat. I stood up to do up the lacings. Behind me Ajanna lay unstirring. Cloud and Scudder, shadowy from the mist, stood together companionably. I pulled my catskin cloak around me.

Finally I turned to look at Ajanna. He lay on his back, so still he might have been asleep, or even dead, but his eyes were open wide, staring up into the mist. I did not think he could have seen anything *there*, even had there been something to see. Yet he saw *something*. I could only think that I had no wish to know what it was.

Seeing the white, puckered skin of the scars everywhere on Ajanna's body, I remembered how even when he lay freshly wounded, torn and bleeding, with the animal life of his body running out upon the ground, he yet survived. I remembered also how he fought Lamma to a standstill when he could hardly stand himself. Oh, I had helped him, in ways he could not have helped himself, and it was my doing that he had not died or healed worse. He took that for granted, as he took everything he needed. If it had not been me, it would have been something else. He would not have failed.

I dared say I was much the same, and I had been tried

perhaps even more variously and subtly than he had. So thinking, I stared at him and finally saw that he stared back at me, grinning.

I shuddered, finally understanding that in this last test of the mad wind I had survived something truly awesome— and brought Cloud through it also; that by that very token I was myself, or had briefly been, something extraordinary.

But Ajanna . . . I looked at him consideringly. Ajanna had not merely survived but *used* the mad wind, taking some portion of it into him, where it yet blew.

"So the two of us survived," he said, repeating what he had said earlier.

Survived.

A great, shuddering sigh swept me. Survived. Nothing was new. The vast, indifferent beings we now were, we had always been—it was only grown a little clearer than it had been. Under the weight of this realization I shifted uncomfortably and felt a stabbing pain in my shoulder. The buried poison that sometimes lay quiescent for long periods rekindled to remind me that I could never be new, but could only go on.

Ajanna grunted. He pulled his leggings to him and stood to put them on.

Something moved at the corner of my vision. I swung around. I had heard no sound, but that form in the mist was one I knew—there was none I knew better. It was Halassa on Starwind.

Gladness leaped up in me, such as Ajanna had not called forth, and I realized I had accepted Halassa as lost, thinking him less than Ajanna or myself. His arrival brought back joy and lightheartedness into the storm-cleansed world. "Halassa!" I called eagerly, running to him.

There came no answer. Instead of growing more solid, the dark, shadowed shape seemed to dissolve around the edges as it approached.

"Halassa!" I cocked my head, straining to hear his greeting. I swung around and saw that Cloud and Scudder stood as before and gave no sign of hearing Starwind's approach. The shadowed bulk receded without acknowledging me. I cried out in frustration.

"What is it?" Ajanna called.

"Halassa. But he doesn't stop. Here he comes again. Don't you see him? What ails him?"

Surely it was Halassa! Despite the veiling mist, I knew him by the set of his shoulders and the way he held his head. I could not be mistaken! But if it was Halassa, how could I feel such dread at the sight of him?

"Do you see Starwind as well?" Ajanna looked where I pointed. "I see nothing. Listen: there's no sound. It's wraiths you see, Oa. The mad wind took them and teases you with wraiths."

"No!" I cried, trembling.

The mist was lifting. A rock loomed over the pond. I scrambled up it the better to watch for Halassa. The surface of the rock was cold and sharp, and cut my hands. Kneeling at the top I twisted my fingers together to warm them and comfort them. "Halassa!" I shouted.

Only echoes replied: "Lassa, lassa, la, sa, sa."

I shouted again, more wildly. The mist took my words and transformed them into noise without sense.

"Oa! Come here!" Ajanna shouted, and his voice, too, echoed about, coming at me from all sides.

"No! No!" I cried. I would not yield up Halassa! And I would not fear!

Again I glimpsed Halassa circling us. When I called to him the thinning mist again said, "Lassa, lassa," but more softly. Halassa still said nothing.

The mist grew ever less. The jumbled rock of the Broken Lands took on solidity in every direction.

"Halassa," I called softly, longingly, despairingly.

There was no longer even an echo.

Windsteed hooves clattered on rock. "It's clear enough to ride," Ajanna said, on the level with me, mounted on Scudder. Cloud nickered anxiously and crowded between Scudder and the rock where I sat. "I shall ride," Ajanna repeated.

I scrambled from the rock to Cloud's back. I sat almost as high as on the rock—on nearly as good a vantage point.

Scudder trotted off quickly over the broken ground. Cloud followed of her own accord. I lifted my hands once to stop her and let them fall without doing it. We crossed Halassa's circling course. He came so close to me, I thought, this time he must know me and will join us. But he kept going, passing between Ajanna and me without looking to either side. His posture was unnaturally stiff, and his face strangely shadowed and expressionless. Though the mist was almost gone, I could not see his eyes at all. Hiding my face in my hands, I wept. I thought of Halassa's caressing, easy laugh, of his quiet solidity and assurance. I clung to such memories of him to avoid the horrible present in which his joyless wraith mocked what he had been—and what I was, surviving him.

Ajanna's hard voice intruded on my thoughts. "You rode near to lords of Sky, Oa. You saw for yourself their carelessness, which some call cruelty. The mad wind is a challenge they set. Halassa could not meet it. You and I are made of different stuff."

"But—but I loved him!" I mourned. Yes, I had loved Halassa, though I had so often left him to follow where my own willfulness, or Ajanna, led—though I loved Halassa, I was a windrider.

"Love!" I knew Ajanna must be grinning, though I did not look up to see. "What can such as you and I know of love?"

His words stung me unaccountably. Didn't I give up Empire for love of Jily? I protested incoherently. Ajanna snorted and drew ahead of me once more.

Again and again I looked back, and I thought I saw that veiled, silent form of windsteed and rider in the shadows of the rocks of the Broken Lands. But I rode away, following Ajanna. Truly, I thought, the wraith was not Halassa: Ajanna was right, about Halassa—and about me. *I* lived. I must therefore ride.

The day's heat soon burned away the last of the mist. With it, the wraith rider finally disappeared, and I saw it no more. Ajanna and I rode across the glittering rock and came out upon the plain.

CHAPTER

13

When my catskin cloak slipped forward over my shoulders once again, I pushed it back impatiently. Even with it hanging by the laces tied very loosely, the fur prickled my naked back where sweat ran down in rivulets. I twitched my shoulders against the itch. Except for my twitching, nothing seemed to move anywhere, so borne down were we and everything else by the weight and heat of the drought.

"Let the next stand forth!"

Murrila's voice snapped out the ritual words of the Ranking as firmly and clearly as ever—just as if he expected the usual answer.

A large branch fell in the bonfire and sent a shower of crackling sparks upward into the night. The air was so hot already I could not feel any additional heat from the fire, close to it as I stood. I shifted my weight, restless from being hemmed in by the motionless, silent crowd. The windriders' naked skin was slick with sweat and oil, and gleamed in the firelight. Their faces seemed to look otherwhere, beyond the drought. Envy twisted the faces of the housebound in only their usual sullen expressions.

No one answered Murrila's call. Time passed, more than enough for Braha to have come forward and spoken the words of the ritual, had he only been there. I strode forward. I could not fail to offer myself for this lottery, when I knew I could hold the rank against challenge, though it was a chief's rank and much above any I had taken before; I knew I could hold it, because I was . . . changed . . . by the mad wind. And I wanted—I did not know what I wanted. More change, anyway. Any change. I cast my token before Murrila.

As for Braha, he had never returned from the High Plain. By that mischance of crossing Ajanna's path and mine in a desolate grove of plainwillow trees and being unable to turn aside from Ajanna's mocking invitation, Braha was lost in the mad wind. His rank, with a minor chief's House, would now go by lot in this autumn Ranking.

Others came up behind me, tardily, as if released from their stillness only by my movement. They did not matter. I stood aloof while they threw down tokens after mine.

"Hail, Oa! Windrider and chief!"

Murrila confirmed my rank very quickly, I thought, hardly bothering to look to see that my token had indeed come up in his hand—convinced by my assurance, perhaps. I grinned and lifted my arms in triumph. I was a chief, a herder no longer to ride at anyone else's bidding. For now it was over. Not until midwinter would I have to fight for the rank.

The rites went on, the many other minor chiefs' ranks, then the high chiefs'. The high chiefs were stripped for once, only for the heat. There had been no indication any of them would fight. Halfway through their ranks people began to talk and move about, the heat driving them here or there almost without their noticing.

Ajanna's voice rang out above all other noise. He spoke nothing more than the ritual words claiming his rank, the rank that no one had challenged since he killed Lamma for it. But I turned back toward the Ranking ground, hearing his voice: there was something new in it.

No one challenged. Murrila confirmed Ajanna's rank in the usual way, but Ajanna did not leave the ground. "I challenge the next!'' he called out. At that, everyone quieted.

How like Ajanna, I thought. "The next," he said, as if he did not know who it was that held the rank just above his. The other high chiefs spent years picking and measuring an opponent before issuing a challenge.

Murrila said dryly, "Shall we allow Osia to declare his rank before he must hear challenges?"

Ajanna took one step to the side, in token compliance. Murrila did not push the point. I looked from Murrila to Ajanna, both standing free of the crowd. They were much the same size. Each well knew his great strength—and that of the other.

Murrila's head was grizzled with approaching age. His massive body, revealed by his cloak flung back on account of the heat, glistened with oil. It looked solid, if no longer sleek or lithe. Of us all, Murrila stood closest to lords of Sky, and for his rank we both owed and paid him great reverence. He had been chief of all chiefs for so long that we thought his steady, impartial manner the only one possible for the position. We saw him veiled by our awe and our need, all save Ajanna, who had challenged Murrila at the Ranking when I first arrived on the plain. In a generation's time there had been no other challenge to Murrila.

Ajanna, too, was becoming an object of legend. Lords of Sky had favored him as they favored very few, with the size and strength to take a high chief's rank. He had gone beyond what he was given, surviving the terrible cat wounding, challenging lords of Sky clear to the High Plain, which was their special place. Though Ajanna was young compared to Murrila—in truth, not so many seasons older than I was—his scarred, misshapen body and his unbounded will set him apart from his contemporaries. There was envy as well as awe for Ajanna: he was the windrider all aspired to be, though none would willingly endure that which had made Ajanna what he was.

Osia declared his rank stridently. No one else moved. Murrila nodded to Ajanna.

At the same instant, with a bellow of rage, Osia jumped Ajanna. I thought at first that Osia took Ajanna quite by surprise, for Ajanna did not respond. I had not seen Osia fight before. He was certainly powerful and very quick for being so large. I thought he might prove Ajanna's match. He did, after all, outrank Ajanna. And still Ajanna did nothing.

Osia hammered away at Ajanna's worst scars, what should have been his weakest points, but the blows had no effect; and gradually I realized Ajanna was fighting back—but differently. After the rivercat wounded him, he had not fought with any grace, winning over Lamma only by his weight and will. Now he put me in mind of the irresistible power of the mad wind. He moved as smoothly and surely as water or wind flow over land. His will seemed freed of all hesitations and obstructions of the flesh, so perfectly did he handle Osia—and yet so sparely we were hard put even to *see* what he did. With the inevitable unfolding and resolution of a rite or a dance, Ajanna brought the bout to a close, and Osia lay on the ground, defeated.

"Confirmed," said Murrila. "Next." He said nothing more about Ajanna leaving the ground. Matches among such high chiefs were rare enough that they could set their own customs. Much was at stake when high chiefs fought, and everyone was already on edge from the drought and the excitement of the Ranking. Murrila would not want to inflame the situation further. And it must have seemed to Murrila, as it did to me, that Ajanna had established his claim. Even those above him must now take their ranks from him—if at all.

Three chiefs held ranks between Osia and Murrila, and had since long before I had come onto the plain. And were large, powerful males, fearless and experienced. One after the other they came out upon the ground, and Ajanna threw them one after the other.

The rest of us watched in breathless silence, understanding what must follow, waiting only to see it done. But with the rank of chief second to Murrila, Ajanna stopped. Murrila confirmed his own rank, ending the rites. We continued to stand waiting. We knew Ajanna must challenge Murrila. Why did he delay?

Housefolk offered drinking skins; I took one without noticing. I drank, and the sour liquid, burning hotter even than the weather, shocked me into some sense of what had happened: the contest between Ajanna and Murrila *had* started, but we would not see it end this night. Unspoken, the challenge was a weapon Ajanna would use against Murrila day by day until he thought Murrila was ready for taking. Ajanna would not again make the mistake of underestimating Murrila.

Meanwhile, Braha's erstwhile herders were jostling around me, come to swear me the herder's oath. For I myself was a chief! I looked them over, seeking in their eyes some measure of what it was to be chief. I spread out my arms expansively, trying the feel of it. "My House will be worth your while," I said grandly. I knew the herds were small and the housefolk few, but such as they were, they were *mine*: beasts, housefolk—and now windriders. I took their oaths—I took all who came.

"Why do they rush to a chief by chance?" someone muttered behind me—doubtless some chief ranked near me, I thought, not turning to look. I should now have to learn the minute distinctions among minor chiefs.

"I doubt she'll hold the House in a fight!" another said more loudly.

I did not deign to answer. Such probing and needling never ceased among the minor chiefs. My new-sworn herders addressed each other with proper scorn. "Do you hear someone calling the lottery chance?"—"Must be a child or housebound to doubt the lottery expresses the will of lords of Sky"—"It's clear that Oa, who rode the mad wind, is beloved by high lords of Sky!"

The last, of course, was unanswerable; like Ajanna, I had come out of the mad wind. The chief, Naglia I think it was, gave up and moved away.

Others came: Samma, Tisla, Haida, more; young windriders first ranked in recent seasons, come to riding life after me. They knew me foremost as a windrider who had killed a rivercat and ridden the mad wind. They took my different coloring and appearance for granted, as something they had always known. Of other aspects of difference—my unexplained arrival on the plain and mysterious origins—they knew nothing, or so little it was a glamour to enhance my chiefdom. They were not much younger than I was, and it was not so many years ago I first came among them that they could not have remembered, but windriders let the past dwindle rapidly behind them. Nor did they look closely to the future. With Braha's windriders there were more than a dozen who swore me the oath, more than my rank warranted or my House could likely support. I took them all. How could I not? I *was* a windrider.

Then Lirra came toward me, swaying on her long legs, her eyes bright and glittering. "Lirra the windrider swears allegiance to Oa the chief!" she shouted.

I felt within me the rush of a high wind, though the drought-heavy air did not stir in the least. Was I then such a chief that windriders would leave Ajanna for me? I raised a drinking skin high above my head. "Lirra!" I saluted her.

She leaned toward me, laughing. I caught at one of her braids, come loose from the coil about her head. "It wants only Halassa to make our celebration complete," I declared. "Come! We'll ride to fetch him back. Lords of Sky can deny me nothing tonight!"

Lirra straightened up and pulled away from me. In the flickering light of the torches her flat, brown face looked as hard as the dry earth of the drought-stricken plain. "Will you betray him?" she hissed at me. "Is that a chief's deed, to betray a windrider?"

I spread my hands in astonishment. "Betray—?"

She thrust her face close to mine. "Betray! Halassa rode where the winds blew. What is it but betrayal to try to turn him aside from the course he chose? Or will you say he rode on a course he did not choose?" Her voice grew scornful. "You may be a chief, Oa, but don't start thinking windriders and windsteeds are possessions for you to hold like herdbeasts and housefolk! Halassa is not one for your binding!"

I stretched out my hands to her, protecting her hard words. I thought she could not have understood me correctly. "He didn't ride gladly, Lirra. I told you, I saw him—or anyway his wraith. He didn't ride gladly!"

Her eyes flashed. "A windrider asks no more than to ride!"

"What of you and me?" I pleaded. "He was your lover also. Don't you want his company?"

"I won't belittle what was between Halassa and me by calling him mine!"

My own anger flashed. "I will dare call him back for my sake alone!"

"No doubt you will! You don't need my approval. You're the chief!"

"Yes, that I am!"

So, spitting with rage, we glared at each other. I felt goaded near madness by her opposition to me—and by something else, within me.

Then I should have been suspicious of the impulse that had driven me to offer myself for Braha's House; I should have known no good would come of it. By then I could not change what I had done. I kept also to my even more impulsive notion of riding to the Broken Lands to claim back Halassa, but in the end I did not ride that night on that errand. Perhaps I might have done, but Murrila called a council of chiefs, which I had to attend, and after that I had new matters to think of.

Murrila proposed that we cull the herds, because the drought had so drastically reduced the forage. "Unless we slaughter the herdbeasts," he said, "all except the very best, we may lose the herds altogether. When the drought ends the herds will soon recover if we have kept good breeding stock. And if we live at all," he added.

"We'll eat well now," I said doubtfully from my place among the minor chiefs. "But in winter the housefolk will starve if their rations are cut below those of last year."

Even in Ajanna's House, one of the richest, this last winter we had seldom eaten our fill, the housefolk more seldom than windriders.

"So long as there are windriders and herdbeasts, lords of Sky will be served," one of the chiefs, Toda, said sententiously. "Windriders need not concern themselves with housefolk."

I scowled. If there was anything sententious ever to be said, Toda could be relied on to say it. I would not be a chief like him, I thought, but as *I* willed.

"If disease and weakness begin to spread among the herds, we could lose them all even if the drought ended and grass grew tall," Murrila warned. Though it was my objection he answered, it was Ajanna he looked to. Everything, I supposed, would now fuel the rivalry between them. The thought that my fate also should do so steeled me to look to it more closely.

"We must ride where the winds blow!" said sententious Toda, forestalling Ajanna, who had made a slight movement, as if he meant to speak.

But he said nothing.

Everyone looked irritatedly at Toda, agreeing with him only perfunctorily. But the matter *was* serious, and the chiefs soon set to discussing it seriously. One by one the chiefs spoke, counting costs, measuring and discarding alternatives. They were coming close, I saw presently, to the agreement that was necessary for all the Houses to take action in concert.

I stood by silently, reckoning my own cost. I had but a small herd which, from what I could recall seeing, Braha had mismanaged, slaughtering the best beasts to feast his herders with prime meat and to inflate his status—slaughtering the very beasts he should have kept to build up the herd. By the standards of culling that were emerging from this council, I might well lose my herd altogether. My herders would leave me. My housefolk would starve. My House would fail. The obstinacy Toda had stirred up in me became open defiance. "No!" I said loudly.

The chiefs turned to look at me.

"No," I repeated. I would not give up my House. Let the drought take it if it could, but I would not give it up of my own will. So I thought, but I said none of it aloud in council, where it would be mulled over, mangled, and worked into the rest. I only said, "No."

I looked around at the chiefs staring at me in silence. Ajanna fingered his bread, seemingly amused. Murrila finally turned from Ajanna to me. In Murrila's clear brown eyes was again that incorruptible measuring look I remembered from the distant winter night when I first gained a windrider's rank. He forgot nothing—not for long, anyway. But he had already confirmed my chief's rank. I lifted my head higher. I was within my rights. I was doing what anyone would who was in my place.

Still no one spoke. I raised a drinking skin to drink. The liquid sloshed about, for my hand was shaking. If I did not explain and discuss and argue and compromise, the council could not reach a consensus. I was a chief, and they would not act without my agreement. Without my agreement I could not lose my House. I drank. The kwass was bitter, and I choked on it. I threw the drinking skin to the ground without bothering to stopper it.

"This is not fit to drink!" I declared. The kwass gurgled as it ran out upon the ground, for no one moved to take up the skin.

"It's the drought," Murrila said. "The milk is poor—"

"No!" I interrupted. But Murrila was looking at Ajanna again, and though he broke off speaking, he did not look back at me. The look in his face had changed and there was something like uncertainty in his voice.

Here was change indeed—what I had said I wanted. I felt it gathering and threatening—a baleful, palpable presence. I thought I could hold my own course. I swung about and thrust my way through the close ranks of the assembled chiefs. No one tried to stop me, but I felt no more free when I got clear of the crowd. The hot, heavy air still confined me.

I must have been more drunk than I thought, for I mistook my way, and instead of coming to the herd of windsteeds in the bottom of the valley, I came out on the bluff overlooking Ocean. Even Ocean was quiet under the weight of the drought, near as quiet as the stricken earth.

I overtook and collided with someone moving slowly through the darkness. "Raun!" I exclaimed. I taunted him cruelly: "Is this a night lords of Ocean will speak?"

"You know that better than I," he said softly.

Unreasoning rage took hold in me. "I am a windrider! Like any windrider I live only from my first Ranking! And if I do remember anything else, still I don't deign to alter the truth: *I have no message!* I never did. I know nothing of your lords of Ocean."

"You may not know," he agreed. "The message may not be for you. But you bear it nonetheless, somehow."

His resisting me rendered me speechless with outrage. With Wiela's own madness, with Ajanna's willfullness, Raun persisted in this search for something to make meaning of his failed life—and persisted in involving *me* in the search. In a low, hard voice which sounded strange even to my own ears, just to punish him for hounding me, I said, "This one time I'll speak. I don't know if windriders truly forget their previous lives, or if it's only a convention to say so. But you're right that I haven't forgotten. In fact, I remember quite a lot of my sojourn upon Ocean. Ocean showed me no more favor that it has you. Ocean storms drove me hard and left me for dead. You know that for yourself. *You* found me. You know the condition I was in and the housebound life I then led—" I broke off, glaring at him.

But I was not quite done. Before he could answer I said, "I didn't come *from* Ocean at all. I only came over it from another plain, where people live much as here, upon the increase of herds." That was true enough; but the herds of the Great Houses of Empire were made up not of beasts but of the Conquered Peoples.

"Do the people ride?" Raun asked quickly. "Like windriders?"

"There are no windsteeds," I said. "No beasts to ride."

But that did not bother Raun. He had long ago given up hope of riding. He wanted only to live. "And among themselves do they set their ranks by fighting, as windriders do?"

"They don't fight naked and openly, certainly. They fight with their wits and possessions and anything else they can hit upon. There are many kinds of people there—more than here. The rankings among them are subtle and various and always shifting."

Even in the darkness after moonset I saw Raun's eyes shone. He whispered, "Lords of Ocean sent you to tell me this. There, on this other plain you speak of, among so many, lords of Sky can't hold all power. I, who can never regain their favor, could make my way without it!" He smiled at me. "I'll go with you when you return across Ocean."

"Nonsense!" I said testily, seeing how my words had gone astray. In speaking of Empire and the Imperial City I had meant to show, by the ordinariness, the hollowness also of Raun's notions of lords of Ocean. Instead I had given him a new goal. Tartly I added, "I can't go back anyway. How could I retrace my path over Ocean? And if I could, I would not. I left by my own desire."

"But—why? A place where there was everything? Where you must have been a high lord yourself?"

I gasped. All that I had described to Raun had seemed to me very remote. With his question my own place on that other plain suddenly came alive within me. In my mind I saw myself in the bustling markets of the Imperial City; myself surrounded by the Conquered Peoples from every corner of Empire; myself crossing the wide, dusty tree-lined streets thick with shadow and promise; entering the old, stone places of the Great Houses: the labyrinthine apartments and hidden courtyards filled with beauty, luxury, splendor, mystery; and Jily.

Raun's eyes fixed on me with the intensity of Ajanna's own; hungry; bottomless as the night; grasping at all I was. I shook my head helplessly and strode past him along the edge of the bluff. The dry grass crackled and hissed under my feet. I seemed to be walking on that other plain with the city behind me. I thought I had only to turn my head to see it—to see all that I had forsworn and fled. I heard a faint noise. If I turned, I thought, I would see lying still before me the old choice I had fled rather than make so many years before. I dreaded it as nothing else . . . but I *would* not stand aside from any challenge! I turned—finally—to face this one

I saw only a dry, dimly lit slope rising to a small hollow set with dry grass and scrubby salt brush. The noise came again. It was a giggle. The shadowy mass at the back of the hollow was a couple embracing and giggling—a flat conclusion indeed to my momentous effort of turning.

"How dare you? Who are you?" I shouted

They fell apart and turned to face me. "Oa—" a silken voice said uncertainly.

I took a hasty step forward. I knew very well it was not Jily; I could not make *that* mistake again. And yet I would give anything to see Jily once more, to touch her. My blood ran tumultuously with the memory of her flowery, sleek body in my hands. The pulse pounded insistently at my temples, and I felt faint.

"I'm Coory." Her voice sounded frightened.

I paused. "Yes, I know," I said. I glanced at her companion, who stood his ground boldly. A youth, likely first ranked this night, thinking Coory would set the seal upon his manhood. Well, I wanted her for myself if I could not have Jily. He would have to give her up to me this night. I reached for her.

"Oa—" he began. Coory put her hand on his arm. He broke off and turned his head toward her, and I saw how she smiled into his eyes.

Just so Jily had turned from me to smile at some other. I made a harsh sound in my throat, thinking of it, and Coory backed away from me fearfully, retreating up the slope behind the hollow, so she was set off by the first light on the eastern horizon. Actually, she looked nothing like Jily, it was only her voice that was a little like. Coory was bright and golden-brown, not blue-white and mysterious. And Coory was losing her youthful slenderness and freshness. The prettiness with which she had enticed me in previous years was blown and fading.

Rage and desire alike ran away from me and left me empty of feeling. Jily must also be aging. Had I left Empire for such foolishness as the fleeting beauty of a false lover? For the first time I thought I might choose more easily if I had the choice truly before me still. After all, Jily had betrayed me. She could not have expected to survive it.

And I now knew I could control the High Dance—had I not done so in every Ranking these many years? I could have spared Jily even if I had Danced. What I would have been in Empire if I had so controlled the High Dance at my very initiation! I would likely have challenged the Dynast by now, and perhaps ousted him and taken his place as I used to dream of doing.

But the old choice was *not* before me. I regretted the

impulse that led me to talk to Raun of Empire, and once again break my resolve to keep the touch of Empire from this plain, except only as I needed to use it myself. I had left Empire behind, and I did not even know for certain now in which direction it lay. I lived on a different plain.

The sun was all but risen. Land and sea were alike flat and colorless, but fully lit. The motionless air had stayed warm all through the night—again. It had not moved for days. The kwass I had drunk, the evil-tasting kwass that did not even get me properly drunk, was heavy and sour in my stomach. There was a dull ache of poison in my shoulder even though I had not fought this last night but taken my rank by lot.

Without another word I left Raun and Coory and her young windrider. I walked on up the slope, crossing the line of listless herdbeasts rimming the valley, and came down into the camp. Nearly as listless as the herdbeasts in the grip of the drought, my windriders stood about the small cluster of tents belonging to my House: Lirra, Tisla, Haida and the others.

"We ride!" I called out to them. They turned to me at once, brightening. Yes, that was the answer: keep moving. Like herdbeasts and windsteeds, windriders were bred to move. If I kept moving, the past must stay in its proper place behind me.

CHAPTER

14

"This is the best place," Tisla said—without much enthusiasm. I grunted while I surveyed the bluff that ran down to the nameless river. The bluff was very steep and partly undercut. Downstream the canyon widened quickly where the river curved around a sand bar to meet the sea; the bluff there was steeper yet, all rock, washed bare by storm waves.

"I searched upriver half the day," Tisla added. "Nowhere was there anything better."

"We'll have to use ropes to get the herdbeasts down," I said. "On this first stretch anyway, past that overhang. Farther down they might be able to fend for themselves." Then there was the river. It could be swum. I looked across it to the far wall of the canyon rising up to the plain again.

"Looks a bit better," Tisla said, following my gaze.

I grunted again and stretched, lifting my long braids away from my neck. In the slight breeze that rose off the river, my skin quickly cooled where it was damp with sweat. Once more I looked down the route we had chosen. It was only what I expected. The canyons growing so much deeper at their mouths was the very reason why no one ever used this coast route—and that was why the pasture along it was better, that and the dampness of the sea air. I swung around dropping my braids so they swirled out around me, to face Tisla standing beside me on a little terrace perched just under the lip of the bluff.

Tisla was one of the best of my House, I thought, though he was not so much to look at as some of the others, not so graceful nor so strongly colored. He was sturdy for his height, which was about the same as my own. His hair and skin were alike a soft nut brown, his eyes being lighter, with a touch of yellow, and very bright. His eyes were the clue to his nature: he would do anything I asked of him in just the same way I would have done it. "I call that a drawback," Lirra had said tartly when she saw it. I thought it no drawback. I liked it that my sworn herders should be like me. I grinned, meeting Tisla's eyes, seeing how he looked at me rather as I would look at a windsteed. I liked being a chief, riding high on the awe of my herders.

"Let's get to it," I said. Tisla nodded, and together we climbed the short distance to the others waiting for us with the herd. Cloud came to me at once, nickering; I scratched her broad face absently while I gave the orders.

It took us the rest of the day to get down to the river, slinging the roped herdbeasts one by one down that first, difficult stretch. We used ropes braided from windsteeds' manes and tails. A strand no bigger around than one of my fingers was far stronger than the heaviest rawhide rope, strong enough to bear the weight of a herdbeast. Even after we loosed the beasts to scramble down the lower slope, we decided to keep a windsteed close on either side of each one to make sure they did not fall far if they tripped. There were over a hundred herdbeasts and a scant dozen to work them: hard work for all. No one slacked. No one *could*, we were too few. I knew most had sworn to me in search of adventure. It surprised me more they seemed to think they were getting it, for so far this journey was little but hard work.

For myself, I liked the work, the testing of myself against bluffs and rivers, the physical hardships of the coast route. It was a change from contending so long with forces less material, less certain, and internal. Here was simply resistance, without trickery. By exertion alone I could overcome each hinder of rock or water. And then there were the windsteeds. On this route we had found aspects of intractability in herdbeasts no one had dreamed of, but also new powers in windsteeds. And in this taxing, complex work we found also new bonds with our windsteeds. More than ever Cloud and I became aspects of a single being.

I set Cloud at the bluff for the last time after pulling up and coiling the last ropes when Tisla, halfway down, loosed the last herdbeast. Cloud seemed to dance in the air, finding footing on nothing in the least substantial on this steep slope. Indeed, she was playing, I realized, and I sent her on more directly to join the others waiting below on the narrow beach that fronted this side of the river.

We had the river to swim, swollen now with an incoming tide. I decided not to wait for the water to go down. The extra distance was worth the lessened risk of herdbeasts being carried out to sea. The herdbeasts swam well enough— they seemed hardly to distinguish between water and land, in fact. And they had no better sense of direction in water than on land. Of themselves I doubt they could have found the opposite shore of the narrowest stream. As always they must be herded.

I gave the signal. The herders moved to bunch the herd tight and drive it into the water. I sent Cloud to one side at the rear. With her moving against the cool salt water, a medium so much thicker than her native air, I could clearly *see* as well as feel the great power in the bunching and thrust of her muscles. All too soon she was driving up the far bank, streaming water from her sleek hide.

The sun was near setting. I looked away along the toe of the bluff, a wider shore here than on the other side of the river, with a bit of marsh and a sandy beach that curved around the end of the bluff some little way along Ocean to an old rock fall. The bluff looked gentler than the one we had just descended, more earth than rock, but work for all that. I hailed the nearest rider over the bustle and bellowing of the herdbeasts excited after the river crossing.

"Haida! Take some others and go search those rocks for shellfish. We're going to spend the night here on the beach."

Haida cocked her head, straining to hear me, then understood, and nodded, and wheeled on her windsteed, braids flying. She hailed some others. Together they swept over the level sand toward the sun. I watched a moment before I turned back to the task of settling the herd.

The marsh was mostly saltgrass, which the herdbeasts would not eat; there was a little sweet around the fringes and they finally turned to cropping that. We riders came down from our windsteeds then to build up a bonfire of driftwood. When the fishers returned laden, we feasted.

I went myself, late, to sleep upriver of the herd. I set no other guard: if a rivercat came in the night I doubted any could keep it from taking what it wanted. I was lucky, and not tired.

In the morning we drove the herd up the bluff to the plain and went on, ever south, at a slow pace. The herdbeasts began to look better with the care I demanded for them. I culled them in a small way, taking only the worst and weakest for butchering. After all their work my herders did not even often eat well. They did not complain; not to me, anyway. They had bound themselves, by their oaths, to do all that I ordered.

Not until the very eve of the midwinter Ranking did I lead my House into the camp in the Long Fen. Housefolk looked up from their work, silent and sullen as ever, to watch us ride by. Windriders nodded a spare greeting. Toda the sententious one came out of his chief's tent as we rode past it in a long line, heading for our own place, which should lie beyond. When I greeted him, he turned his back to me, in token that he remembered my intransigence in council, I supposed, briefly amused. But when other chiefs did the same, I knew many had fared worse than I had. I only lifted my head the higher in defiance, saying to myself that if they had followed the route I took, they could have gained as much.

No snow had fallen as yet; nor had the ground frozen. For all one could tell by the weather, it could have been an autumn Ranking we prepared for. The fen hardly deserved its name any longer. Dry, it revealed new unpleasantnesses: the mud became a powdery fine dust, foul smelling and strangely clinging, which soon coated everything in the camp and all of us. What water remained at the bottom of pools was scummed over with strange growths; it, too, smelled bad, and it tasted even worse.

My housefolk had set up my tents very near one of these ponds. The miasma that came off the stagnant water seemed a palpable assault to me, standing in front of my chief's tent, stiff with distaste for the smell, naked, while my housefolk made me ready for the rites. They coiled my braids—as long now as any other windrider's but still the color of none—and oiled my skin, and painted symbols of rank over the fine, pale lines of my Imperial tattooing. Stiffly, alone, I strode through the camp toward the Ranking ground. Shunned by the others or not, I would now be alone in any event: the Ranking tested each individually.

Of all who crowded out upon the ground to cast their lots before Murrila, it was Kirbana who came against me. Kirbana: Murrila's herder, Murrila's champion. I glanced at Murrila where he sat bulking large with the bonfire behind him. The flickering light of it distorted my vision so I could not read his expression. Lords of Sky set the test of the Ranking, or so we always said. . . . I wondered as I swung my gaze back to Kirbana, who was coming for me.

Like everyone else I had watched Kirbana's swift, sure rise through the ranks these last few seasons. He might be young to be already aspiring to a chief's rank even as low as mine. He was growing so quickly it was clear he would be one of those to reach the size and weight of a high chief. He had something of the air already—unlike ill-fated Braha.

He should be able to take me easily.

He came to meet me with the cruel grace of the young who have as yet no notion of limits. He looked flawless: his muscles sleek and full, his skin golden brown, gleaming, and nowhere marked. He carried himself as lightly as a skittish windsteed, his head high and fine, his dark hair tied close and smooth. His eyes shone brightly with assurance. Thus Ajanna and Rauna must have looked at that age, I thought suddenly; before I knew them—just so strong and bright. No longer, either of them.

Kirbana came to me and set a hand on my shoulder as gently as a lover.

All windriders were young, of course; I was young myself, though not so young as Kirbana—young enough I could think I need not be bound by any limits I had yet seen. I was strong—all my body was muscle, very lean, leaner with every season the drought endured. I was not unmarked. The Gandish pallor of my skin had finally taken some color in the years of riding and herding. It was a flat brown hue, on which scars and bruises showed up strongly, especially the long, streaked scars of my cat wounds. My pale hair, near transparent, braided as tightly as Kirbana's shed a faint glow about my head. My eyes, paler than my skin, a color no others had, unnerved many, I well knew. I narrowed my eyes, measuring Kirbana. I was nowhere near his size. I knew I ought not to be able to beat him. But I would stop at nothing to win.

I stepped in close, under his hold, where the wild, sweet scent of his youth, stronger than that of the rancid oil that overlay it, filled my nostrils. Coldly I struck with hard chops at those points of separation I had learned not from human bodies, but from the butchering of herdbeasts. Kirbana grunted, feeling my blows; he was slower than he doubtless meant to be in moving away. When he took too large a step, I was ready. I threw him to the ground by his own weight. He fell heavily but thrust himself upright at once and came after me.

If I was to wear him down, him with his youth and strength, I had a long task ahead of me. And he, of course, had no mind to give me the time. He was wary of me from the outset and became more so; he drove me hard. Pressed, I gathered the Dance about me like a shield.

Deeper than I had ever gone before I sought through my heritage of Empire that I had never dared discard, to dredge up the will to beat Kirbana. As in no bout yet my own flesh was inadequate; the Dance lifted me into a high, spare region where flesh was of little account, where the knowledge and cunning of Empire held sway. I—I was the least of it, I knew that. The old compromise I had struck when I first came to ride, whereby I *rode* free of Empire, I had indeed to strain. I did not like it. I had no choice, if I was to win.

The long life of House Gand flowed strongly through the conduits of my nerves and blood, close to the plain, around Kirbana, and at last he Danced to the bidding of my will. He came to me meekly like a beast willing to the slaughter. My hands settled near his head, above the Death Points. Dance—the High Dance—held me as closely as it did him and came then to the very core of me, where I was a windrider. I remembered Ajanna's old warning that winds and windsteeds would not take up a killer.

I knew the warning was not literally true. I had long ridden now, though I had killed in Empire, and I had seen Ajanna kill upon this very ground and ride again. But I would take no chances where it touched on riding. I turned my will against the Dance, against my own nerve and sinew and straining muscle. Slowly, terribly slowly, I won free. I raised my hands and let Kirbana fall. I stood over him, breathing hard, and waited to hear Murrila confirm my rank once again.

Murrila's words came slowly; reluctantly, I thought, and they did not come before I turned to question his delay. I met stern eyes fixed on me. With the keenness of the Dance still strong about me, I saw more deeply into Murrila than before, and saw how it was his assessment resembled the awesome, testing gaze of the Dynast in Empire: Murrila looked not only to see what I was but looked also out from his care for his people, caring as the Dynast did for his Empire, judging me against an equally absolute and incorruptible standard.

I shared no such standard. I went always some way only of my own, as I had also in this fight with Kirbana. And I had won. Sure in that knowledge, I met Murrila's gaze, and finally he spoke the words the rites—and I—required. But I thought he did it against his will, and I threw up my head angrily as I turned to leave the ground.

Windriders and housefolk crowded close. Their very gathering, the rare relaxation, with the rites, of boundaries of caste and House, manifested as never otherwise the standard Murrila held to. I felt myself set apart by it from all others. Suddenly I could not bear to stand among them.

I looked about me, doubtless wild of eye. Near the edge of the crowd my gaze caught on my own herder Tisla—he who had ridden so closely after me all the long trek south. I called out his name imperiously, "Tisla!" My voice snapped across ritual; my willfulness forced all to acknowledge me.

People moved uneasily, murmuring. Tisla turned his head to see me and stood stone-still, staring at me, more now as if he saw a rivercat than a windsteed, wary—and eager. I rode that look of his like a wind out of the sky. I smiled at him—challenging. His eyes gleamed yellowly at me, brighter. He came quickly to me—making my meaning clear to all as he fell in with it. I tossed my head, still defiant, and led him out of the crowd, out into the night, leaving the others to their rites.

In the morning I came out of my tent feeling lazy, my leathers laced loosely. The air was mild and pleasant as it should not be at midwinter, but all the same it *was* pleasant. And I felt pleasant, all my rage of the night quite soothed.

The camp was strangely in a ferment, windriders striding about as keyed up as if the rites had never been, housefolk looking fearful. Ease fled me. "What is it?" I demanded. My own housefolk, crouching about the cooking fire in front of my chief's tent, started in alarm at my voice. They looked around at me but they could not meet my gaze. Wordlessly they shook their heads.

Some way off I heard Ajanna bellowing in anger like a herdbeast, his voice rumbling with power and threat. He had not yet fought, I thought—I could tell by his voice. Over Murrila and all the rest of us he was still holding his challenge unspoken. On that account the rites could seem to have been of no avail, the Ranking come to nothing, windrider about to turn on windrider. Or it could be on account of the drought. How could any of us be easy while we saw the very earth shriveling about us?

Ajanna I could do nothing about, but I had some notion still of dealing with the drought. I called back over my shoulder to Tisla inside the tent, to bid him fetch the herders of the House from wherever they had ended up during the night. Them I sent to cut our beasts from the massed herds milling about the perimeter of the camp. Then we ran into the Long Fen.

We found dry ground everywhere we went. The trees still held their leaves, for no frost had come to drop them. With another year as dry as the ones just past, the trees would likely be dead, but for now the dry foliage was better forage for the herdbeasts than any pasture remaining on the plain.

Seeing what I had hit upon, other Houses came out after mine, but by doing first I got the most benefit. Through the quiet forests of the Long Fen, I moved south steadily in front of all others—days; and came finally to a vast, slow-moving river whose farther shore was scarcely visible. Many more days we ran then upstream—east—along its bank. We could see it was impassable. No herd could swim it. It was the Flod, I guessed, running out of Empire. I looked at it and wondered and then shrugged. I could not know for certain what river it was; nor was I at all certain I wanted to know. Whatever river it was, the drought did not look to have diminished it: the water ran full to the banks. It was only the streams from our plain, which should have watered the fens, that had failed.

A little rain did fall, very late, after we had turned north again. On the fen trees the last dead leaves of the old year turned brown and limp. The trees did not look to be leafing out with any new shoots this year.

I brought my House into camp in good time for the spring Ranking. Others, foraging, mistook the time now there was no change of season to tell it by. The crowd was thin of windriders when we assembled for the rites. Many ranks would have to go by lot.

I saw Raun among the housefolk crowding onto the ground to cast tokens in lottery after lottery. He got no rank. Passing near me once when he left the ground unsuccessful, he averted his face to avoid my gaze. With scant, wry amusement, I wondered if he thought I would hold it against him that he took this chance with lords of Sky after all his talk about Ocean and Empire. He did not know all I had done, to ride.

He limped worse than I remembered. He looked thinner and much older. None of the housefolk looked very well. The drought bore down hardest on them. In more than one House chiefs stinted even windriders for food, and the small wild creatures that usually supplemented housefolk fare were themselves decimated.

Only the windsteeds were not affected by the drought. Of course we gave them the pick of everything. Considering their size they did not eat much; they seemed able to live on the very wind that was their natural place. I glanced away through the shadowed trees where the windsteeds wandered. In the darkness pale-colored windsteeds like Cloud showed up as shapeless glimmerings. The others were invisible presences, only felt. I wondered why I stayed here in this camp among the defeated when I could ride. The bonds that held me to other people were growing thin indeed. I was a herder no longer. But of course I had sworn a chief's oath. . . .

Looking around at my fellows, I thought more than one of them looked to be feeling as I did. Ajanna was openly impatient with the rites, broken as they were again and again by lots for unclaimed ranks. But he, too, stayed.

Mere children sought rank. I marked one with astonishment, thinking her the youngest ever, a mere slip of a thing, hardly waist-high to me. On her face, which was so young her features were not yet fixed, I saw a look as hard as any windrider's. I stared, calculating the time. Six, no seven, years it must have been; this could be Wiela's child . . . Ajanna's child, born that first winter after I came out of Empire. Boldly indeed she walked onto the ground and cast her token.

And the child took her rank to hold without contest until the next Ranking, chosen by the lots to fill an empty rank. She proclaimed herself Groa, and Murrila accepted it. The face she had! Seeing it, I could think Wiela had worked her twisted will in this child of Ajanna's begetting. Wiela herself paid the child no heed; she also took a rank by lot.

When my own turn came, I once again faced Kirbana across the emptiness of the Ranking ground. I thought it could not be by chance he came to me twice running, and if Murrila had altered the lots this time, likely he had also done so before. Little though I had ever heeded lords of Sky, something in me went cold at the thought that Murrila dared to try me in their name. With a new grimness I faced Kirbana. He looked hungrier than he had a season since, not so young or so graceful; I beat him all the same, more easily in fact, for I was less willing than ever to be beaten. If the Rankings could bend to anyone's will, I meant them to bend to mine.

Seeing my win, and the thriving of my herd, more windriders came to me, from many Houses. This time I picked and chose among them and did not take them all; now I had gone to some trouble to hold my House, I did not mean to undo what I had accomplished by burdening my herds with the support of too many mouths.

I watched with no small curiosity to see that Groa was one of those who came to swear the herder's oath to me. I said no. She drew her dark brows together over unchildish eyes and turned away from me without a word. Later I heard Murrila took her.

And still Ajanna did not speak his challenge against Murrila. We made no pretense of celebrating, that night. Sober, we rode out of the camp early the next morning.

Already what little grass had sprouted on the plain was withering; no one could think much good would come of the year's drive north but we had to go: we were windriders and we could not stay still.

Standing high over my windsteed's neck, feeling the wind blow full in my face when I got free of the last trees and knowing it had blown over the plain for days to reach me, I felt the old exhilaration as if for the first time. I raised my right hand above my head. Reaching their places, my herders turned, one after the other, to watch me. I brought my fist down smartly.

Cloud lunged forward with the other windsteeds. I kept my weight on my knees pressed hard against her neck and rode easily. Calves squealed and their dams lowed reassuringly. By my touch and will the herd began to move out from the fen onto the plain. The power of the enormous herdbeasts coursed through my body.

Almost at once the right flank of the herd bunched and

swung out. I sent Cloud nipping at the rumps of beasts to straighten them out. The bull that had caused the mishap stood his ground, head lowered. Cloud danced around him, playful, until, bewildered, he lumbered after the others. She trotted past him briskly, full of her own importance. I felt the stretch and surge of her stride in my own muscles.

The wind gusted stronger and swept up the cloud of dust raised by the moving herds wherever they passed. As I could not see past the nearest beasts, I pulled my cloak around my face for protection. I soon threw it off again, hearing another commotion in the herd.

A score of beasts, taking fright, ran blindly away from the rest. Beyond them a windsteed and rider loomed out of the dust cloud. I jogged forward, irritated, marking how the windsteed came on at a broken pace. None of my herders rode such an old, decrepit windsteed.

Wiela's high-pitched voice came through the noise the herds made. "Oa! Hail!"

I rode up to her. "What are you doing? Why are you scattering my herd?"

She looked around, wide-eyed. "I scatter a herd?" Her eyes narrowed as her gaze returned to me, and her tone grew sly. "You don't need to teach Wiela how to herd beasts!" She gave a wild laugh, and the herdbeasts, which had been returning to the herd, went off again. Cloud also started at the sound, but Wiela's own windsteed stood dumbly still, taking no notice. It was old Madder, whom I had ridden when first ranked. He took no notice of me now.

"What do you want, Wiela?"

"I've come to inspect you, to make sure my revenge against Ajanna goes forward, though you no longer ride with us. I'm ready to see it concluded." She spoke with a quiet seriousness that belied the madness of her words.

"I have no grudge against Ajanna," I said coldly. "I won't be a tool for your madness." I remembered the uncanny child Groa and added, "Anyway you have the child—"

Wiela did not seem to hear me. "Raun took you up from Ocean, Oa, and I set you on the winds. Now you'll do something for me. You wouldn't be a windrider but for me—and Raun, of course. And you're still something besides a windrider. When Ajanna finally sees what it is you are, it'll bring him down, for he'll have to acknowledge that you're something greater than he. Then I'll see him lie at my feet and hear him acknowledge defeat!''

I stiffened, not that I could think Ajanna needed protection from me or anyone else, but to hear Wiela speak so openly of what no other would dare, what no other even knew for sure, what I had brought onto this plain and kept alive all these years because without it I could not ride: Empire. Then I realized she could not *know*. "You're raving!" I said roughly. I thought also how Ajanna had already seen all I was—and used it for his own ends; I didn't tell Wiela that.

I urged Cloud to round up the straying herdbeasts before they mixed with neighboring herds still close so soon after setting out from the winter camp. Wiela, shouting, drove Madder after me. Leaving off her preoccupation with Ajanna for the moment, she taunted me: "I see the care you take with your House—with its herds and possessions! Take care, Oa, that your House doesn't grow so vast and powerful that it binds *you*. You wouldn't ride so free and haughty then!''

I grew hot with anger, but I set myself to ignore her. I got the beasts moving away from the next House's herd, and moved to the rear to watch for strays. The dust only increased now all the herds were moving faster. It was difficult to see far, and I did not want stray calves to slip between my herders and get lost in the other herds.

Viciously Wiela jabbed poor, ancient Madder to keep up with Cloud. I felt sick that my old companion, with whom I had first ridden the wind, had fallen into the clutches of Wiela's madness. But I could do nothing for him, for Wiela had won on the Ranking ground the right to ride him. All the while Wiela shouted ever wilder threats and demands at me.

Another figure loomed out of the dust. Even before I could make out his face I knew by his bulk it was Ajanna on Scudder. I turned Cloud to head him off.

"Your herd is straggling along this flank!" I called to

him sharply. "Keep your beasts together, or I'll take them with mine!"

"Very well," he said mildly, angling Scudder's course to do as I asked, moving back into the dust and becoming shadowy. Wiela followed him at least. I stopped to watch them go, to make sure Wiela did leave without wreaking more mischief.

Gusts of wind blew dust at me crazily from all sides, so I closed my eyes and buried my head in Cloud's mane to escape it. She ran, and for an instant we soared upon the wind, alone, free, and flawless. But soon again I tasted the dust of the drought, and I seemed to hear faint peals of Wiela's mad laughter on the wind. I rode on feeling burdened.

CHAPTER

15

I rode through the fire of a relentless sun, across a dry plain that reflected up its own color into the vast, brassy sky overhead. The dry air leached life away. The very earth looked brittle, so the least thing might cause it to crumble. I felt as brittle, nerves snapping, sleepless, skittish. A single word might break me. I brooded over Wiela's words to me. Not those about Ajanna, those I was used to and hardly heard: I brooded over what she had said about me—what I was coming to see as truth.

In taking Braha's House, what had I done save set around my own self stronger bonds than those I chafed at before? The care for my herd and House bound me more closely than it did the least of my housefolk.

And there was worse. Even when I was housebound, I had dared to scorn the claims of Empire. But to hold my House against the likes of Kirbana, I had given myself over without reserve, yielding up freely what I must of my self to wield Imperial powers—exactly what I had forsworn Empire in order to be able to refuse. Here indeed was the old unresolved dilemma! Here was the old choice still before me.

So I brooded, but found no more answer than ever before. A windsteed came alongside Cloud, seeming pale and insubstantial in the searing afternoon light.

"Oa—?"

I didn't answer. A tug came on one of my long braids that fell to mingle with Cloud's lank mane. Just so Halassa had once tugged my braids when I brooded. Tears started to my eyes, from my thinking of Halassa; blinded by my tears I could not at first see who it was who rode beside me, but I knew it could not be Halassa, and more tears flowed.

"Oa!" came Lirra's voice again, startled now. "Are you hurt?"

The dry wind drank my tears, and I saw Lirra rode beside me on her white Moon. She looked near as wraithlike as Halassa had, her soft brown color gone flat, even her eyes, from the wearing down by the drought. Her windsteed, coated with the dust of the plain, had the same lusterless color. All the years of our close companionship ran together without distinction, a background shriveling like the plain.

"Halassa—" I began in a tight voice, wanting him and all else in my life that had been so free and easy before . . . before what? Whatever else I might also be, I was too much the windrider to alter the truth. Truly, when Halassa rode among us, I had often left him, wanting more. Dumbly I looked at Lirra, and saw her expression had hardened. Because I had spoken of Halassa. She would not speak of him.

I shrugged and turned from her, brooding again, over Halassa now as well as myself. Day by day I brooded, and drove my beasts and herders ever harder, northward . . . and eastward.

One of the herdbeasts collapsed. The other beasts started away from it in alarm. When the herders checked them, they snorted uneasily and stamped the ground, leaving a clear space in which the fallen beast lay, crumpled and twitching. From Cloud's high back I looked down upon it. An old cow it was, likely past bearing more young; we would have butchered her soon in any event. I motioned to the windrider nearest me, Haida.

She swung down from her windsteed, drawing a long, white-bladed knife from the sheath on the outside of her leggings as she approached the herdbeast warily. It could not rise; it could hardly breathe; desperate with fear it still struggled. The lunging of that great head, or those flailing forelegs, could kill a person.

Haida flicked her long braids back over her shoulders with a toss of her head and dove, driving her blade across the throat of the beast, swinging past it in the same motion, out of harm's way.

She had struck true. After one mighty heave the beast lay still. I went myself to drive those still living downwind, where their dust would not blow across the camp we would set up beside the carcass. Several herders went to help Haida with the skinning and butchering, others gathering fire fuel, the dry dung and clods of dead grass that were all this spot afforded. The meat must be quickly smoked if we were to keep any of it in this heat. We had our work cut out for us for that day.

But we feasted that night, on the liver and tongue and other parts that must be eaten fresh. Afterwards we lay lazily around our little fire, passing a skin of kwass from hand to hand in the balmy stillness of night. We could think it such an evening as we had not had since the drought came. Even to us sitting right beside it, our small fire was the merest speck of light in the unseen vastness of the silent plain. That was as it should be.

"Look at the stars," someone said.

We all turned up our faces and gazed into the black night sky from which the stars hung low and glittering. By their positions I saw midsummer neared; I had no more time for my brooding. Or for herding. I stood up, finally decided.

At my movement the windriders turned to me. "In the morning, turn back with the herd toward Ocean." I said to them. "You'll have to hurry. You may be hard put to get there in time." Only now did I bethink myself how far we had run. I might already have delayed too long, and still not come to a clear course. Now I had to risk my rank along with all else. "I will catch up to you," I promised—and hoped that I would.

"Oa! What do you mean?" Haida cried, sitting bolt upright, clutching a drinking skin with thoughtless strength. Someone else leaned over her to fasten the stopper before she spilled the contents. But they all looked as uncomprehending as she did, even Tisla. Looking slowly from one to the other, I doubted they could understand me.

My eye caught on Lirra's. She at least had some inkling of what I would be about. I looked at her long, pleading. Abruptly she turned her head, breaking our locked gaze. I stiffened, understanding *her*. Just so she had turned her head that day Halassa rode away with Ajanna and me to the High Plain. Implacably she refused to see or hear what might impinge on her too much. That was well enough for her, I thought. Not for me. There were several matters I had turned from overlong. It was they I would now ride to remedy. Without another word, I went.

Cloud came to me out of the night, unbidden, a huge, pale, amorphous mass, moving slowly. I swung up to her back and tied my catskin cloak to the gear strap behind me. I had a long knife in a sheath along one leg, a shorter one at my belt. I took nothing else: if I did not come back, I would not short the others food I might not be able to use anyway. So much care I had for my House—no more.

I locked my feet under Cloud's throat and she moved off, gliding slowly through the mass of resting herdbeasts, being careful not to alarm them. When we were free—alone—she stretched her stride eagerly into the too-warm night. I slept, wrapped in her long gray mane to keep my seat. I could sleep better windsteedback than elsewhere; I could sleep more easily now I had finally decided my course.

What I would do when I reached my destination I still did not know.

Cloud ran through the night and into the morning. The sun came to meet me, casting a slanting fire down the bulwark of the Broken Lands, the rock face that rose in giant steps to the High Plain. Here was my goal. From wind and rock I meant to demand the return of Halassa. *That* was the end result of my long brooding: simply to face all that I had ever turned from. Empire I could not easily reach. I would start with Halassa. It was madness, one could say. But was it? Who knew what the mad wind was? Or might give up to a determined will?

I directed Cloud at the rock. Her footsteps clanked loudly when she left the dusty plain for bare rock, and echoed as we wove into the maze of canyons.

Walls of rock rose on either side of us, brightly-colored mineral hues, colors of no living things; we went on and found a break where Cloud could clamber up to higher ground, a terrace, which rounded the slope and entered yet another canyon. The sun blazed everywhere, dazzling me. All was open to view, and Halassa was nowhere. I kept on doggedly, and late in the afternoon came so high only a single scarp remained above me, sharp against the empty sky, and I thought beyond it the High Plain lay. I wondered if I need also go there: there was where Halassa was lost; only a wraith had wandered in the Broken Lands.

All day the hot sun had beat at me, from the sky and again from the glittering rock. I was dazed and worn by it, wandering from sense. While I craned my head upward, trying to think, Cloud picked her way delicately along the narrowing terrace, and turned a corner into sudden coolness and shadow, a canyon so narrow its arching walls nearly roofed it over. In the grottoed depths a spring trickled into a mossy rock basin. Gratefully I slid down to the rock, slid to my knees on the cool moss, and bent to drink from my cupped hands. Cloud lowered her head beside mine and slurped the water noisily.

I leaned back on my heels, grinning to think of the sight we must present huddling so greedily over the little water. When Cloud had drunk her fill, she nuzzled me with her moss-soft lips. I lay back quietly on the cool, shadowed rock to rest, just for the moment.

Voices sounded, suddenly and loudly, echoing about the rock so I could not tell their source. I started up, hardly daring—but unable not—to hope it could be Halassa come to me so easily to be found. The voices did sound familiar; there was more than one, I thought. Puzzled, I circled behind Cloud and headed for the entrance to the canyon.

Half a dozen figures came into view around a jutting rock, not ten paces distant from me, so short the canyon was. Their voices broke off at the sight of me. For a long moment they and I stared in open-mouthed astonishment.

I saw it was no wonder they had sounded familiar: they came from my past, as Halassa did, but a far more distant past. Though I had never actually seen them before, I knew them instantly for what they were.

Red bordered their identical drab kilts and jackets, red laced their boots and helmets; not the bright, true Lusian red, but a darker hue, just as famed; two females and four males. They were soldiers of the Hereditary Army of the Red, that renowned force that had been gone from the Imperial City for generations' time, advancing Empire ever eastward—within sight, it had been said before I left the city, of world's end.

Though I thus knew who these persons were, I yet stared at them uncomprehending, for how had they come here from the eastern borders of Empire? And they stared back at me as astounded; seeing, I guessed, a lean, leather-clad figure standing beside a beast of legendary stature. They must have wondered how I came to be in this wilderness of barren rock. Then I grew angry and ceased to wonder the hows and whys of them: they came of Empire, which I had meant to forswear; they came onto *my* range, on which I had always determined should come nothing of Empire save myself. I drew myself up.

"What is the meaning of this intrusion?" I demanded.

They gaped; and I judged from their astonishment how stilted my speech had grown. By now I spoke wholly in the windriders' accents and theirs would sound strange. They gaped—but they also acted. They raised their pikes to bar my exit through the narrow mouth of the canyon.

"You must yield," the leader among them warned me, a fair-skinned, brawny male with small, pale eyes. His tone inflamed me.

"Be gone from this place at once!" I said fiercely. "I, Oa, order it!"

Cloud came up beside me with a clatter of hooves on rock, made edgy by my tone. I grasped her mane and swung onto her back and stared down from that height at the soldiers of the Red.

They stood their ground. They had seen many strange

things in their long history, if never a windsteed. They were immune to wonder, and they were disciplined.

I touched Cloud with one hand, a signal to go. She was willing. She had no knowledge of weapons or soldiers or of any danger to herself, save perhaps rivercats. She could not know how near kin a soldier was to a rivercat, and I had forgotten

The soldiers of the Red set their pikes. I was steeled to overleap them and Cloud was moving before I saw what they were about. Only a windrider could have been so slow to see so obvious a tactic—a windrider who could not conceive of injuring windsteeds. They meant to disable Cloud, thinking then to have easy prey of me. I saw it so late there was then nothing for it but to throw myself bodily between Cloud and the soldiers.

From a pike I took a glancing slash along one arm. I hardly felt it, expecting as I did likely Cloud's whole weight on my back. That did not come: she stopped, throwing herself back upon her haunches so hard that her hooves squealed for purchase over the bare rock. Her forelegs, flung up, swung wide, missing me but knocking aside one of the soldiers, who lay still then where she fell, whether dead or only stunned, I could not tell—and did not care. I cared for nothing save that my windsteed was endangered. Had a pike touched her, I would have killed them all, or died trying. As it was, I had a good mind to.

The five remaining soldiers rallied and advanced.

I could only think I must safeguard Cloud from them. "Stop!" I cried. "Fools! Will you attack a near-heir of the Imperial House?" So sorely pressed, I took what came to hand. My voice remembered the accents of the Imperial kin. The soldiers of the Red heard it and came to attention by ancient instinct. They grounded their pikes. Still they eyed me suspiciously, ever more so as the minutes went by. I could understand it: how could a near-heir be here or look as I did?

"It's not for us to decide such matters," the burly leader muttered at last. "You must come with us to the commander."

The slash on my arm stung, goading my anger. "Must?

Must? Will you talk so to *me?*'' I demanded, thrusting my face forward into his.

The soldiers' eyes widened, seeing thus at close range the pale Imperial blue of my eyes and my many tattooed lines of rank. Then they dropped their gaze, yielding allegiance, and I stood back, with time finally to take thought.

I thought how these were only six—a scout unit, the merest token of the vast horde that was the Hereditary Army of the Red. ''What is the meaning of your presence here?'' I asked again, with less anger and more determination.

''We march at orders,'' they said woodenly.

I could see them as they had been described to me long ago, the thousands in their ranks moving like a flood tide. ''Here?'' I said. I could not see them *here*, not on the High Plain. Or on the true plain.

The burly, bold one looked up at me. ''Here,'' he said disgustedly. ''Rock and brush we fight, we who conquered a hundred peoples. Weeks we've marched and never seen a single living being. Sometimes not even very many bushes. But always rock.''

Over the High Plain they had come, then, through the nameless mountains west of the Imperial City, I guessed. For such a campaign the Army of the Red had been recalled from the east? *''Why?''* The question burst from me.

The soldiers of the Red stood silent. They could not know the answer, they were but common soldiers who had known nothing but service for generations.

''Who commands?'' I asked.

''Hallek.''

So Hallek held the Red now. Hallek of Lus. I knew him: middle-aged and dour, coming to the Imperial City so rarely that he was always out of fashion and we young heirs made sport of him. He had been in the High Command of the Army of the Gold then, occupying the rich, walled cities of the Southern Shore. I pictured him in my mind, red-haired like all Lusians, but his skin was not so ruddy, diluted perhaps by Imperial blood and pallor.

''Where is Hallek?'' I asked. ''And the headquarters?''

The bold one gestured upward, toward the High Plain, someplace nearby, and my impression that this was a solitary advance unit faded. When such as Hallek of Lus commanded, there must be also the bulk of an army. Seeing Hallek through all I had learned since I had last seen him, I better reckoned his worth: he would not easily be turned from his purpose.

But what *was* his purpose?

I stared at the five of the Red. The sixth lay where Cloud had flung her, likely dead, to be still so long. The five stood automatically in a straight row, evenly spaced; parts of a unit, not persons at all, as I thought of persons, not even so much as housefolk. I chewed my lip, considering.

In a thousand years, I knew, no army of Empire had ever turned aside from its ordained goal. Oh, armies had been beaten, broken, even lost. Our records did not lack such occurrences. The armies had always recovered and gone on. Everything, they had taken. That they meant to take also this land I could not doubt. It made no sense to me, however, for the plain was empty of plunder and almost of people. The threat could not seem real to me. How could Empire hold windriders or windsteeds? I could not think what to do. I chewed my lip and did nothing

I heard a noise. My head came up at once, questing. In these canyons noise was thrown about every which way and its source disguised. This was an evil noise: a soft, even beat, echoed, repeated over and over without change— maddening.

Cloud shivered at the sound and shifted her weight restlessly from one foot to another, wanting to be off. I did myself, but I curbed myself, and considered.

I realized the five soldiers of the Red were not reacting to the noise. Yet they must hear it, as I did. It was not all that loud, perhaps, but it was very distinct. Then I knew: the noise was not strange to the soldiers because it was theirs. Not the rocks gave it that inhuman evenness: that rhythm was real. It was the marching feet of the Army of the Red. Those were people—no, they were not *people*; they were an army, a thing apart, with a life of its own. A monstrosity.

Cloud sensed my recoiling horror and leaped, faster than

the soldiers could react—their indecision about me slowed them anyway. I leaped, too, my fingers scrabbling in the windsteed's long mane; clawing my way to her back even as I tried to tell myself there could not be the Red coming in all its thousands at once. It was likely only another small detachment, which I could face down.

So I thought, and told myself, but I made no move to check Cloud's leap over the soldiers or her headlong run from the canyon over the blood-red rock. Whether we moved by her decision or mine hardly mattered—the same instincts moved us both. We did not stop even when night fell.

Sometime in the night we reached the plain, and Cloud quickened her pace yet more, though all sound of her footsteps was now stilled in the deep dust of the dry plain. She might truly be flying. Oppressive as was the hot air over the plain, I welcomed the great empty expanse of it. Now Empire also loomed over the plain, the drought seemed to me to be a lighter matter than I had thought it hitherto.

We ran finally neither away from any particular thing nor toward anything else, but just to be running and riding, Cloud and I one with each other and the wind that blew.

In the night, on open plain, I heard a hungry rivercat howl. I sat up suddenly on Cloud's back, marking how near it sounded. Startled by my movement, Cloud broke her pace and came raggedly to a halt. She was willing to go after the rivercat. As soon as I realized that, I turned her head and urged her on.

Soon I saw it: a great, flowing shadow in the night. It growled, a low rumble more vibration than sound that ran all through me and left a chill in my flesh. I had brought down a rivercat once before, but not easily and not alone.

Cloud went on gamely and the cat turned. Still I let Cloud continue. A windsteed might be a rivercat's prey in the confines of a canyon, but on the open plain the windsteeds' unmatched speed gave them some safety; and Cloud's hooves, with her weight behind them, could well damage larger foes than the soldier of the Red she had killed.

The cat stood its ground roaring a challenge. Though I had to think it might leap, I made no move to turn Cloud. And the cat turned first, running low, twisting evasively. Playing, Cloud paced it closely. I made no move, curious to learn what she would do. I had never heard of a windsteed hunting thus like a windrider.

Then I sensed the void of a canyon yaw ahead; in the dark I could not see how near. I was not willing for the cat to escape, nor for Cloud to run yet greater danger. I leaned far out from Cloud's neck and dropped onto the cat, hardly even falling before I met its bulk and my fingers sank into the hot, rich fur and sought purchase. My nostrils filled with the rank, wild odor of the beast.

The cat doubled back at the feel of my weight, forgetting Cloud in lust for me. Nearly as swiftly as a windsteed could move, it rolled to reach me with its fangs, which glistened evilly in the night. Its green gaze caught mine. In another instant, I knew, it would bring its claws upon me also. I cursed, seeing too late what I had come into: here was no fight such as I had wanted, fair trial and release. Here was no proportion. The rivercat would kill me without thinking. I must kill it or die, and kill it at once or not at all.

I shoved my knife at the green glow of those bestial, hate-filled eyes. The blade ran in cleanly and deep, missing bone. The cat fell heavily with me, knocking the breath from me

Cloud danced around the cat's carcass snuffling, her whistling breath as wild and lustful as any hunter's. I scrambled to my feet and stood feeling dazed, though I was not hurt and should not be tired; all had been over in an instant. The impulse that had set me after the cat died with the beast. But Cloud would not be still; not even when, unnerved by her strange, high excitement, I scolded her.

I gave up any notion of skinning the cat. I doubted I could manage the job by myself, and I could hardly school myself to close work with Cloud as she was. But before leaving I knelt down and hacked with my knife the claws from one forefoot, curved talons longer than my widest handspan. Some token I must have, lest I should come to doubt what had passed was real.

Then I mounted Cloud, and we went on. Running, Cloud settled down.

CHAPTER

16

I came to the River-that-ever-changes from the easy side, where the plain ran down by gentle stages to the wide, cobbled bed that was so much wider than the water's reach even in the wettest year. This year the river was lower than I had ever seen it, and young riverwillow grew between the dry-caked stones of the cobbling, a sign that the river had long not flooded. Herdbeasts were grazing on the green sprouts of riverwillow; some of the herdbeasts looked like those that had been mine. I looked across the river, up to the rock-toothed ridge there, and found the smoke of cookfires rising in several thin columns very straight into the still air. I set Cloud at the river, to go to discover why windriders lingered here at their ease with cookfires, and herdbeasts looking lazy, when they were likely overdue clear across the plain at Ocean's edge for the midsummer Ranking.

Cloud ran into the water, casting up long veils of spray on either side of her. She did not have to swim: nowhere, any longer, did the water rise as high as her belly. She took the far bank in the first of a series of bounds that carried her clear to the ridge and one of the cookfires, where sat Lirra, Tisla, Samma, Haida—all of the herders sworn to me, and some other windriders as well. The windriders' gaze fixed on my arm, on the blood-stained strip of leather bound there, and their greetings died away unspoken.

"Hail," I said.

"So you, too, found a fight," Lirra said. "I might have known."

I grunted, irritated to get only such words by way of greeting. Abruptly I felt weary, and my arm ached. I guessed it was no use to run farther. I slid down from Cloud's back and touched her on the shoulder absently to release her. She glided away, in among the strange rocks of that ridge, as large as windsteeds, where loomed also the shapes of the others' windsteeds.

"You shed blood, Oa? On the plain?" asked another voice, harsher than Lirra's, wilder. Naglia it was, chief of a small House. She ranked below me, just barely. She was a chief, and none to be scorned. But I was not used to her talking to me thus.

"Not on the plain, no," I said. "In the Broken Lands. And only my own blood." I remembered the soldier of the Red who had lain unmoving even when I rode away. I added, "My windsteed killed, I think."

Someone gasped. I cut off talk with a sharp gesture. "Too?" I questioned what Lirra had said. "What else?"

I looked at Lirra, and *she* looked at Naglia and said uncertainly, "Windsteeds and riders wounded . . . killed, by . . . by *housefolk* who appear on the plain out of nowhere—" She could not fathom the words she spoke. But I knew: skirmishers and scouts of the Army of the Red must be moving down through the Broken Lands onto the plain. Windriders had met them. "Naglia—" Lirra prodded.

Naglia started as if she had been struck. Her voice was high-pitched when she spoke, wilder than before, sending a shiver down my spine. "All my herd—my House! —gone." Her eyes, darting around as if she thought yet to *see* some explanation, crossed my gaze. She recoiled. "But I never killed . . ." she said in a new, pleading voice—she who had been a chief! Her eyes went blank. She did not see anything, I realized.

But I did. I had been right, both in thinking this plain was not of the same quality of reality as Empire, and in dreading the intrusion of Empire into it. There *were* two realities. They could never be reconciled, but they were meeting. The battle so long waged within me, heightened recently by my need to beat Kirbana, was about to become general to all. Naglia was but the first to be borne over by it. I sank down to the ground. Tisla handed me a drinking skin, and I drank deeply of the foul kwass that was all we had had to drink for so very long.

Windsteeds clattered over rock—many of them. Windriders swung down and strode toward us. Surya I recognized by her tawny hair, bright even in the flat light of the drought-hazed sun. Behind her came Kiia and Bretta and others of Ajanna's herders. There came Ajanna also. He crouched down and reached for one of the passing skins. A shadow fluttered behind him, unable to settle: that would be Wiela. I turned my gaze from her; I would not deal with her.

"Hail, windriders," Ajanna said in his deep, wild voice.

Others answered him back. We *were* windriders; the touch of Ajanna's voice reminded us of that. The drinking skins passed more quickly. I drank from each and handed it on to Lirra beside me. The drink burned in my gut and coursed through my blood, turning it to fire. I sat up and looked around at the glittering eyes that stared back at me from flushed faces. Voices sharpened as the blood ran hotter in us all.

The day ran into dusk, then darkness; all the while we sat drinking, abandoning ourselves to the frenzied wind of drunkenness. Windsteeds cried out from the night, and their hooves pattered on the rocks just out of reach of the firelight. Someone—Surya, I think, too red in the fireglow— jumped up over the fire and taunted the rest of us: "Dance! Dance, then!"

Others rose, pulling with them laggards who had stayed for one last pull from a drinking skin. I stood and took a deep draft of the night air, tasting frenzy like a flavor on my tongue. I took up the chant that someone started.

Stamp, kick, clap, bow. No subtly patterned Gandish Dance was this, but the expression of blood and heat.

Leap, twist, bow. Faster. Faster! Locked arms held me up when my feet were swept off the ground by the whirling circle of the dance. I gasped for breath while I chanted.

Someone fell, breaking the circle, and all of us tripped into a piling mound of bodies. A shout went up for the drinking skins. I crawled away from the fire to retrieve one from where I had seen it tossed at the outset of the dance. I took an immense long swallow of the thick, almost furry liquid. It soothed my parched throat. I took another swallow.

Pass it on! Stand up. Dance. Laugh. Drink. Dance! Build up the fire. Multi-colored flames licked into the sky. Our voices soared above them, crying out to lords of Sky. My limbs flexed and twirled as if of their own accord, with seemingly tremendous power, and I thought I could run through the very sky without a windsteed. I knew it was mostly the drink, but I pulled free of the dancers to stretch out my arms to the night sky. I floated free of the revels; then I fell through silence to the hard ground.

Someone dropped down beside me. I heard the gurgle and swallow of drinking and sensed a heated, quivering body. I propped myself on one elbow and swung my other arm through the dark until my hand felt soft, bulging leather. I pulled the drinking skin to me and felt for its mouth with mine. Kwass flowed thickly down my throat.

A hand ran roughly across the taut skin of my neck, stretched back to drink. I stoppered the kwass skin with care and laid it aside. A head bent close to mine, and a husky voice whispered nothing I could make out. I was not even sure whose voice it was—none of my herders'. Hands caught mine and pulled so I came to my feet and into the embrace of a lithe body, the heat of which I felt even through our thick riding leathers; or perhaps it was the heat of my own body fast rising. A mouth met mine. I seemed again to float free of the earth, upon an upswelling of desire. I leaned back, savoring it. It was not so high a feeling as the other, but high enough.

The mouth broke away; a voice demanded; and suddenly I felt affronted. "What is that?" I demanded. For answer came only a low chuckle and a scrabbling at my laces. "Kiia? No. Bretta." I stiffened, remembering that night long ago when I first saw the Ranking rites and the scrabbling lust of windriders in the aftermath. In my mind, very clearly, I saw Bretta's face and the drunken insolence of him bringing down a housewoman at his fellows' feet in Ajanna's chief's tent. That housewoman could have been me—then.

Bretta—if Bretta it was—tore at my leathers. My ardor cooled further. He seemed to think he could have me at *his* will, even now; he thought he could have what he wanted, windrider that he was.

But I lay only with whom *I* chose. I twisted his grasping hands away, so he cried out in surprise and pain. I scrabbled away from him on all fours. Then I got my feet under me. But I did not run: I danced, a dance of my own, a cruel dance, to taunt him.

His footsteps sounded here or there in the darkness where he twisted and turned, seeking me. "Oa!" he shouted. "When I get you—"

I danced close and hissed, "When you get me? Then what?" He stopped short, stammering, sounding frightened. I laughed and danced on. The sound of him faded, and I forgot him. I spread my arms wide and spun around again and again.

The star-blazing sky swung past me at an odd angle. I greeted it companionably and danced on along the crest of the world on the great sharp, clean rocks so high above the plain my head reached among the very stars. This was more like, I thought. I called out to lords of Sky to dance with me. I searched all through that sky that blazed with such a cold light: abode of incorporeal lords of Sky. Them I did not see, however; only the vast, slow wheeling movement of the heavens over the face of the earth. Through the entire universe I looked, and found everywhere the reflection of myself.

That was the answer to Halassa, who once said to me, reprovingly, a windrider need not be hard or cruel. Halassa! He faded to a wraith at the uncaring touch of lords of Sky manifested in the mad wind. Ajanna had the right of it, always: seeing nothing beyond his own life, he had claimed it for his own and fashioned reality around him in his image.

So I did also, but for the one ancient compromise with

the power of Empire, whereby I gave it exercise—and the unexpected effects of that seemed like to endure as long as I did. I held myself stiffly erect against the sky and swore I would yet pluck all taint of Empire from me. Soon now, I swore. Then even lords of Sky would yield me homage.

I looked down on the world disdainfully, and I saw someone there, with a presence as large as that of the night—large enough that I could notice. Interested, I went forward. It was Ajanna, of course. Stars and rock seemed to whirl crazily together when we met, all time in flux. I knew I was very drunk. And yet, all I drunkenly perceived seemed to me also to be real. Anything might happen, I thought. I wanted Ajanna: that would be true in any case. I reached for him through an increasing roar and turmoil.

"Oa?"

A high, clear voice called me elsewhere. I turned my head, listening, not yet turning my steps.

"Oa?"

That voice was the pivot on which all my life had already turned, and turned again, and seemed like to turn once more. Through any chaos I would have heard it clearly. It was Jily calling me.

A different time gripped me and held me fast. I did not now confuse Coory with Jily, for I was caught very surely in a time before I knew Corry—though I knew also the time was past. I *saw* Jily: her pale, perfect skin glimmered like the shining, white petals of a flower unfolding in the pure light of dawn. She touched me very lightly with her sleek, silken hands; her touch was as slight as a dream. My limbs loosened at her touch, yielding. My breath stopped, and my sight grew dim. She smiled obliquely past me toward some other. I supposed it was true she betrayed me, but I did not feel it, for just then I became aware of the Dynast sitting somewhere behind me. Was it *him* Jily had looked to? I turned and looked to him myself, questioningly.

"Do you understand?" the Dynast asked me.

I stiffened: that had not been the question. Of course I understood! He had offered me Empire but required a high price. He had set me too hard a choice, and I had fled. It was all done, long since—no, not done, I corrected myself;

but past, put out of reach. And yet here it was, and again the Dynast asked, "Do you understand?"

And finally I *did* understand.

His pale, probing gaze had never looked at *me*—only at Empire, to see how to shape it and hold it. Nothing had been as I thought. Jily's betrayal had been irrelevant, perhaps even fabricated; the Dynast had made what he wanted of us all. Truly he meant me to Dance. He wanted to see if I could do what no one had ever done before: control the Dance while yet Dancing—but only for the sake of his Empire. Only because I would thus be bound inescapably to serve Empire, by my very power and participation in it.

Jily had merely been cast to her fate. But by the chance that I so loved her, something very different had come from what the Dynast intended. I had forsworn and fled Empire—I, who could in fact control the Dance, and had done so now many times.

Truly I did love Jily! Her body felt very sweet to my hands even in this flux time where she was likely not real. My hands on her lay over those points that were the same in every one of us, the points that at the slightest pressure betrayed the life of the body; within my hands was Jily's destruction—the old choice.

She lay very still. Perhaps she was *not* real. Yet I had the choice—

"Oa, if it's what you will do, then do it."

At the sound of Ajanna's voice, my breath, which I had been holding, came out with a rush. "What—?" I asked, bewildered. Where was I? "Ajanna—"

Years passed. I was truly no longer a young near-heir in Empire, but a seasoned windrider. The contest remained, however; eternally; in me, except not Jily but Ajanna lay under my hands. "Ajanna!" I cried. "Long ago you said you would neither fight nor lie with the likes of me. You had better have kept your word!"

"How could I stand aside from you?" he asked softly. "I who never stood aside from anything?"

My breath sobbed with the effort of keeping my hands still. I thought I would never dare move for fear of killing him. I had controlled the High Dance. I had spared Wunna and Surya and all the others after them. But I had never come this close to dealing death, nor so wholly of myself. Here was more test than the Dynast ever knew, I thought.

For *I* wanted Ajanna alive. By a convulsion of will, I threw myself to one side without putting the least weight or pressure or even thought on those points where my body had been suspended over Ajanna. I pulled my death-dealing hands away at last and held them stiffly at my sides.

Ajanna took them very gently in his enormous hands and drew them to his mouth and kissed them. We were not yet done with each other, Ajanna and I.

At times during the night I thought we never would be. Our contest became more ordinary, however, though never without larger aspects. For in his great bulk and strength, enormous and unyielding as nothing but the earth, Ajanna seemed more than any ordinary male. Nonetheless, where any aspect of him was real, it was nothing that my own body was not competent to meet.

Dawn glowed in a colorless sky. I lay stiff and chilled on bare rock, my arms held at an uncomfortable angle. Ajanna lay beside me on his soft catskin cloak, curled to face me.

His eyes opened, met mine, and grew wary. "You're no windrider," he said softly. "You've made yourself what you should not be."

"I?" I snorted. Stiff and tired I was, but also strangely light and free—a match even for Ajanna. I said evenly, "I am a windrider. You've seen me tested on the Ranking ground yourself, again and again. And by the windsteeds. Do you doubt that the will of lords of Sky is expressed in the Ranking or any of the other tests? Do you think anything else matters?"

"I doubt you even acknowledge lords of Sky . . .," he began, speaking slowly.

I began to grow angry—but even more puzzled: I had always thought of Ajanna, but never wanted to say, what he now said of me, or something like. I rolled away from him and stood up, stepping gingerly on my bare feet to escape the prickles in the hollows of the rock, though in a way I welcomed that petty discomfort. I suddenly wanted everything to be quite ordinary—and it was not. "It was but a night's play," I muttered. "Like any other. You make too much of it." I pulled on my leggings and began to lace them.

Ajanna snorted.

"It was the kwass," I insisted. "It's bad. From the drought." Indeed, my head ached unspeakably. How could I have thought I felt well? I wondered. And I wondered what had happened in the night. Beyond the obvious, that was. Confusion and upheaval I remembered—were they real? I knotted the lacings of my leggings, muttered an explanation—many explanations—all at hazard. I sensed Ajanna was not attending. I broke off speaking and looked around.

Wiela stood there. She ignored me and stared down at Ajanna's naked, misshapen body lying upon his catskin cloak. A triumphant smile bloated her face. She leaned forward and hissed, "Look at her! Ah, Ajanna! Oa has bested you, but it was I who made her do it. Didn't I say I'd see you brought low? Well, I see it now!"

Ajanna lay unmoving under her taunts, his great, scarred body seeming powerless. Wiela kept after him. "You can't deny it, Ajanna. Through Oa I have shown you what even the rivercats and the mad wind could not: there is a limit to you, proud, hard Ajanna!"

I doubted he really heard her words, but his windrider's arrogance kindled at her tone. He got to his feet slowly, his eyes fixed on Wiela with something of the fascination with which I had seen him face the mad wind. He raised one hand menacingly.

"Yes," Wiela said eagerly. "Kill me, Ajanna. Then I'll bind you even more surely than Oa has yet done. I'll bind you to the earth by my blood, and you'll never be free again. Kill me. *Kill me!*"

Her sudden shriek seemed visible in the air as tendrils of yellow sky that wrapped about me, jarring my already pained head. I turned on her, crying, "You're mad! Your raving is suited only to housefolk and not fit to speak before windriders. Take yourself away until you can behave like a windrider if you will call yourself one."

Wiela gave no sign of hearing me. Ajanna took a step

closer to her. Wiela watched him come, gloating. "I've got you now. In Oa I finally found the weapon to take you!"

"No!" I shouted, stepping between them, goaded beyond reason by Wiela's claim she had formed me and could use me. I thrust my face into hers, and she saw me at last, and fixed those enormous, fathomless eyes fully on me. This time I did not quail. I stared her down. She stepped back, quieting.

"Go," I said to her, implacable. She blinked, and frowned a little, as if confused, and walked away into the still early morning that lay so quietly on the land.

"She's right," Ajanna said, behind me. I whirled on him. He stood very still, and I relaxed. "How can I run like a windsteed," he asked, "with senses empty and open to the sky, when you, Oa, ride in my way?"

I sighed and shook my head. I put on my shirt and laced it up. Had something happened? Was I suddenly something more, or confirmed in something I had more gradually become? I supposed I would find out soon enough: I had the feeling of many things closing in, faster than I could possibly follow. Ajanna was not the least of these, nor the least troublesome, for all he seemed so strangely wary—almost deferential.

"I have no wish to interfere with you," I said tartly, casting about the rocks for the little plant we called the lovers' flower. With my knife I pried handfuls of its bulbs from the hard ground and ate them despite the bitter flavor of their poison. One thing was sure, and I would not rely solely on my Dancer's controls to avoid it. I shuddered to think what monstrous child could have come of that night just passed.

But nothing could have been worse than what did come, and nothing I did but made it worse.

CHAPTER

17

At first, to be sure, there seemed to be nothing: only a still summer morning in which everyone felt at loose ends. No one made any suggestion of riding on. I went along the ridge aimlessly and was surprised to find how many windriders were camped here or there in the clearings and small terraces among the great rocks that ridged the crest: half of all the windriders seemed gathered here.

Around noon a cloud rose on the horizon, as of night or storm, but it was not the hour for the one nor the season for the other. Empire, I thought: the Army of the Red was on the move. But I felt no urgency, and it turned out to be Murrila and several other high chiefs with herds still large who came to the river out of that cloud, late in the afternoon. Soon after, a young windrider from Murrila's House rode along the ridge calling chiefs to council.

I went, to find most of the others before me, those in the valley, that was: the best and the largest of windriders, well-built males and fewer females. Their faces had a parched look like the plain, a blankness. From the dust their riding leathers and even their hair, braided one way or another, had much the same color as the rock they sat on. I supposed I must look much like them, what with the dust as I anticipated the news Murrila must be bringing. For he had come in from the east, from the direction of the Broken Lands.

Osia, one of the high chiefs who had ridden in with Murrila, spoke first. He had only met up with Murrila the day before, it seemed. Before that he had been running along the very border of the Broken Lands, and there he had met Empire. "*Housefolk* walked out of the Broken Lands, in among the herds as if by right. They cut out herdbeasts without leave and slaughtered them. When I forbade it, they drove me off with barb-tipped spears. . . . We stampeded the herd. . . . Over distance these strange housefolk move as fast as a tired herd. They came among us again—we ran, and finally we outran them. . . ." Osia's voice trailed away.

Others took up the tale—the same tale. There was nothing as bad as what had befallen Naglia; some herdbeasts lost, a very few windsteeds and windriders wounded. It was enough to confirm the Red had come out onto the plain, had there been any doubt.

And it was a tale I had heard many times before—from the other side: the advance of Empire over yet another people. I thought of the pikes those five soldiers of the Red had set against Cloud with such determination. I knew what it was to go on foot into a herd. I knew the soldiers of the Red could never have seen the like of herdbeasts. But they faced them. These were but small instances of the discipline of the Red, but they were telling ones. Windriders were bound only by their own will and the single fear that a windsteed might not take them up to ride. This one bond was very strong: it had to be, for the survival of an entire people dependent on the single resource of the herdbeasts was precarious. Empire counted no costs at all; windriders counted the one, and it had to give them a terrible vulnerability.

In the fading daylight I stared away over the deslolation of dry, cobbled rock in the wide riverbed far below me. The sun was setting into distant meanders of the River-that-ever-changes. The water seemed to be running away into the red fire of the sun; so our very lives would shortly also do, I had to think. The chiefs' voices went on in soft murmurs that blended with the rustle of the distant river. I hardly noticed when they were done speaking

"We must take counsel what to do," Murrila said then briskly.

I started and turned to look at him. His great shaggy head, with his many thick braids hanging down over his chest blended imperceptibly into the dusky twilight. Only his eyes were bright, from some last reflection of sunlight off the river. I saw care and concern in his clear eyes—and determination, and an idea. Hope flared up in me only to flicker away again at once. How could Murrila hold off Empire? He could not even hold me at that last council on the question of culling the herds.

Toda spoke up confidently, "The plain is endless. We will ride."

Toda could always be relied on to say something sententious—to make the very truth seem trivial. It was he above all others who had driven me to intransigence in that other council.

The others seemed to think much as I did. Osja answered for many: "One end has been set to our range. We can't run far enough to get away from knowing that."

"Are we to stand, then?" asked one of the lesser chiefs. "To fight? To kill?"

"To shed blood on the plain—?"

Again a silence fell. A wild cry broke it: "What blood? What blood? Of housefolk who strike at windsteeds!" It was Naglia, who had been sitting rather apart from the group, but now drew all attention to her. She twisted her head back and forth as she spoke, so her braids snapped about like serpents. She looked as dangerous as any serpent.

Several chiefs agreed with her slowly. "These housefolk aren't human. They are vermin . . . for the killing. . . ."

None denied it; nor could any easily accept it. The chiefs remained undecided, some leaning one way, others another. Looking around again at Murrila, I thought he looked to be remarkably satisfied with the way the council was unfolding, and again I began to hope he knew what he was doing and knew something to do.

Hope was quickly dashed—as Ajanna shouldered his

way to the center of the gathering. He came to the council only now, late. I had felt him coming. I had stayed out of his way all day, obscurely dreading to find what might be between us, come of the last night's meeting, and lingering. Now he stood quite near me, within reach of my arm if I stretched it out. He was intent on Murrila. He did not seem to see me at all, or even to be aware of me. I felt relieved—I thought after all there was nothing out of the ordinary.

And I thought also of what I had heard only that afternoon, what one of Ajanna's herders, Kiia, had told me.

Like so many, Ajanna's House had also had a brush with the Imperial forces. They had surprised a party of soldiers of the Red camped far upstream along the River-that-ever-changes. The soldiers had taken up their pikes at the sight of Ajanna's herds and herders, and formed up to oppose their passage. Of all the herders, Kiia himself had been nearest the soldiers, and had turned aside, believing they would harm his windsteed. Ajanna had ridden straight on, as if he did not even see the soldiers, keeping Scudder on her course. At the last minute, when Scudder seemed sure to drive onto the pikes, the soldiers had scrambled aside. Ajanna rode through their camp, and all his House followed after.

Before Ajanna, it seemed, even Empire gave way. It seemed to me there should lie some chance for us in this occurrence—but I could not see how to use it. I could be sure, too, that Ajanna would scorn to. But Murrila? Murrila with those measuring, stern eyes of the Dynast himself would surely use what came to hand for defense. I looked to Murrila, sitting quietly before Ajanna's advance. I was watching Murrila when Ajanna continued, "It's the Ranking that we should be concerning ourselves with. It's midsummer."

"No!" I cried instinctively, responding mostly to the sight of Murrila's face tightening, his eyes finally darkening— but night was thickening. He said nothing.

"Look at the stars!" Ajanna said, unmoved. Murrila only looked at Ajanna. Doubtless Murrila already knew very well what day it was. And only the first few stars were yet out, none of those that tell the seasons. Set and determined though Murrila's face remained, it yet seemed to lose what had inspired hope in me.

The other chiefs were greatly relieved by Ajanna's interruption. The Ranking was a challenge they understood and welcomed. They turned at once to considering the arrangements for the rites, and did not even see the contest that was unfolding in their midst between Ajanna and Murrila.

Only dimly did I see what Murrila might have done to alter tradition and set a new course in which windriders might survive what was coming. From his great care, which reached beyond his own self to all the life lived on this land, windrider though he was, he had forged notions of forethought and strategy. But he *was* a windrider. Ajanna's challenge was, of course, against Murrila personally, and Murrila let it distract him. If he could beat Ajanna he might take up his larger purpose once more, but for now, I saw, he put it aside. That I saw—and tried to think I did not.

"Here," Murrila said, gesturing around him. Between the rocks there was a level place large enough for a Ranking ground. "Tonight."

Ajanna nodded. I tried to think he had gotten all he wanted.

And that was the end of the council. The other chiefs stood, seemingly content. Barely half our number were present, but those who were absent could hardly object to the decision, and those who were there saw no cause to. And despite my deepening sense of doom, I found I shared the general feeling. I strode back along the ridge with a lighter step than when I had come.

An unfamiliar noise rose out of the valley, which was swathed in darkness deeper than yet held the ridge. I stopped short. The high, squealing cry of a windsteed sounded again and again, as if the windsteeds were fighting among themselves, something I had never known them to do. I heard the shouts of windriders going among them, and presently the windsteeds quieted. I went on, but I could no longer pretend anything was as it should be.

* * *

I stripped off my worn riding leathers. Around me, the windriders who were sworn to me as herders did likewise. We had no tents in this makeshift camp, or housefolk. We piled our leathers to one side of the cooking fire. We oiled our bodies in watery, evil-smelling grease rendered from the carcasses of the sickly herdbeasts we had been eating these last days. The pike wound on my arm, which was still fresh, stung maddeningly. I could hardly stand still for Lirra and Tisla to braid my hair.

"Sh-h-h-h," Lirra hissed softly, intent on arranging my braids, as if that task were the only thing there was to concern her. I eyed her sidelong, saw the lean sureness of her body, the set expression on her face. I would have done better to have patterned myself on her from the outset, not on Ajanna. She was very right to concern herself always only with what was real and before her. *She* was immune to Ajanna. But she was not, I thought belatedly, wholly immune to me.

Tisla was slower at his work. When Lirra was done with one side of my head, she pushed him aside to do his work over better and finish it. I caught his eyes and smiled at him, a little wryly, and motioned him around where I could reach to arrange his braids. He moved under my hands willingly enough. I touched his sleek, oiled body with pleasure, as I had so many times. He seemed to have no sense of me this time; that was as it should be, with the Ranking upon us. I checked my wayward thoughts. I, too, was a windrider, though lately I seemed to be straying from it.

"There, that's done," Lirra said. She bent to dip her fingers in the soot of the campfire to paint my signs of rank on my face. I finished with Tisla's braids and did the same for him and then her. Unused as we were to these tasks, in the end they were done. We went to join the others on the ground where we had held council; even with all there were, we made no great crowd.

From the beginning nothing went right. The sacrificial animal bleated piteously when Murrila cut its throat. The skimpy fire of what little brush we could find, and herdbeast dung, was not hot enough to burn the offering cleanly, and an unpleasant odor of singed hair and flesh settled over the makeshift Ranking ground. There was none of the flamboyance or excitement of other Rankings. Dust raised by the opening rounds stuck to my oiled skin and itched. Lirra had coiled my braids too tightly, and my scalp hurt.

For all we were so few, the rites seemed interminable, slowed and broken by the many unanswered calls to absent windriders. No few of those who were there had taken their ranks in the last Ranking by lot. As they now ran no risk of losing to rankless folk, there was much shuffling about, what with the newly ranked looking higher and older windriders resenting those so recently housefolk ranking by chance above them. No one challenged the child Groa, however, I noticed.

My turn came to walk out onto the empty ground. The crowd was silent, as it mostly had been all evening. The emptiness of the ground seemed to extend without end, so that I spoke my claim into a void and hardly expected any answer. But someone came at me from the darkness.

By instinct I crouched and circled, seeking my opponent's eyes to take their measure. There was not enough light to see.

The other took advantage of my heistation and leaped at me. I fell hard, but did not feel it. I got to my feet. That long-limbed, lean body could be almost anyone. I feinted and circled to get what light there was behind me. I found then it was Naglia I fought. She met my gaze squarely. For all the light on her face, however, I could see nothing in her eyes. Unnerved, I could not settle what to do.

Naglia stepped in closer to me. She counted no cost and took no care, for she thought she had nothing more to lose. I should have been able to beat her easily even without the Dance, but the awful emptiness of her eyes dragged me down, and when I finally looked for the Dance, I could not find it.

Naglia raised her arms swiftly, caught mine and twisted, and then I lay where I never had before: on my back on the unyielding earth of the Ranking ground, with the weight of a victor pinning me.

So this was defeat, I thought wonderingly. It did not seem particularly bitter after all—only numbing.

Murrila confirmed Naglia's rank and mine. I got to my

feet. I was still a chief, by virtue of Naglia's former rank, but of nothing, for her House was lost.

The rites went from bad to worse. Wrangling over precedence delayed the succession of matches. The fire went out. We scurried around in the dark to fetch more fuel, but after that the fire merely smoldered with smoke and a stink and not much light. The ritual was confused and too long. Sourly I said to Lirra that lords of Sky must have more patience than windriders were usually thought to have if they stayed to watch this Ranking.

Finally Murrila called the ranks of the high chiefs, and I thought we might at last breathe easily. Surely the high chiefs need not fight! Murrila listed the ranks hastily, scarcely giving any the time to step out to claim them. Murrila confirmed Ajanna's rank without hearing from him at all, and went on to his own rank, and then he paused.

A murmur rose in the mass of windriders and moved toward the Ranking ground. Voices spoke sharply but I could not make out the words. I felt the unmistakable mass of Ajanna's enormous body pass close by me. He was heading for the cleared ground where Murrila still stood. My numbness lifted.

"Ajanna! No!" I cried, grabbing his arm, hardly knowing why: on my own account nothing could matter. I suppose I did feel in that moment something of a true chief's care, what mostly drove Murrila, and the Dynast in Empire. Murrila must not be lost! I thought. No one else—certainly not Ajanna!—had the least chance of making the windriders over into something that could survive Empire. "No!" I cried again desperately; my hands clung to Ajanna as if I believed I had the strength to hold him back.

He hissed, "Tonight I can take him. I can't stand back from that challenge. In this, at least, you shall not stand in my way, Oa."

My fingers went slack with the thought that it was just *because* of what had happened between us that Ajanna moved *now* to take the rank that would surely come to him in the end—if any survived Empire. He easily escaped my suddenly nerveless hold and went on beyond my reach.

This time Ajanna and Murrila fought in silence. They were far beyond taunts or jeers. They fought almost companionably, without calculation or ambition—as the expression of the capabilities of their being, much as windsteeds ran because that was what they were formed to do. The fire soon went out altogether, and they fought in darkness, unseeing and unseen.

And in darkness we others stood motionlessly by. We did not need to see or even to hear to know what was happening. We also were windriders, if not ones of such high perfection as those two.

Murrila was aged. His frame, still massive, had become hollow from within. He fell and did not rise; dead. The last faint scuffle died away. It was over.

There was no triumph in Ajanna. He stood like a mass of rock over Murrila, who lay on the earth motionless and indistinguishable from it as he would be now forever.

We realized Ajanna scarcely knew what he had done, only that it *was* done. He did not think to speak the ritual words that would establish his rank as chief of all chiefs. We waited for him to remember thus to put an end to the rites, but he never did.

One by one we drifted away. That night there was no celebration, and what time I slept, I slept alone.

I sensed Ajanna's approach before anyone else did, even without seeing him. I hunched my shoulders against the assault that was the otherness of him. I looked around at the others, astonished that they did not notice it.

The others, a score of windriders gathered on the slope below the ridge in the light of another still, dusty morning just like so many, were intent on Gabbra, who had just ridden in to tell us that Empire was on the move. That I already knew. I was more interested in Gabbra himself.

He was the sole survivor of his House, himself but lightly wounded, his windsteed unscathed. He rode still—he had just ridden in among us—but he was rankless, his rank gone by lot the night before. Rankless but still riding. . . . I chewed my lip, considering him. I myself was a chief, but of nothing. I had no herders, no herdbeasts, no House. Like Gabbra, I had no ties.

I had only a windsteed.

I looked away from the windriders down the slope toward the River-that-ever-changes. Cloud ran on the level ground near the water's edge with some other windsteeds. Silvery gray, she stood out like a ghost or a vision from the duns and browns of most of the other windsteeds, graceful and achingly lovely. She would allow no other to ride her, she never had. While I lived, I could ride; and I could not count the cost of it, nor the loss of anything else, while I rode.

Indeed, it seemed not to matter at all that I had lost my rank. Did rank then have nothing to do with riding? After all that had passed was *that* what I was to learn? It did not make sense. And truly, I could not think clearly with Ajanna so near, looming . . . as large as Empire.

The others finally noticed Ajanna. Osia rose from where he had been hunkering on the ground beside Gabbra. He faced Ajanna. He stood as tall, but without Ajanna's presence. Half a dozen others stood at Osia's back, Toda and Kirbana among them. In the ill-starred Ranking this past night Kirbana had finally taken the chief's rank he coveted—but not from me.

"What are you going to do, Ajanna?" Osia challenged. "Are you going to leave everything at loose ends? Or will you now confirm the rank you killed Murrila for? Will you be chief of us all or not?"

Ajanna looked back at Osia with an air of indifference to what Osia spoke of. We others held our breath. Would that long contest between Ajanna and Murrila now begin anew, with Osia? Then, abruptly, Ajanna threw back his head, tossing his heavy braids wide, and laughed, a great bellowing shout.

Osia stiffened in rage. Toda sputtered. Others came to their feet, to be ready—but for what, they did not know. And Ajanna only laughed the harder to see them. The noise he made rolled over me, immense and overwhelming. His presence was a flood

I was standing behind Gabbra, a little higher on the slope than anyone else, so I looked to Ajanna over the others' heads. I stood on a level with him, but just barely, and not for long, I thought. I summoned my will hastily, thinking that to survive even another moment I must exert myself tremendously. Over the terrible noise of Ajanna's laughter I shouted, "I will ride!"

He quieted. His and other faces turned to me. Even Gabbra turned, Gabbra who as yet had looked no one in the eye, but likely he turned only by an animal instinct, responding to sound.

I hardly knew what I had said. Wildly I went on, "Ride! Against the Red! I do not give them leave to pass!"

"What new start is this?" Toda cried. "Will you go haring off with no regard for herds or herders? To fight? On the plain?"

"Yes!" I cried. "Yes! I will!" And I, too, laughed, a short, bitter laugh. "Why not? There are no herds or herders now that are mine."

"Fly in the face of lords of Sky?" Toda protested.

Lirra appeared at my side, lean and sure. Softly, she said, "The Red comes off the High plain, which is the place of lords of Sky. The Red is *their* sending—their challenge. We must meet it—ride it—if we will call ourselves windriders."

Looking from face to face I saw her words gave everyone pause. Gabbra's eyes glowed. I looked long into them, past the terrible killing of windsteeds and windriders he had witnessed to a new-forged core. He would ride with me, I saw.

Lirra broke the silence by swearing me an oath, a new oath, such as no windrider had ever before given. Hearing it, I grinned and nodded. I opened my mouth to answer and then, on impulse, delayed.

Others were clamoring in Lirra's wake—not all by any means of those who were there, but enough to lift me up like a wild wind and carry me quickly along the new course I had chosen. Then Groa came riding at me, mounted on the enormous black windsteed Murrila had given her, a small, dark flame in her intensity.

What had Murrila meant to make of her? I wondered. Had he thought, like Wiela, to use her against Ajanna and not had the time? She stared down at me from windsteedback, her black eyes fierce in her uncannily unchildish face.

"No," I said, turning my back on her as I had done once before. "And I will not take all the rest of you either," I said to the others. "Only Lirra and Gabbra." And I added, "And I will not swear even to you, though you swear me an oath. I will not again be bound."

The clamor broke out anew. I shook it off impatiently. A line of windsteeds was running up the slope in the wake of Groa's black, Cloud among them. I stepped free of the crowd where she could see me.

Still people tugged on my arm and begged and demanded. "No," I insisted. "Do what you will. Don't ask me to lead."

Tisla was there, right in front of me, between me and my windsteed, not speaking, only staring at me with those wide, eager eyes, yellow-pale, so like my own in all but color that I could not refuse him. "Yes, you," I muttered, angry with myself for doing it. Him above all I should leave to make his own way; I overwhelmed him like no one else—and his susceptibility bound *me*.

I mounted Cloud and she leaped away, in one bound reaching the crest of that rock-toothed ridge. She raced down the far slope toward open plain, heedless of her footing. Never looking back, I urged her on.

CHAPTER

18

Out of a duststorm we four rode down upon yet another
outpost of the Red. So thick was the dust, we were in
among the handful of tents before we could even see them
clearly. The storm was no mad wind, but it was a strong
one, which picked up the dry dirt off vast stretches of the
plain where no grass grew any longer to anchor it. We
ourselves contributed the aura of madness, more so for
every day that passed while the Red marched west across
the plain.

Horde though that army was, it would not watch all the
plain at once. Once the army had passed, all was as it had
been—except for the thin line of waystations that ran back
to the Broken Lands, over the High Plain, probably clear
to the Imperial City, along which all supplies for the army
must come. We rode around behind the army and attacked
these stations under cover of night or, as now, of duststorms.

Among the writhing shadows our windsteeds' long legs
cast on the screen of dust, we slipped to the ground. The
windsteeds snorted from excitement and from the dust
clogging their nostrils. The wind was loud enough to cover
any noise they could make. Anyway, the Red was not on

watch. The soldiers were in their tents, which were laced up tightly against the dust. What could they have watched for, in this storm? We could distinguish their presence a long way off, but they never knew where we might be.

We drew our long white blades of windsteed bone and slashed the tent lines. We rolled up the soldiers still in the tents. It was not fighting, only butchering. We knew by now we could kill soldiers with impunity; neither wind nor windsteed marked it at all. Nor did the army seem to. It kept on westward while we killed and killed and our spirits grew wild with killing.

Finally nothing moved save the dust. Someone tugged at my arm—Tisla. He grinned ferociously and gestured with his head. I followed him, to a cache of supplies under canvas tied down closely. There was food, which we sorely needed: grain, dried fruit, oil, and wine.

"Load what you can on your windsteed," I shouted at Tisla through the storm noise. He set to work. I moved past him through the dust, peering at the faint shadows slinking there, trying to make out which were Lirra and Gabbra and which were mere fancies of the wind. My eyes stung from the grit in them, and my clothes chafed where dust had gotten inside. Impatiently I grabbed at Lirra's arm, shouting in her ear to fetch Gabbra and assist Tisla—so we could go on.

What we could not carry away we buried in the trackless plain, digging graves also for the soldiers, with their own tools. If we were lucky, the storm would last long enough to hide all trace of this waystation, and when the next convoy came marching, it might lose its way and fall easy prey to us, or to one of the other small bands of windriders that harried the Red as we did.

We rode away into the storm, disdaining even the shelter of our windsteeds' streaming manes, sitting erect with our faces at the wind and the dust, still drunk with killing. The windsteeds raised that eerie, keening cry of theirs once seldom heard, louder even than the storm wind. Between my legs I felt the barrel of Cloud's body tremulous, for all its mass, with the force of her cry.

*   *   *

The duststorm blew itself out, but others followed as another summer of drought shifted into autumn. As that season then advanced the weather grew cold, but it remained dry. We kept at our grim work, my band and the others like it. None of us had beasts to herd—I had lost mine to Naglia, those others had started with soon went astray. Windriders harrying the Red had to keep moving and could spare no time to herd beasts. We made do with soldiers.

And all the while the main body of the horde of the Red went on westward I could see no sign that our nipping at its flanks and outposts slowed it. Gradually it learned to counter us. Perhaps the Red had not before dealt with an enemy at once as haphazard and as ruthless as we were, in concert with the distances and barrenness of the plain. At the very first the army was disproportionately vulnerable to our tiny but very mobile numbers, but the Army of the Red, which had in its countless generations conquered most of the world, was not easily overcome.

The army built roads, scarring the plain the wide swaths lined with rock: the Red had people enough for such a vast labor as that. Where the roads ran, we were hard put to lead any small contingent astray.

The soldiers no longer moved about in small parties. Both advance and supply units kept such large numbers our bands could not easily beat them, or even nip at them without great risk to our windsteeds—the only risk that ever checked us. The small bands of windriders made some attempts to ride together in larger numbers. That was no use; we only ending with fighting among ourselves.

Still, though it cost more and more, we kept at what we had started. Windriders had always been stubborn in their willfulness. In my band, both Gabbra and Tisla were wounded, though not so badly they could not ride. The pike wound in my arm never healed properly and gave me much trouble. I rode anyway. All of us grew gaunt with hunger and effort. Hard as the drought had driven us so many seasons, the Red was a worse scourge.

Late that autumn, finding the Red's supply line ever better entrenched and defended, I led my band west on the trail of the main horde. When presently the dust of passage rose before us on the horizon, I thought we had caught up to the army.

"Those are no persons afoot!" Lirra exclaimed. Indeed, the leading edge of the dust cloud moved too quickly. Windriders, then: but a larger group than any I knew of riding in the area. I sent Cloud on to meet them. They soon veered toward us, doubtless seeing our dust. At a wary distance they halted in a ragged line. Lirra and Gabbra and Tisla ranged silently alongside me, warier still.

A dozen there were: Osia and other high chiefs and some lesser chiefs, including Kirbana—none I had seen since the midsummer Ranking, or even the spring Ranking; these were they who had scorned the new oath and run west, trusting like Toda to tradition to hide them from Empire. The sight of them put me in mind that time was passing, enough for yet another Ranking. I wondered if they had contrived to hold an autumn Ranking; we had not.

I lifted my head, feeling scornful and not a little hostile. "Hail, windriders!" I called across the distance they kept between us. "Do you finally acknowledge what is real? And come to ride against the Red?"

"I acknowledge no such thing," Osia answered sturdily. "*I* am a windrider, Oa. I keep the oath as it was given by lords of Sky, and I keep my herds and housefolk also. I fight on the Ranking ground only."

I laughed. "You have a narrow notion of what a Ranking ground can consist in! All the plain is the ground where I meet the Red!" They looked soft, I thought; vulnerable, as I might once have been but was no longer.

Osia met my gaze evenly. He was still a high chief; for all his softness there were few in any other land who could match such as him. "What do you seek, then?" I called to him with less unfriendliness.

"Not you," Osia said. "Ajanna. He must claim his rank as chief of chiefs and beat me to keep it, or else yield it to me."

Instantly sullen, I gazed away over Osia's head. "You're a fool if you think Ajanna will help you keep your traditions," I muttered. But I was thinking more of how

Ajanna had said I bested him, there on the dry hillside above the River-that-ever-changes. How could he have thought so? Because he saw I could kill him? Because I could have done but did not? Or simply in mockery? More and more it had come to seem to me that he had bested me. Since that night I had not ridden truly free of him. To Osia I said, "I don't know where Ajanna is." I turned Cloud.

At my back Osia called, "Oa, I think you know."

I stiffened, pressing my lips together tightly. Yes, I did know where Ajanna was. Always. And I used that awareness of his presence on the plain only to keep clear of him. I had not seen him either since the midsummer Ranking. And I did not mean to see him now. Or to speak of him.

Cloud picked up speed. My windriders came after me. The others followed as well, I knew, without turning around to look, by the louder rustle of windsteed hooves on soft dirt.

I knew Osia and the rest of his kind had taken Murrila's herds when Ajanna did not, and run south with them on the traditional course. We could have used those herdbeasts here, to keep from starving while we harried the Red. I knew well enough we would have gotten precious little nurture even from those large herds, for we would have lost them. Nonetheless, I turned my head to throw back another jibe at Osia. "You look no different now from us! Riding across the plain so far from beasts and pasture! Are you a windrider now?"

Grimly he answered me. "You may be sure *I* will again be."

I snorted, not deigning to answer him further. I pressed Cloud to go faster. Both my own windriders and these others kept hard on my heels. I refused to regard them and went on just as I had earlier meant toward a river canyon for rest and forage. Pickings from the Red had become slim; we had eaten nothing in two days, ever since we finished the last supplies taken in a raid on a waystation just before we set out after the main horde of the army.

The Red favored canyons for campsites as windriders had never done, for the water and shelter they gave, I supposed. Rivercats did not seem to alarm the Red, though we found soldiers that looked to have been killed by cats. Going down into canyons ourselves, with our small numbers, we had to be alert for both. This time I went boldly as never before. The dozen extra windriders at my back were enough to scare off a rivercat. The Red I was coming to care less about.

Down a long rocky slope to a nameless river the windsteeds slid on their haunches. In the wide, dry-crusted riverbed water barely trickled. I turned upstram and found a pool dammed by a rockfall. I slid down from Cloud's back: here was water for drinking and washing, and warm, balmy air, for all the season was far advanced on the plain. And if we were lucky, here was even food. Gabbra and Tisla went off on foot after any small beasts or fish they could catch, or edible roots and tubers if no better offered.

Osia's people gathered in the shade of a riverwillow tree and built a little fire; from habit, I supposed. It was a habit we had lost, spending so much time in the vicinity of the Red. Osia's chiefs had diverged from habit in other matters, I gathered from their talk. With no one to hold Murrila's House or position, it seemed a number of them held the place jointly. I could not easily imagine windriders riding continually in the intimacy of council meetings. I soon shrugged off the effort to imagine it—I had no wish to know how they lived. I was too restless even to sit among them while I waited for Tisla and Gabbra to return. I went to the pool to bathe.

I stripped off my filthy riding leathers, beat them on rocks, and hung them in a tree to freshen as best they could, remembering long ago performing the service for Wiela. Now as then Wiela rode with Ajanna, together with Groa and some others. Like ourselves they harried the Red.

I sat down on a sun-warmed rock and pulled my braids forward over my shoulders. My pale, Gandish hair reached far below my waist now, in a dozen thin braids that sprang from the crest of my skull in a line from forehead to nape. One by one I loosened the braids, spreading my hair into a shining cloak across my shoulders. Then I slid into the water, diving beneath the thin green scum that covered the stagnant pool. The cool water played like fingers through my loosened hair and slid caressingly along the length of my body.

My head broke the surface. I gulped the fresh air, and swam across the pool. Cloud came to see what I was about making so much noise in the water, disposed herself to play if only I would. I climbed the bank to her, the water pouring off me in sheets. She shook her head with a show of distaste. When I put my hand against her face, she shuddered all through her enormous body.

But I wanted a different game. I turned, and leaned against Cloud's shoulder, to watch Lirra, stripped, dive into the pool, her slim, brown figure as quick as a shadow. She swam under water; a flash of motion was all I could see, for the stagnant water was murky. Her head broke the surface. She threw back her braids. They roiled the water with their swift movement. She grinned up at me. I grinned back at her, and held out my hand.

In two strokes she stood at the bottom of the steep bank below me, in water only knee deep. I bent. She grasped my outstretched hand and let me pull her up beside me. Quickly I slipped my arms around her, pulling her lithe body, so like my own, against me. I slid my hands down her bare back, and her long, hard-muscled flanks. Her breath came fast from the chill of the water, and faster still at my touch.

We moved toward a riverwillow thicket, into shade and a carpet of dry leaves. Lirra gripped me hard, clenching too hard on my arm where it was wounded and never healed. I drew my breath in sharply, from pain, but I did not pull free of her. I was too impatient. Lirra's brown eyes narrowed, looking at me. Wordlessly, greedily, we closed on each other.

Later we lay quiet. I dozed, my head against Lirra's bony shoulder, which was as unyielding as the riverbottom rock beneath me, or the willow trunk against my other side.

I was as hard.

"Oa!"

Tisla called me. I roused, smelled meat roasting, and

woke fully. Hastily I pulled on my leggings and went out still lacing them up, my shirt slung over my bare shoulders by the sleeves, laces dangling, and my hair hanging free but for the tangles come from playing with Lirra. Lirra followed me, silent and withdrawn.

Tisla held out our portions of the little rabbity creatures he had snared and cooked. Gabbra had gone farther, scouting, Tisla said. Nodding, I ate greedily—hungry and not knowing where my next food might come from. Osia's people also ate of the catch and in exchange shared with us some dried herdbeast meat. Once I had eaten such daily; now it had become unfamiliar to me, with so much else. We ate quickly, in silence, and sat in silence afterward. With Lirra and Tisla I no longer often needed words. Between me and these others there could be none. Presently Tisla went to bathe, and Lirra also wandered off.

I felt languid after love and food; I was not disposed to be hounded from my resting place by such as Osia. Ignoring the chiefs who sat silent and wary beside me, I braided my hair anew and then took down from Cloud's gear strap the new knife I was making.

There had been dead windsteeds enough of late we could have all the tools and weapons we wanted to make. I worked at grinding a cutting edge on each side of a flat windsteed rib bone. When it was done I would stretch strips of uncured hide to form a handle, with a ridge to keep my hand from sliding along the blade. When the leather dried I would carve into it the chief's signs I painted on my forehead for the Ranking. The knife was a long one, the full usable length from the rib of a large windsteed. It would hamper my walking if I carried it in a sheath along my leg, for it was a handspan longer than my calf, but I could just as well carry it on Cloud's gear strap when I was not using it.

Gabbra returned, appearing in our midst with no warning save his windsteed's soft nicker of greeting. He was the best among us at scouting, noiseless, all his being seemingly so suppressed that even we who rode with him often had no sense of his presence. Looking up from my work, I pointed at the food we had set aside for him. There was a light in his eyes I knew. I put away the knife and the grinding stone.

"There's a camp of the Red some ways upstream," Gabbra said while he ate with quick gulps. "At a spot where the canyon widens. They've cut all the brush so there's no cover." His gaze flickered over Osia and those who had ridden with Osia. "With so many, after nightfall, we may manage something." I nodded, and myself looked at Osia, questioning him—and mocking.

"No," he said shortly, his eyes hard and angry. I looked over the others. Not a one of them spoke or moved, save Kirbana dropped his gaze, unable to meet mine.

"We'll take a look," I said at last. Lirra and Tisla were ready. We four mounted and rode away upstream by the water's edge, and this time we were not followed.

It turned out the Red was camped in some force, dug in defensively for what looked to be a long term. I decided to let them alone, and we rode back onto the plain.

I did not see Osia or his fellows again. They found Ajanna, I heard later. He laughed in their faces, just as I had done, and said Osia must beat the Red before he could challenge Ajanna. Osia rode south for the winter with the rankings left as they were.

I heard this story from Tisla, who had gone for a time to ride with Ajanna. Tisla came back to me . . . changed. I saw it at once, so soon as we dismounted and came close for greetings. We sat on the bare, dry ground of the plain, the four of us again, without a fire. Tisla had brought a skin of kwass—from where, I knew not. We shared it and talked while dusk settled thickly down through the rising wind.

I peered at Tisla through the uncertain light and could not make out what the change in him was. I doubted he could explain it—I could never have said what Ajanna had done to me—so I didn't ask him. I doubted, too, it could come to much now.

Tisla was full of news and raids. "Hundreds of them we got! They camped at the very lip of a canyon, a deep canyon. The wind had kicked up a lot of dust, and even when night fell the sky remained clouded. After nightfall there was lightning; by it we saw the camp of the Red, tents lined up in rows. The wind began to rise again, the lightnings struck all around us as we rode.'' He took a pull of the drinking skin and grinned to see how intently we listened. Raids on the Red was what we lived on by then, more than on food or water—which we had little of.

"Ajanna called a halt," Tisla continued, "and sent several of us into the canyon on foot, around the flank of the camp. He wanted torches, made of whatever could be had. We waited in a fever of impatience, to be down on the camp like the wind. Finally the people came back from the canyon, and when Ajanna had seen to dividing up the torches among us, he let us go. The lightnings were still coming down, striking the ground in our very midst, but never touching a one of us, though we rode so high on our windsteeds. We lit the torches, and they crackled almost like lightning, for the wind was very high by then. We felt as if we were the wind, I can tell you!''

We three knew it; we felt it ourselves.

"We ran into the camp, waving the torches and flinging them into the tents of the Red. The fire caught, and the wind did the rest. We danced through the very flames, I think, and yet were not harmed, so quickly did we run on our windsteeds. The fire ran across the camp and burned it all. I doubt a one of the Red escaped. We stood between them and the plain, a dozen or so of us, in a wide line. The Red never ran toward us. And the other way, the way the wind went, was only that high cliff into the canyon.''

Gabbra's eyes glowed in the dusk as if they reflected that very fire Tisla spoke of. "What a notion!" Gabbra exclaimed. He turned to me, "Oa, we must be on the lookout for such a chance!''

"Yes, yes," I said, as eager as he. But we did not find the opportunity. The Red itself began to set fires, burning large stretches of what range remained, so we rode often for hours over wasted, blackened ground, and even the windsteeds went hungry. Only winter put a stop to the burning; that winter snow came early in great storms, such as there had not been for years. The winter helped us to harry the army more closely, but it also harried us.

* * *

Gabbra was killed by soldiers' pikes in an ambush we fell foul of, driven by hunger to take chances. After that some others rode with me for a time, but one of them was killed and the others rode south to make their peace with the high chiefs there. Alone, Lirra, Tisla, and I rode on.

About that time the army brought in herdbeasts of its own, the small, docile breeds of Empire, taking a lesson from windriders as to how to live on the plain, perhaps thinking it might be easier to provide the soldiers their food on the hoof. But the Red was hard put to provide food for the beasts—that too had to come in winter from Empire over the High Plain. Anyway, the very introduction of the beasts onto our range roused the windriders to new industry, and we soon got most of them and for a while lived as well as we ever had in any winter. Lean times returned, however, with ever worse cold and snow. More of our number ran south.

I would not run away. I was determined the Red should acknowledge me as all Imperial soldiers would if they knew my rank among them—but without knowing. Thus, the more care the Red took against me, the more wild and desperate became my raids. With some I succeeded; others, not.

When the storms had resumed after the usual midwinter lull in the weather—usual, that was, when there was a winter to the year—I gathered a score of windriders to go into the very largest encampment of the army in the dead of night. A snowstorm, which I had counted on for additional cover, blew over unexpectedly. I knew I could not long keep so many windriders together, so I gave the word to go ahead. Almost at once I was cut off from the others, however, save for Lirra and Tisla, who alone knew how closely to follow me. Between the roused camp and a long column marching in that night by evil chance, we three were trapped.

The soldiers in the camp, intent on the larger number of the other windriders cut off from me, did not, at least at first, realize what they had in me and my companions. That other column, wheeling so smartly into place despite the darkness, marching to orders as precise as any Dance: they knew.

From the threat they were, we three fled in among the tents in a tight pack, our excited windsteeds jostling each other dangerously. A platoon of unsuspecting soldiers trotted toward us down an avenue between two rows of tents. By the light of torches their outrunners carried I saw the surprise on their faces when they saw us. They recovered and quickened their pace. I slowed. Cloud squealed as one of the other windsteeds ran onto her. I glanced back, beyond the windsteeds so close behind me. The Red was there, well aroused. We could not turn back.

Tisla lost his head and ran straight at the soldiers coming to meet us. Pikes flew upward into the belly and throat of his windsteed. The great beast fell, throwing Tisla into the soldiers' midst. Doubtless they had comrades to avenge: they cut into him viciously once they had him at their mercy. I watched him die, unable to look away; watched the breaking of his sweet body, which was still that of the youth who had always pleased me greatly—by being so like me. I knew it was also my own fate that I watched.

But if so, it delayed. Tisla's windsteed, taking longer to die than his rider had, held back the soldiers from me and Lirra, but also cornered us between two tents. I marked the size and ornamentation of the tents and realized they were my goal—Hallek's headquarters. I had meant to fire them. I looked around now for a torch.

The soldiers finished with Tisla's windsteed and overleapt the carcass. A ring of weapons hemmed me in and cut me off from any person who held a torch. Again there was a pause, as the soldiers measured the reach of windsteed hooves and windriders' knives. One soldier with more initiative than the rest ran in right under Cloud's churning feet, startling me so I sat an instant blankly staring when I should have acted.

Lirra's Moon gave a fearful scream even as I leaned over his rump swinging my long knife in a great arc that clove the soldier between neck and shoulder deep into his chest. He fell like a stone, but he had done his work. Hamstrung, the white windsteed's hindquarters dragged helplessly; his great wedge-shaped head turned to me and Cloud, a terrible incomprehension clouding the once free gaze of his eyes.

The soldiers closed in more boldly, reaching for Lirra, who was near falling within reach of their pikes. I caught her, and kept hold of her arm, though it was slick with blood—hers or Moon's, I could not tell which. Lirra's eyes were blank with shock; she was a dead weight hanging from my hold.

"Lirra!" I called fiercely, through teeth clenched with the effort of holding her. "Climb up behind me!"

Slowly, like a dream figure with no will of her own, she threw one leg over Cloud, ranging skittishly beside the fallen Moon, and scrabbled up, such a weight on me, I thought for a moment we would both surely go over. But I held on and held my seat, and she got seated and wrapped her arms around me. Then I leaned out once more, with a quick, hard slice of my knife, to free Moon from his broken body.

All this had taken doubtless but an instant, but already the last open avenues of the camp were filling with the soldiers of the Red. The whole camp must be abuzz with the news of trapped windsteeds and windriders. The memory flashed through my mind of Cloud and me caught in a stampeding herd of the mindless herdbeasts. Then, one beast had died and we had won free. Grimly, I thought this time no single death would buy my release—save my own, of course.

Cloud whirled, too nervous to stand, her forelegs snapping out against the Red to clear breathing space. From the vantage point of her back, I could see, as she turned, that in every direction the soldiers crowded without number.

The taste of my own death came into my mouth. I laughed as a mad impulse came to me, and I lifted myself erect, high on windsteedback above the soldiers of the Red. I filled my lungs and gave voice to the battle cry of the Imperial House—what I had yelled as a child running through the palace gardens, and what had spurred the Red for generations across the face of the earth.

The soldiers could not march against my cry: for too many generations reverence for it had been instilled in their blood. While they stood stopped, Cloud bounded with great leaps over their heads and carried Lirra and me away into the winter night.

I laughed; but all the same I knew that I had seen my end. It could not be long delayed. All my band was gone now, save Lirra, and her windsteed was lost. I had taken some toll in soldiers, but only pricked the army. We had wreaked havoc this night next Hallek's very headquarters, mocking his most secure fortifications—but done no real damage. It was only a gesture, like all we had done. And it was a gesture Hallek would not let be, I reckoned from what I remembered of him. He would follow me, and in the end he would take me.

He would have done so in any event; I was glad at least to have given him cause.

Lirra stirred at my back. I gripped her hands where they were passed around me, knowing what she must finally have thought through. "Let me go," she mumbled thickly.

I would not allow it. Long as she had followed me, she had always kept a reservation of herself, insisting on her own terms. This time I would not allow it, and weak as she was, she had to submit to my will. After a while she gave up struggling, too weak from shock and wounding to insist on death. She laid her head against my back and slept.

Three days we ran across the white winter plain without stopping, under clear skies the pale, cold color of Imperial blue. We did not see the Red, but I knew it was there, below the horizon, coming on inexorably. It must be.

Hills rose suddenly above the white frozen plain in a sharp-toothed line I did not at first recognize. Then I saw it was the heights that guarded the River-that-ever-changes from this side. Climbing, Cloud suddenly lifted her head and nickered her greeting to windsteeds. And an answer came from beyond the ridge. She topped it, and I looked down on a camp of windriders—a considerable number, likely all there were still living of those who had ridden against the Red.

There were windsteeds, too, of course, but not so many as there looked to be riders, I thought. I knew Scudder at once by her great size. Ajanna must also be here. I had known some little time that he must be. I had felt him ahead of me just as surely as I sensed the Red behind me.

But I was in no hurry to see him. I slowed Cloud as windriders came in a crowd to greet me looking light-hearted—strangely so, for I could see at a glance they were in much the same pass as Lirra and myself.

I handed Lirra down. She was dazed, from shock or fever, talking wildly; I thought she had no sense where she was. Some windriders carried her away. Sliding down to the ground from Cloud's back, I felt no small part dazed myself, such was the air of celebration all about me. The windriders greeted me with light words and laughter, and yet the snow was deep, faces were pinched with hunger, and riding leathers were bloodstained and ragged. Someone pressed a drinking skin into my hands. Automatically I lifted it to my mouth and drank and found, not as I expected the thin, evil-tasting kwass of the drought years, but a sweet, creamy drink such as the best kwass had never been.

Kiia, who it was that had given it to me, laughed at my astonishment. "We have herdbeasts of the Red still," he explained. "Cows in milk that give such quantities as ours never did, for all they were so much larger. And rich meat, too; you'll see, Oa. Come."

I drank some more kwass and went with Kiia toward the one small fire in the center of a ring of ragged tents. Fuel looked to be scarce, but there was roasted meat as Kiia promised, and it tasted as good as he had promised. Among the rocks below the ridge I saw a makeshift corral; it held only a handful of the little Imperial beasts, and there were no others elsewhere that I could see.

"We feast only this once?" I asked Kiia.

His face changed. Though he said nothing, I understood he and all the others felt the end approaching. They were windriders, facing it with defiance, feasting and celebrating.

"Then let us feast!" I said cheerfully. I was also a windrider. I went with Kiia to help with butchering the last few herdbeasts. Others brought out all there was of kwass and firefuel. The windriders crowded around and we set to feasting in earnest.

Ajanna came, as I knew he must, with the slow, awkward gait left of his rivercat wounds. His thick black hair hung in hanks around his face, obscuring it as fully as his long fur cloak did his misshapen limbs. Only his eyes showed sharp and clear—farseeing as a windsteed's eyes. Abruptly his eyes fixed on me. I swallowed hard.

His presence was as large and oppressive as ever upon me. I had no more thought of avoiding him; I *could* not, to any avail. "Hail, windrider," I said softly, and he replied the same, his dark eyes gleaming. If I had bested him, he had come to terms with it, I thought. But I—! Ajana only smiled.

And that was all, before the noise and bustle of the crowd separated us. I could not think it was all there would be, but for the time others claimed me, and I let them. I joined in their light, careless talk.

But the feeling in the camp was not wholly—hardly could be—without darker elements. Groa was one of these. She had grown quickly, but she was still very much a child, at least in the flesh. Her enormous dark eyes had looked upon too much for any child: Wiela's madness, Ajanna's willfulness, the drought, the Red. She wore a strap across her chest from which dangled half a dozen short, wicked blades. With these she fought, someone told me, slipping around camps of the Red like a shadow. Ajanna and others of the band, fighting more openly, held the soldiers' attention, and Groa got them from behind. She was very proud and sure, I could see—but of death only. But only a little more so than anyone else. I put my mind to drinking.

Presently I went to see how Lirra did. She lay in the best shelter the camp afforded, a tent that had once belonged to the Red. Her mind was clear enough, but she was very still and quiet—more insubstantial-seeming than ever, as if her being had been honed nearly to pure spirit. What little could be done for her had been done. I just sat with her, silent as she was; not really *with* her, for she was not with me. She had gone a long distance away—ahead, where we others would also follow. I stood up and took off my catskin cloak and settled it around her. I could not follow her just yet.

"And what will you have?" she whispered, protesting.

"This is only half the skin, remember," I answered. "I

think perhaps the whole should have been mine. And I know where to go in search of it.''

Such she would not discuss. I left her—but I only returned to the fire, delaying still. Quietly those who remained shared the last skins of kwass with me. Mostly by themselves, windriders slipped away into the night one by one, dulled enough finally to sleep. I knew already where Ajanna had gone—how could I not? At last I followed him.

He lay in the open, in the snow, with only some cold rocks for screen against the wind, but wrapped around in his great cloak of catskins, their fur nearly as long as my hand. There was plenty of room also for me.

We said not a word, either he or I. Our bodies spoke for us clearly enough, now we were so near losing them; they found us a place of refuge and delight as remote from ordinary life as our fur bed in the snow. And, after all, I found all was easy.

The army reached us before dawn. I woke to the rhythmic tramping of its march and started out of my resting place, it was so loud: I thought the soldiers of the Red actually surrounded me. But they were some way off; the preciseness of their steps gave the noise of them great carrying power. Just now, they were in fact moving no closer, but turning to encircle our position on the ridge, crossing through distant gaps to meet up with another Imperial contingent deployed across the river. Day was near enough I could make out the forces clearly: it was not the whole army by any means, no endless horde. But hundreds, many hundreds; perhaps thousands. Against a few score. But we had one of the few defensible positions on the plain.

I stood barefoot on one corner of Ajanna's catskin cloak and pulled on my worn riding leathers. Carefully I tightened the lacings. I coiled my braids as for fighting in the Ranking, and Ajanna fastened them against my skull. I helped him also with his.

I slid my two knives into the sheaths on either calf of my leggings; the one was too long, but I would not walk so far that it could matter. I thought I would not bother to fetch my catskin cloak from Lirra. I was not cold, and it would hamper my arms' free swing, fighting. Last I snubbed short the strip of leather around my neck on which five cat claws hung. I would not remove them for this fight, but I would not, either, leave them dangling where someone might catch them. Then I was ready.

Ajanna and I looked at each other, likely for the last time. We still had no words to speak. Nor any more caresses. We were windriders going, in a way, to rites, alone as always.

The others came out past me silently, ready as I was. The Red resumed its forward motion—upward now toward us near the ridge. By unspoken agreement we spread apart from each other among the rocks of the highest saw-toothed ridge. The light kept increasing, though the sun had not yet cleared the horizon, and the vast bowl of the sky remained as white as the frozen earth. The air was utterly still. There was no sound or movement except the marching, and occasionally the bark of an order, so near now, we could distinguish individual voices. The rhythmic sound no longer frightened me, I realized. I could meet the Red.

There was another pause. The forces behind us seemed to be having some difficulty crossing the river. Perhaps the many windsteeds milling on the low ground on our side of the river gave them pause. I watched over my shoulder until I heard a windrider scream, high and long like a windsteed, and then I turned my gaze quickly forward again.

Flourishing a knife that glowed brighter white against the white sky, a figure ran down the slope so far from where I stood that I did not know her except by the voice. It was Wiela's mad voice

Here, at last, her madness was fitting.

In that instant I understood that Empire's existence, so at odds with ours, was impelled by a madness not unlike Wiela's—sort of a possession that likely only madness could stand against. We had gone mad ourselves, but that was only destroying us one by one. Even if we prevailed against Empire, we could not have remained windriders. I understood—but I did not accept. There was no time: the scene before me was running out toward its end.

Wiela ran against the mass of the army, which recoiled a little and clotted at the point of her impact. Under her white knife the edge of the mass crumpled; bits—bodies—fell away from it and lay on the ground unmoving. The knife Wiela waved high one last time was stained dark. Then she was gone, and the mass flowed on as before.

Others ran against it, as vainly, and were finished. Then I was also at that edge, and I could see only what was immediately around me.

Time stretched and shrank oddly. Spears rose with interminable slowness. But when they reached their apex, they came down swiftly at me, again and again. Everything became a single whirl of motion. I had no chance to speak words of challenge, but anyway this was like no fighting ever on the Ranking ground. Nor was it even like hunting, for there one sought out an individual creature for prey. Against this mass of the Red I did not so much fight as hack and slash at the myriad creeping extensions of a single monstrous being that was malicious but hardly sentient. I soon lost all sense of where or who I was beyond the slasher at spear-thrusting arms and wicked, closed faces.

The confined space among the jutting rocks hindered the swing of the Imperial pikes, and my shorter knives had an advantage. I fought free. I looked up at the sky. The light had not changed. I had no idea how much time had passed—if any had passed at all. I was exhausted. Every muscle in my body ached. I set one knife against a rock and leaned on the hilt, my breath heaving, closing my eyes to concentrate on catching it.

"Oa! Are you hurt?"

I looked up and found Lirra stood before me, grasping two bloodied knives. Her riding leathers were stained red as well.

"I'm all right," I said. "And you?" She grinned. Her eyes glowed with the strength of the will that drove her wasted body on. There was no point in her telling how she was; I could see she hardly *was* at all. A fire ran in my own veins, just from seeing her gallantry.

"Now we have taken to killing, we'll do it with a windrider's abandon!" I declared, and she laughed. Behind her soldiers poured through a narrow passage in the rocks, raising spears as they came.

"Beware!" I cried, lunging past Lirra, my knives high, my exhaustion forgotten. Lirra whirled and flailed at the outstretched spears. Side by side we advanced, one step at a time, chopping away at Empire.

But somehow Lirra was gone, and I stood alone, chopping, chopping, until no more spears came through the rocks. Bodies piled high on either side of me. The light seemed less than it had been. Had the entire day gone by? I pulled one forearm across my eyes in weariness, and my vision cleared. Then I thought perhaps only minutes had passed since the start. Momentarily confused, I stared at the blood dripping from the point of the knife I held and disappearing into the dirty snow to form another stain like so many others.

I pulled myself erect and glanced behind me: most soldiers there had yet to cross the river. I looked to either side of me. The thin line of windriders still stood. Soldiers of the Red were falling back, taking up their fallen. I stared, trying to comprehend that we had after all halted the advance of Empire.

But of course we had not: the line of the Red reformed and came on again. While I waited for it to reach me, I caught my wind. I found Ajanna standing on a rock apart from any others. He stood easy and relaxed, as if he had not just spent an eternity fighting and been about to spend another dying. His leather riding dress hid the deformities of his cat wounds, but even naked he would have looked perfect, I thought: it was the force of his will. It made an aura about him that dazzled me. His gaze moved disdainfully over the scene and met my eyes. Lazily he smiled at me. Once, I remembered, he had owned himself less than me. What then was *I*?

But I had no time for puzzles. The soldiers of the Red were upon me again, goading and jabbing with their pikes. I raised my knives and chopped and hacked at whatever came at me.

But from time to time I also glanced along the ridge where Ajanna laid about him tirelessly with two knives. Spears kept coming at me, distracting me, so I would forget him, but always I remembered and looked once more and saw him.

Then one time I saw only a close pack of the soldiers of the Red; a last concerted rush must have carried them over the rock. Ajanna was gone. The Red did not flow forward unchecked, however, and I knew by that Ajanna fought on, though I could not see him—only that knot of soldiers held in place

More spears came at me, more than one reaching through my guard to pierce my body. I did not feel it much; I just lifted my knives to chop and stab. The noise about me was deafening, more of an assault even than the Red. In a lull I recognized the sound of my own voice. I realized from the rasp in my throat I had long been yelling. I closed my mouth.

The din retreated outside my skull at least, but still another spear rose at me. I struck it, over and over, but always it came whole and advanced. It was like being on foot in a herd of crazed beasts, knowing there was no escape. I knew I must soon be borne down and trampled . . . but first I would, one last time, lift my knife—

Our line snapped. Soldiers came through in so many spots that their rush carried with it all of us who remained standing. I struggled to keep my feet. I could not get my knife free of those who hemmed me in. Nor would I have dared to strike, for I saw there were windriders mixed in the mass of soldiers. And then there were windsteeds.

The whole tangle of soldiers and windriders poured down the slope, to the nearly level land on the riverbank. The windsteeds ran there, crazed, crying eerily, louder than any roar of battle.

I was swept into the midst of the herd of plunging windsteeds. Windriders around me leaped upon windsteeds and whirled away. I cried out warnings, remembering the Red held the river and all the land across it. None heeded me—likely none heard. Cloud came chirruping anxiously before me, a pale, shining blaze, dancing on her light feet. I lifted my arms to her to take me up.

A gleaming pike shot from behind me to lodge, quivering, in Cloud's chest, the gray metal color of the haft almost disappearing from sight against darker gray blotches in her silvery hide. She started to fall, crumpling toward the ground, unable to reach me, her clear eyes clouding with confusion.

The noise of the battle seemed to explode within me—my heart bursting; and all went dark.

CHAPTER

19

Opening my eyes, I found, very near, the face of Hallek of Lus, dour-featured, red hair cropped so severely its color hardly showed. His eyes were brown, the color of many windriders'. He was speaking loudly to someone behind him whom he blocked from my view.

"She is most certainly Imperial kin," Hallek was saying. "Near-heir by the evidence of these tattoos."

The one behind him answered, "We got such a report, remember, last summer, from some early scouts in the badlands. We thought it impossible—"

Hallek grunted, not attending to this other now he finally saw my eyes were open and that I heard. Deep into my eyes he stared with his brown, Lusian eyes—and saw some little way into what I was, I thought. He said softly, "And I think I know *which* near-heir: the child-heir, Oa, who disappeared some few years ago. You don't look so old but what you could have been a child still, some six, seven years ago. Such a hue and cry there was! I heard of it, even on the Southern Shore. Torturings and executions on both sides of the river, but never a word of Oa's fate. I think I understand now . . . several things . . . that had puzzled me about the purpose of this campaign, and also about the way it has gone.''

I heard Hallek's words quite distinctly: his speech was not so strange to me that I could not understand it. What he spoke of seemed beside the point, however—trivial. After all, he could not have seen very far into what I was, I concluded. But what *was* I? And where—? The questions stumped me. I tried to consider, but my thoughts were too unwieldly to control. Puzzled, I stared up at Hallek. He rose and stood away from me.

Then I realized I lay in the open, on rough, icy ground. And then I knew: I had been beaten. I had lost my windsteed. So gaily I had ridden out against the Red at midsummer, lightly hazarding my life and my windsteed, thinking I need only face the Red to conquer it! But I had lost.

Hallek was speaking again. "I never thought to find Imperial kin in this wasteland," he said. "You'll understand, Oa, that we have no fit accommodations for you—'' I looked at him. I listened. I did not speak. I did not care.

His face changed, growing narrower and harder, his eyes taking on a cast no windrider's ever had—a slyness I could only scorn. I thought he did not even know he had beaten me. But what could that matter to me? Steedless, rankless, I was housebound.

At Hallek's gesture some soldiers of the Red came forward and lifted me up. I saw a wider view then, of the banks of the River-that-ever-changes and of the slope rising steeply to the ridge on this side of the river: the last Ranking ground. All was still, a large expanse of dirty, trampled snow, empty save for scattered mounds and lumps, mostly dark-colored. Belatedly I realized what were those still, sodden lumps: windriders and windsteeds. Dead, there was nothing about them whereby one could know what they had been.

The soldiers carried me across the battlefield, passing near one small form I recognized: Groa, lying with her soft, childish head thrown back at an impossible angle. She looked now only to have been a child, her fierce spirit gone as if it had never been. All Wiela's mad efforts had also come to nothing. Doubtless Ajanna had been brought low, as Wiela wished; but never by her. No longer did I have any sense of Ajanna.

The soldiers carried me toward a camp already springing up in orderly rows of tents, into a spacious shelter: Hallek's own commander's tent. Under Hallek's supervision the soldiers handled me very carefully. They need not have bothered: I could not feel pain, or anything else.

Hallek's own physician came to tend me, and could hardly do so for her exaggerated respect for what I had been so long ago—what Hallek and she thought I still was. I gathered that I was sorely wounded: that was why I could not move. Hallek said worriedly he would not run the risk of moving me. Yet he had the region still to subdue, he said; he seemed truly not to understand that he had already won. He ended with leaving most of the army at the river camp to guard me and taking a small force west.

The drought ended. Storm after storm swept across the plain, layering it deeply with snow. When spring came and the snow thawed, rainstorms followed. The grass grew thickly, as it had not done in years, already knee-high while it was still pale green with its first growth. It was beginning to ripen with summer's heat when Hallek returned to the encampment by the River-that-ever-changes. He had run clear to Ocean and then south along the coast, all the way through the Long Fen to the banks of the river Flod, building roads and waystations and garrisons. He brought herdbeasts and prisoners in his train, but no windsteeds nor any windriders. All the windsteeds were dead, he said; and any who had been windriders were now housebound like myself

Imperial arts had healed my body and even counteracted the poison in the rivercat wound in my shoulder. I was well enough—and ever more bitter to be so. When Hallek came to me I demanded that which no one had yet answered me: "What are you doing on this plain? Why did you come here?"

He blinked, taken aback. "I claim the Dynast's due," he said finally—as if it should have been obvious; or as if I tested him. "All must acknowledge his Empire, for he is lord of all earth."

"Lord of Earth!" I exclaimed. "So I called the mindless herdbeasts on this plain!" My bitterness burst all bounds. "But indeed, mindless is what the Red is!"

Hallek watched me, frowning. "Why did you come to this plain, Oa?" he asked. "If not to take it? As the representative of Empire." Truly he sounded puzzled.

Reminded of what I had brought of Empire among the windriders, I turned away, speechless. Then I bethought myself that worse than my using the High Dance to take windrider's rank, worse even than my succoring Ajanna or my headstrong self-will, were the drought and the Imperial invasion—these things had done the real damage, and these things *I* had not wrought. I looked Hallek in the face once more. "But *why*? What is this empty plain to the Dynast that he should send the Red to take it?"

"There was nothing else left to take," Hallek answered simply. "The armies have come to the ends of the earth, to open Ocean, beyond the northern tundra, beyond the nations of the Eastern Plains, beyond the walled merchant cities of the Southern Shore—on every side save across the mountains west of the Imperial City on the Flod." He shrugged. "And when the mountains bloomed after these last years of unprecedented rainfall, the Dynast concluded the time could never be better to cross even there."

I reined in my bitterness in an attempt to understand. I was not brought so low, I thought, housebound though I might be, that I would not acknowledge whatever was truth. But what *was* the truth? I started with details. "You say the nameless mountains bloomed?" I asked.

I remembered the dark rock into which the Flod ran in cataracts. Such rock could sprout and flower? It had rained, Hallek had just said, unprecedented amounts. Our rain, I thought: the plain had shriveled while those mountains bloomed.

Hallek seemed anxious to keep me in conversation. "Those mountains are nameless no longer," he said. "They're now called the Mountains of Pleasure. Those who can, build retreats and pleasure grounds in the mountains."

That I shrugged off. "After the mountains you crossed the High Plain?" I asked. I reckoned it must be so, but to imagine it was something different. "You did not encounter a . . . strange . . . wind?" Perhaps the mad wind did not always blow.

"A wind? Is that what you call it? Nothing so commonplace, I think! There was an oddness in the desert plateau that dragged unpleasantly on the mind."

I was baffled. "The army marched through a mad wind?" I could not understand it: the merest soldier of the Red could withstand what Braha and Halassa could not? In my mind I tried to see the soldiers of the Red when they marched. I heard them, the rhythmic tramping; the monstrous, inhuman rhythm. Then I understood. Not because the soldiers were more than windriders had the Red come safely across the High Plain, but because they were less, their minds well insulated by the discipline that had so narrowed them in the generations of their service. Truly I began to grasp what Empire was then, and how it had beaten the windriders.

Hallek continued talking. He seemed bent on conciliating me—I thought it strange, soldier that he was, who held me captive

"It's true," Hallek said, "this plain is little practical use to Empire, and I think the Dynast suspected that would be so. He warned me to expect desert terrain and barren mountains. But he ordered me to go to the end of the earth and to take whatever I might find there." Hallek paused, considered, and went on. "I think he knew, or hoped, *you* would be here, Oa. He has taken all earth, but he can't take all time, and he's finally looking seriously at the succession—and he doesn't like what he finds around him."

The Dynast. Though I stood in Hallek's tent, the entrance flaps tied open so I could feel the soft summer breeze of the true plain and hear the purling murmur of the waters of the River-that-ever-changes, in my mind I could see the Dynast as clearly as if I stood before him, and he was watching me with the impenetrable pale blue gaze of those eyes that were ancient before I was born. Did they finally near their end? Perhaps I would not now find them quite so impenetrable. Hallek said the Dynast *knew*. Did he know *all*? My life on this plain? Had *he* arranged it, to test me? Even that I became a windrider?

At the thought, I grew angry. I would not have it! But what could I do? And at that moment, I came nearer acknowledging the Dynast's power than ever before. All my life seemed to me as nothing, a vain struggle to escape him. He had me now.

"Anyway, I've done all I was ordered to," Hallek said. He gestured through the open entrance of the tent at a traveling chair standing ready, six runners beside it. "Now we can return to the Imperial City."

I stared at the chair, answering Hallek bitterly, "So I'm to be carted back to the city like booty of conquest!"

Hallek stared at me in surprise. "How else would you travel if not by chair?"

I had forgotten the lords of Earth have no windsteeds, that they are lords of earth only. More and more I come to understand my fate, I said to myself. I let Hallek hand me into the chair.

Day by day we inched our way across the plain. Runners' best speed was a crawl compared to windsteeds. The once-pale grasses swelled and darkened as the year advanced. Delicate flowers sprinkled the ground and winked out after their brief time. The sun grew hot and stared down at us unrelentingly. The ground baked until it sounded hollow under the footsteps of the runners. Never was there sign of herdbeast or windsteed or windsteedrider.

I came to understand my fate! Bitter did I find it. Days I sat in the cushioned traveling chair while my guard of the Red trudged alongside. Nights I lay in a silken tent, on the plain still, but with every detail and illusion of Imperial comforts. Hallek persisted in according me every attention due a near-heir. In his every courtesy I saw only mockery of my captive, housebound status.

The morning finally came I looked out of my tent and saw the sun rise over the red rock scarp of the Broken Lands. Today we would reach the end of the plain. I turned back into the tent; captive that I was, I could only turn my back.

"Will you have breakfast, Oa?" asked Hallek at my back. Without waiting for an answer he set up a small folding table. Slaves entered with dishes. "May I join you?" Hallek asked.

I grunted a graceless assent and came to sit on one of the carved campstools set out on either side of the table.

"I'm pleased to see you've put on the summer robes I gave you," Hallek murmured while he served the food. "These last days the heat has been intolerable—" I looked up to discover why he broke off speaking so abruptly. "How did you get such a scar?" he exclaimed.

My fingers felt the rough skin that filled the four slashed lines running parallel from my neck to my armpit, partly bared by the low-cut garment I had put on. Imperial arts of healing had not quite removed the scars. With long months of confinement, my skin had paled to its natural color; the cat wound scars were the same white, but a roughness of texture still set them off.

"A rivercat—" I said, remembering the hard, wild bodies of both the cat and Ajanna. As I remembered them, the two seemed much alike. And both were now dead.

"Ah, yes. I believe I've seen the skins and some claws of such creatures on some of the captives." Hallek smoothed his tone to the courtier's style he used most often with me.

"No doubt," I said coldly. Then I added, "I—and one other—hunted the cat that did this. With knives." My fingers toyed with the faint unevenness of the scar.

"And you killed it, no doubt," Hallek said drily.

"That one, and another one also," I agreed. "The second one I brought down alone, without letting it mark me."

Hallek looked at me for once with something more than courtier's gaze. "You came near taking the army, too," he said with feeling. "You were behind those raids, weren't you? No mere barbarians could have kept at us so long. You wore down the morale of the Red as I couldn't have thought possible. And that last mad raid, on my headquarters, was some finishing touch! I was almost ready to believe what the troops did—that you were something immortal, unnatural, invincible. The sight of those monstrous beasts—and their riders—dead in camp the next morning was hardly enough to get the army moving again. And the Dynast complains that the near-heirs are gutless beings! He may change his mind when he sees you. Single-handedly you made the Red pause.''

I only shrugged. Doubtless Hallek had the right of it, but what did it matter? I—and one other, Ajanna—were largely responsible for the harrying of the Red. I had not thought it had done so much as Hallek now said. And how could I care if I had almost won, when I had in fact lost? I was still enough of a windrider to deal only with what was real and before me. I went on eating and drinking all the while Hallek spoke, staring past him at the silken wall of the elegant traveling tent he had furnished me. The sun rising behind it made the red Lusian silk glisten like new-shed blood. Outside housefolk bickered—captives and soldiers.

"You there! Barbarian! I want a word with you."

"Who do you think you're talking to? You're housebound the same as I am!"

There came a snort from the first speaker. "The difference, barbarian, is that you're a barbarian captive and I'm an Imperial guard."

Housefolk meant nothing to me. Their lot could be no worse in Empire than it had been on this plain.

Hallek's tone sharpened with irritation that the captives dared talk back to the soldiers. Amused, I listened finally more carefully to what the people outside the tent were saying.

A voice spoke in the accents of Empire—a soldier: "—you were at the battle? When the barbarian line broke and they leaped upon their beasts? What a sight—!"

A second Imperial voice—the one that had been needling the captive housefolk, I thought—interrupted, "I told you before, I spent the whole campaign at this very station. But listen: yesterday I was out in back of the station, and I saw an enormous beast. It moved without a sound. I tell you, it was on top of me before I even saw it! And the rider! He stared right at me, but I'll swear he didn't see me. He looked right through me! And I'm pretty solid, wouldn't you say? It must have been one of *them*,

don't you think? One of those windriders? I was just going
to ask these barbarians about it.''

"Naw, it couldn't have been. They've all been cleaned
out. We took care of that. This country is as clean as a
whistle. You can't have seen a windrider!''

"It was broad daylight, I tell you,'' the other continued.
"Just yesterday. Now how could I imagine such a thing?
You explain that to me! You there—barbarian! Doesn't
what I describe sound like one of your windriders? It was
an enormous dark male with a great black beard. He was
hung about with skins and heads of monstrous beasts.
Looked filthy. Wasn't that what you call a windrider?''

Wasn't that a windrider! I was on my feet crossing the
tent even as the words sank into my awareness. It was
Ajanna! It could be no other. He would be wearing his
catskin cloak with the one-eyed head, still stained with our
blood, of the cat we killed together. Scudder was the dun
color of dry grass, so the stupid soldier would not have
seen her running right at him over the plain. I laughed
aloud to know a windsteed yet soared above the plain and
a windrider sat her back feeling at one with the sky.

"Ride free, Ajanna, windrider and chief. Ride with the
wind.'' Without thinking I murmured the ritual words of
the chief of chiefs, which Ajanna himself had forgotten to
speak at the end of that last, fateful Ranking.

I rode in that instant with him. Pain, confusion, guilt,
bitterness: all dropped away from me between one footstep
and the next. They were no burdens any windrider could
have fashioned, or set upon me. The windriders who were
gone had all gone freely to the fates that were theirs. They
would be amazed—outraged—to think that I had tried to
take their fates upon my head. No windrider held back
from any challenge, come what may.

And Ajanna still rode! I had not known it; I had not felt
him—not as I once had. But he *was* there. Now I looked, I
felt the touch of him, light and easy, but sure—part of
myself. I reached the entrance of the tent and jerked aside
the silken door covering. Somehow I must have expected
to see Ajanna himself riding there. The contrast between
that and what I did see could not have been greater.

Soldiers of the Red, seeing me, fell back and hung their

heads, thinking they had disturbed me. The captive housefolk watched me sidelong, warily, like captives everywhere—as they had been always—fearing new humiliation, dumbly hoping to find something that could be called an advantage.

I waved my hand in a sharp gesture of disgust at the cowering. All scattered but one. I swung around to see who it was that did not heed me or fear me.

Glittering black eyes blazing with a passionate certainty met mine and did not fall. I gasped.

Ajanna!

No, of course not: it was Raun. He took a step toward me. "It's true," he whispered. "It's all true, just as I always thought. You're a high lord sent to me by lords of Ocean to lead me to freedom."

I stared hard at Raun, dark-skinned, black-eyed, harsh-featured, self-willed. So like—and unlike—Ajanna. I laughed aloud at the irony of it. "Yes, Raun, I'll lead you to Empire," I said, surprising myself but not him. "I would like to see what you can do with it."

I cast my thoughts forward to the city, the Imperial House, the near-heirs, the Dynast. I had learned to control the High Dance. I had passed the Dynast's test. What now awaited me in the city?

I had cheated the Dynast of Jily's life. He would have to settle for the life of an entire people—a people without name or identity, to be sure, a people that refused to be ruled, counted, or mourned. A people that chose death before Empire and rode freely into death. The Dynast need not know these things, however; nor that I kept back Ajanna from the bargain. Yes, I thought: the Dynast could count as paid the price I had refused before. Now I thought of all Hallek had said, which I had hardly regarded, and I decided: I would be no captive. I would take up the prize I had paid so much for—Empire itself.

Hallek came out of the tent behind me. He touched my arm, wondering at my sudden start from the table. I glanced down when I felt his touch and saw the soft folds of silk that clothed me, the robe he had given me. It was somber-hued soldiers' garb with a narrow trim of garish Lusian red interwoven with darker army red. It was in no way suited to my blue, pale Imperial coloring—or to my Imperial ambitions. Before entering the city I would have to send ahead for my own clothes—

The detail of Empire—luxury, intrigue, power, illusion intermingled—swept over me in a flood. I cried out, remembering also the free, soaring flight of a windsteed, now denied me forever—

The price I had paid!

"Oa! What—?"

I should need much to compensate me! Empire—the world was not enough. It was what I would have, however, to start. I turned blazing cold eyes upon the Lusian commander beside me. At the sight of him measuring me so slyly—and so inadequately!—I knew how much more I was than his captive. I saw his unctuous words had been no mockery. I saw what his conciliations aimed at. I snapped, "You may have had some notion, Hallek of Lus, to use me to make your future. But I say you shall not! I shall rather use you."

And Hallek dropped his gaze before mine. I smiled a little to myself, seeing it. Even he was infected with discipline, high commander that he was; his will was flawed and made malleable by the habit of giving up something of himself. Of all on earth, only I was not bound or bounded. The Dynast may have meant to test and hone me; I had become rather more than even *he* knew.

I strode out onto the plain, leaving the waystation and my escort behind, too impatient to stand still. The wind played over the tall, waving grasses, drawing currents of shifting subtle colors over the plain, which stretched west, seemingly endless. But all that plain was simply the flat floor of the sky.

I lifted my head to the vastness of the sky. Some little time I had ridden there between earth and sky. I closed my eyes and felt myself become one with limitless space. Against my raised face the wind came, laden with the sweet smell of ripening grass, gusting and sighing, moving freely, passing by me on its way to the Imperial City.

I would overtake it. Like a new Gandda coming out of the legendary Land of the West, I would sweep down from the newly named mountains upon the city. The windriders' life had contained me a time; Empire had smashed that life and left me nothing, I had thought. I had been mistaken. Empire had hardened and then loosed me—freed me.

And Empire, like me, was newly complete. The naked might of armies of conquest had finished their work. Now subtler forces would take their place, forces of will honed like mine. I could take Empire now, and hold it.

I spun around, so quickly the long grasses whipped at the bare skin of my arms. I turned my back to the plain that looked empty and set my face toward my future.

DAW

DAW BRINGS YOU THESE BESTSELLERS BY MARION ZIMMER BRADLEY

- ☐ CITY OF SORCERY — UE1962—$3.50
- ☐ DARKOVER LANDFALL — UE1906—$2.50
- ☐ THE SPELL SWORD — UE1891—$2.25
- ☐ THE HERITAGE OF HASTUR — UE1967—$3.50
- ☐ THE SHATTERED CHAIN — UE1961—$3.50
- ☐ THE FORBIDDEN TOWER — UE1894—$3.50
- ☐ STORMQUEEN! — UE1951—$3.50
-    TWO TO CONQUER — UE1876—$2.95
- ☐ SHARRA'S EXILE — UE1988—$3.95
- ☐ HAWKMISTRESS — UE1958—$3.50
- ☐ THENDARA HOUSE — UE1857—$3.50
- ☐ HUNTERS OF THE RED MOON — UE1968—$2.50
- ☐ THE SURVIVORS — UE1861—$2.95

Anthologies

- ☐ THE KEEPER'S PRICE — UE1931—$2.50
- ☐ SWORD OF CHAOS — UE1722—$2.95
- ☐ SWORD AND SORCERESS — UE1928—$2.95

NEW AMERICAN LIBRARY
P.O. Box 999, Bergenfield, New Jersey 07621

Please send me the DAW Books I have checked above. I am enclosing
$_____ (check or money order—no currency or C.O.D.'s).
Please include the list price plus $1.00 per order to cover handling
costs.

Name _____

Address _____

City _____ State _____ Zip Code _____
Allow 4-6 weeks for delivery

DAW

The really great fantasy books are published by DAW:

Andre Norton

☐ LORE OF THE WITCH WORLD   (#UE1750—$2.50)
☐ HORN CROWN   (#UE1635—$2.95)
☐ PERILOUS DREAMS   (#UE1749—$2.50)

C.J. Cherryh

☐ THE DREAMSTONE   (#UE2013—$2.95)
☐ THE TREE OF SWORDS AND JEWELS(#UE1850—$2.95)

Lin Carter

☐ DOWN TO A SUNLESS SEA   (#UE1937—$2.50)
☐ DRAGONROUGE   (#UE1982—$2.50)

M.A.R. Barker

☐ THE MAN OF GOLD   (#UE1940—$3.95)

Michael Shea

☐ NIFFT THE LEAN   (#UE1783—$2.95)
☐ THE COLOR OUT OF TIME   (#UE1954—$2.50)

B.W. Clough

☐ THE CRYSTAL CROWN   (#UE1922—$2.75)

NEW AMERICAN LIBRARY
P.O. Box 999, Bergenfield, New Jersey 07621

Please send me the DAW Books I have checked above. I am enclosing
$_____ (check or money order—no currency or C.O.D.'s).
Please include the list price plus $1.00 per order to cover handling
costs.

Name _____

Address _____

City _____ State _____ Zip Code _____

Please allow at least 4 weeks for delivery

DAW

Do you long for the great novels of high adventure such as Edgar Rice Burroughs and Otis Adelbert Kline used to write? You will find them again in these DAW novels, filled with wonder stories of strange worlds and perilous heroics in the grand old-fashioned way: